The Leading Edge of Now

The Leading Edge of Now

Marci Lyn Curtis

KCP Loft is an imprint of Kids Can Press

Kids Can Press gratefully acknowledges the financial support of the Government of Ontario, through the Ontario Media Development Corporation.

Published in Canada and the U.S. by Kids Can Press Ltd.
25 Dockside Drive, Toronto, ON M5A 0B5

Kids Can Press is a Corus Entertainment Inc. company

www.kidscanpress.com
www.kcploft.com

The text is set in Minion Pro and Golden Plains.

Edited by Kate Egan
Designed by Emma Dolan

Printed and bound in Altona, Manitoba, Canada in 6/2018 by Friesens Corp.

CM 18 0 9 8 7 6 5 4 3 2 1
CM PA 18 0 9 8 7 6 5 4 3 2 1

Library and Archives Canada Cataloguing in Publication

Curtis, Marci Lyn, author
    The leading edge of now / Marci Lyn Curtis.

ISBN 978-1-77138-999-0 (hardcover)
ISBN 978-1-5253-0139-1 (softcover)

    I. Title.

PZ7.1.C87Lea 2018   j813'.6   C2018-900384-7

FSC
www.fsc.org
MIX
Paper from
responsible sources
FSC® C016245

For the strong, the kind and the compassionate —
the gentlemen in my life. Paul, Talon, Blaise and Merle.

One

Here I am.

Standing at the base of Rusty's front porch, where I've been for probably a full minute, trying to find the courage to move. Over the past couple of years, I keep having moments like these, where I come to a sudden halt, look around and ask myself, *Grace Cochran, what were you thinking?*

The answer is always the same. I was not thinking.

Sarah, my caseworker from social services, is beside me, watching carefully. Back in the day, she was a Troubled Teen on Drugs, but then she went to rehab and cleaned up and found God and etcetera, and now she's trying to make the world better, one troubled orphan at a time. Which probably explains why she's looking at me as though I might spontaneously combust. Having once been a Troubled Teen, she's in tune with such things. "Take your time," Sarah says. "It's probably a little overwhelming for you, coming back to your uncle's."

"You have no idea," I say.

Which is absolutely true.

If Sarah knew what had happened the last time I set foot in New Harbor, she wouldn't be so keen on carting me back here right now.

My heart races in my ears. The instinct to run is sharp and physical, as if some lunatic is coming at me with a knife. I close my eyes for a beat, trying to reel myself back in. Rusty is family, the only blood relative I have left, so as screwed up as it is, I belong here. This place is home — or as close to home as I can have right now. I breathe in deeply and drag my suitcase up the porch steps, both my bravery and my feet stopping before I get to the door.

Sarah clears her throat, glancing at Rusty's house and then back at me. I have the distinct impression that psychoanalysis is about to occur, so I busy myself by idly swatting away a mosquito. Sarah starts in anyway. "I'm sure you'll fall into a routine here. Reacquaint yourself with your uncle. Rekindle some old friendships." She pauses for a moment, waiting for me to reply.

I do not. I'd sooner talk about how sausage is made.

"Your uncle tells me you have an old friend here," she goes on in a low voice, and then she elbows me, just barely. "Even a boyfriend, at some point?"

And just like that, my lungs start closing up. I can feel my pulse banging in my ears, my fingertips, the backs of my knees. I imagine a field of sunflowers — something my therapist told me to do when I feel like I'm losing control.

It doesn't help.

Slowly, methodically, like I just bought my mouth and I'm not yet sure how to use it, I say, "Owen and I were together for, like, a few months. We broke up, and I haven't spoken to him since." Looking down at my hands, which are knotted together in a white-knuckled clamp, I talk myself down. Everything's going to be fine. Owen has already graduated from high school, so he'll be heading off to college at the end of the summer. All I need to do is avoid him for a couple of months. I can do that, can't I?

Sunflowers.

Heaps of sunflowers.

The freaking planet, covered in sunflowers.

"Did I say something to upset you?" Sarah asks.

"It's just — I don't know," I say quietly, working to keep my voice calm. "It's everything, I guess. I'm finding it kind of overwhelming, being here."

"Look," Sarah whispers, her eyes on mine, steady and firm, "I know you're upset with your uncle for leaving you in foster care for so long. I get that. But you need to understand that this is a big change for Rusty, and it's better that he took his time and made sure it's the right decision. It was the responsible thing to do."

With great effort, I restrain a snort. The last time Rusty was a responsible human being was never. His brain is a tossed salad of Michelob, Cheetos and nearly half a century of adolescence. So I don't reply to Sarah. I just let out a loud exhale.

Sarah stares at me for a tick. She's probably only five-two, but the way she carries herself makes her appear six feet tall. "You've got this, Grace," she says, loudly enough that I wince, and before I can stop her or say anything else, she steps forward and rings the doorbell.

Footsteps clomp through the house.

Oh, God.

I try to breathe. In through the nose and out through the mouth. In through the nose and out through the mouth. In through the nose and out through the —

Rusty throws open the door in a grand, animated gesture, like he's presenting himself onstage. He was a singer, way back when, and he never quite adjusted to life without performance. "Grace!" he hollers, his voice, as always, several decibels too loud.

I don't know what I was expecting. Red-rimmed eyes or pale skin or a guilty tilt to his brows, maybe. Or some other tangible evidence that the past couple of years have been as hard on him as they've been on me. But Rusty hasn't changed one bit. He's still all lopsided grin and cowboy hat and exuberance. He launches himself over the threshold and crushes me in his arms, holding me hostage for several breaths. He smells just as he always has, like Old Spice deodorant and cigars and the first few days of summer. Pulling away, he holds me at arm's length. "Holy hell, G, you look great!"

Anxiety and panic sear my stomach, even though I know there was a time that I felt as safe with Rusty as I had with my own father. "Thanks," I say, backing out of his grip, the word coming out pricklier than anticipated.

His smile falls, just barely. Which should make me feel vindicated. But the fact is, Rusty's smile used to be one of my favorite things, back when I had favorite things.

We stare at each other. We breathe. He shifts his weight. Sidestepping the awkwardness, Rusty turns to Sarah. "Ma'am," he says. He tips his hat and winks, his trademark move with the ladies. His fourth wife called it charming.

But, Sarah, she just gives him a curt nod.

Silence.

I clear my throat. "Right," I say finally, wiping my palms on my clothes and doing my best to smile like a seventeen-year-old whose entire life hasn't been jerked out from underneath her. "So I'll just …" I gesture to the doorway, which Rusty is mostly blocking. My big idea to get past him is to step around him a little. Like we're chess pieces: he's a knight and he can't move to my square. But he wraps a meaty arm around me and half squeezes, half drags me into the living room, where he and Sarah talk "guardianship" and "custody" and "rules and regulations," during which I do not open my mouth or form a syllable or communicate in any way.

I was afraid that — after everything that happened the last time I was here, after Dad's death, after my two-year absence — Rusty's house might've drastically changed. But it still looks the same, like it's never been formally introduced to the new millennium, all avocado-green appliances and outdated couches and dusty, taxidermized animal heads. In the kitchen, the edge of which is just visible from my perch, I see the ancient wooden table that's always functioned as a landing strip for unopened mail, car keys, beach towels and Solo cups. Rusty would clear it all to the side in the evenings — with a giant swipe of the back of his forearm — to make room for boisterous, legendary games of Spades. My gaze roams back to the living room, to a picture of Dad and me on Thanksgiving, several years back. To a framed invitation to my eighth-grade violin recital. And, most notably, to the lucky bamboo plant Dad gave Rusty.

A sudden pang pierces the hollow of my chest. I blink a couple of times. My vision blurs and clears. Dad was ridiculously superstitious. I used to find St. Christopher statues wedged in his glove box and sand dollars dotting the house. I was gifted with rabbit's-foot keychains, lucky-penny clocks and horse-shoes in all colors and sizes. This bamboo plant — it was Dad's Christmas gift to Rusty a few years ago. Currently, it's sitting on a small, round table by the front door, looking droopy and ignored. "Have you been watering that?" I blurt, pointing to the plant. There are so many questions I should've asked Rusty — Why did it take you two years to sign my guardianship papers? Why didn't you come to Dad's funeral? Why haven't you even *called* me? — and yet here I've opened by grilling him on his horticultural skills.

Rusty leans back on the couch, kicking his legs out in front of him and crossing them at the ankle. His smile is back full-force, and the entire living room seems brighter because of it. "Huh? The bamboo?" He peels off his hat and scratches his head, nearly taking out a lamp in the process. "Yeah. Of course I water it. Every other week, I s'pose? Once a month?"

And the state of Florida thinks it's a good idea to leave me in his care.

Still, though, Sarah is serious and respectful as she hands several papers to Rusty, who holds them out as far as his arm will allow, squinting. He needs glasses, but he's always despised wearing them. Most people look ridiculous when they squint. Rusty just looks more like Rusty. And as I sit there, watching him read the guidelines for my care, I realize just how much I've missed him over the past couple of years. But then Sarah says something to him, and he laughs, full and rich, like things are completely normal, and I think about all those nights I spent in foster care. Like a reflex, I turn away from him.

Two

Something you probably should know: I got kicked out of my first foster home.

All right, so that's a smidge theatric. It isn't as though I was acting up or cussing or doing drugs, or anything. My foster parents didn't toss me to the curb, my suitcase flying out behind me. And the truth of the matter is that I actually liked Heather and Thomas Danielson, my first foster parents, who were perfectly nice and kind and friendly.

Who I did not like was their twelve-year-old son, Phillip.

Now, I'm just going to come on out and say it: there's nobody meaner than a twelve-year-old boy. In fact, I'm reasonably certain that somewhere in a psychology journal, there's a chapter revealing a scientific study that quite explicitly states that twelve-year-old boys are — and I might be paraphrasing here — spawns of the devil. They have an uncanny ability to find the one thing you're sensitive about — the one thing you're aware is your very worst feature — and then tease you about it mercilessly.

Like, they make fun of you *honestly*.

This is a trademark move. It's virtually unavoidable, because what they are saying is true. And how can you argue with the truth? In my case, I'd probably lived with the Danielsons for a day, tops, when Phillip started in on my largish nose.

Can you smell what's for dinner tomorrow?

Does that thing influence the tides?

Stop breathing up all the air in the room.

Here we are, just the three of us.

Everyone take cover: she's gonna blow.

And so on and so forth. He was relentless. Keep in mind that I'd just lost my dad. My mind was a tangle of what had happened with Owen the last time I was in New Harbor. I was living in a house with virtual strangers. I felt like a tree that had been uprooted and then stuffed back into the ground in a foreign country, where everyone spoke a different language and ate weird foods. I won't go into details, but eventually Phillip just wore on me until I snapped.

I lasted a whopping three weeks.

After that, I lived with the Marios, where I rode out the rest of my time. The Marios lived smack in the middle of Tampa in a five-story condo development, of which Mr. Mario was the super. So I dubbed him "Super Mario," which is probably the laziest nickname ever.

The Marios were sympathetic and soft-spoken and keen on giving me whatever I needed. Thing is, I wanted something they couldn't give. I longed for the life I used to have. I wanted this one memory of sitting on the couch in Rusty's living room. On my lap was a plate of pizza, which I ate while Rusty and Dad, on either side of me, watched a baseball game, lulled by the sounds of the game and the garlicky smell of pizza sauce and the weight of the thick sea air. After a few minutes, Rusty became bored with the game and took a giant bite of my pizza. *Sorry*, he said, though he was smiling. I jabbed him with my elbow, pretending to be annoyed. Dad laughed and stretched an arm over the top of the couch, squeezing my shoulder. It is such a normal memory — totally ordinary, actually — but even so, we were more a family then than ever.

Now, years later, as I sit on that same worn plaid couch, I realize that I know exactly what I want, because, once upon a time, it was mine.

Three

It's the middle of the night, I'm glaringly awake, and I have just one prevailing thought. Maybe it's more of an observation than a thought, but regardless, there's only one of them.

It's hot.

This is early June in Florida, after all, so while the rest of the free world is enjoying cookouts and camping trips and back-yard croquet, Floridians are walking around on the surface of the sun.

For the first hour, thinking about one thing is sort of heavenly, because there are many unpleasant thoughts I'm currently avoiding. But after a while, my one thought becomes so dominant and so miserable that I swing my legs to the floor and sit on the edge of the futon, which, for the record, is also uncomfortable.

As far as I can tell, the futon was part of a room-renovation project that never actually came to fruition. Gone are the bed and the dressers and the lamps that used to clutter this room.

Now it boasts a futon, a television, a desk and a mini fridge. And that's it. Most girls would've chosen to sleep in the other spare room, which hosts real furniture with a real bed. Not me. Nope. I claimed the futon room immediately and without deliberation. And to fully understand the brilliance of this, you'd probably need a PhD in The Science of Horrible Mistakes.

Hoping the living room is cooler, I pad down the hall, where I find Rusty's cat, Lenny. I do not actually notice him lying there, not until I step on him and he hisses at me. Scraggly and muscly and enormous, Lenny is a rescue. Not a rescue as in *We need to find this fluffy, adorable kitty a new home so he can brighten someone's day* — a rescue as in *We'd better get this cat adopted ASAP, before he goes Shawshank and starts picking off all the other cats.*

According to Rusty, Lenny is a "bobcat mix," though I suspect the only thing he's mixed with is another bobcat. His defining characteristic is his long, prickly, above-the-eye whiskers that function as eyebrows, which effectively express his dislike for mankind. Due to the fact that Lenny has a nasty habit of rummaging around in the neighbors' trash cans, he's restricted to the house.

As in: house arrest.

So he's miserable and foul-tempered and despondent, and I figure it's only a matter of time before he pulls out a sharpened toothbrush and crams it into my neck, prison-style.

"Sorry," I whisper to him as I walk past. "I didn't know you were there." No clue why I explain myself to him. It just seems like the right thing to do.

Rusty is asleep on the couch, lit up in the bluish light cast from the TV, his Stetson pulled low over his face — like he's napping against a tree out on the prairie while his sheep graze around him.

To be clear, Rusty is as much a cowboy as that guy in the Village People.

Folding my arms across my chest, I watch him sleep for a moment. The two of us hardly spoke after Sarah left, and when we did, it certainly wasn't about anything of substance. But then, we've never talked about anything serious in all our lives, so maybe it makes sense that every time I start to ask him for explanations, my words lump up in my throat. Now, though, with him asleep, and without my initial shock at being here, I can almost pretend that this whole thing isn't going to turn out badly. That maybe he actually wants me here. He came for me, after all. Which is something, even though I don't know what prompted it — whether his guilt finally got the best of him or he just grew tired of Sarah's emails and phone calls. Now that I'm here, my suitcase in my room and my violin propped against the desk, it will kill me if he walks away again.

Shaking my head to clear it, I slip outside to the front porch, where it feels maybe one-fiftieth cooler than it did in the house. The wooden porch slats are warm and familiar under my bare feet as I curl my palms around the banister and lean forward, turning my face to the sky. For what feels like the first time since I set foot in New Harbor, I exhale.

Dad and I used to come here for long weekends and holidays, and I've spent most of my summers in New Harbor, Dad remaining at home during the week to work and then making the fifty-five-mile drive south to Rusty's for the weekends. Rusty's neighborhood stretches up the beach, on the land side of a skinny one-lane road that faces the ocean. It's on a point, actually, where New Harbor proper ends and where undeveloped land takes over, dissolving the asphalt into bumpy dirt roads. The houses here are ancient beach cottages, Rusty's at the very end of the street, where everything peters out abruptly into seagrass, sand dunes and craggy trees that are whitewashed from their proximity to the ocean.

Tonight, the sounds are all waves sweeping ashore and breezes flapping at distant wind socks and wind chimes tinkling. Out of habit, I look past the Simons' house next door, past the long string of lifeguard towers studding the beach, to the dark silhouette of the McAllisters' house, about a mile away.

Janna McAllister used to be my best friend here in New Harbor. More often than not, she'd be waiting on the steps of Rusty's front porch when I arrived — her knees pointing in together and her chin propped on the heel of her palm — ready to haul me off to the beach. We'd lie on the sand here for hours, swapping stories and eyeballing lifeguards and acting like complete idiots. She took a ridiculous amount of pleasure in teasing me about my dislike of swimming in the ocean. "C'mon, Fruit Cup, get in already!" she'd bellow, knee-deep in the waves, looking ridiculous in her wild smile and her bright-yellow throwback swimsuit, her flaming curls waving around her head like she was conducting some sort of antigravity experiment.

Janna was one of the biggest reasons why I loved New Harbor. I spent so much time at her house that her parents automatically set an extra place for me at the dinner table whenever I was in town. I had my own pillow in Janna's room, my own shampoo in the bathroom, my favorite granola bars in the pantry.

And I had Owen.

Janna grumbled and carried on and generally acted put out

when she discovered I'd been crushing on her older brother. "Why does it have to be *Owen*?" she moaned. "He's going to break your heart. Or else you'll break his. And it'll be our friendship that suffers because of it." At the time, I thought she was being dramatic. But the thing is, she was right.

I rest against the railing and close my eyes. I knew that coming here would unearth all sorts of nasty memories. And just standing here, I'm hit with a multilayered emotion that's heartache and shame and panic, my past suddenly so close I can sense it brushing against the tiny hairs on the back of my neck. Slightly unnerved, I spin around to head back inside, stumbling a little in the entryway and giving just that fraction of a second that Lenny needs to shoot outside. I lunge at him, missing his tail as he dashes across the porch. Paws skidding on the wood, he darts off into the night.

Crap.

I consider leaving him out here. Creeping around in the dark after a homicidal cat isn't my idea of fun. But it was my fault that Lenny escaped, so I feel a sense of duty to retrieve him.

Okay, fine: I don't want to wake Rusty to tell him the cat ran away.

I don't want to talk to Rusty at all, actually.

And so, cursing under my breath, I creep barefoot down the porch steps and wince my way across the gravel driveway into the dark, shadowy area between Rusty's and the Simons', where cats that shouldn't be house pets lure seventeen-year-old idiots to their death. It's silent and eerie and creepy as hell, but I'm committed now, so I keep going, praying that I find the cat quickly and that my jugular remains intact.

I hear a sound — not a loud sound, just a little crash-thump

— and I flinch and jerk to a stop. "Lenny?" I yell-whisper, my nerves completely on edge.

This was a really bad idea.

Another thump, followed by a crunching sound.

I hum a few bars of Bach's Violin Partita no. 2. I imagine my sunflowers. I wrap a protective hand around my throat. I step forward, tripping on my own fat feet and pitching headlong into somebody.

"Oomf," the Somebody says in a low, masculine grunt.

Now, I'm not sure of the verbal protocol for barreling head-long into someone in the middle of the night while chasing a maniacal cat, but I'm relatively sure that it isn't "Holy shit! I didn't know anyone was here!" I jerk backward, causing a motion light on the edge of the neighbor's house to click on. And there, wearing a University of Florida T-shirt, a pair of earbuds and an expression of absolute shock, is Owen McAllister.

Four

There's a moment when I do not breathe, when my heart rate goes volcanic, when the distance to Rusty's house seems so wide and so impassable that it will take me hours to scramble back.

Owen is staring at me, eyebrows crashed together like he's trying to solve a particularly difficult crossword puzzle. It's an expression I know well, seeing as how I've spent half a lifetime watching him stand in the garage, gazing at his projects as though he were unraveling the greatest mysteries of the universe.

I want to turn around and run.

I want to slap him.

I want to burst into tears.

What I do, though, is stare at him. He looks the same now, only different. While his dusty-blond hair has been cut short, his eyes are the same — still clear emerald green, big and serious, with lashes as long as palm fronds. He's probably grown a full two inches since I last saw him, and he's broader across the chest. On his right forearm is the small diagonal scar he got back in the third grade, when he tried to build a birdhouse for an endangered owl. I always considered that scar one of the things that made Owen *Owen*. But now it looks misplaced, inappropriate. I have to resist the urge to try to scratch it off. I close my eyes, like maybe I can erase his presence that easily. But he smells so familiar — like sawdust and coffee and soap — that this particular action only makes him more real.

I open my eyes again.

Owen plucks the headphones out of his ears. "Grace," he says slowly, like he's trying to remember how my name is pronounced.

Now would be the proper time to speak. But I'm pretty sure that my mouth has been blown apart and then reattached backward and inside out, a couple of miles north of my vocal cords. So I just continue to look at him.

A few decades pass.

I want to ask Owen what he's doing here in the middle of the night, and I want to ask why his hair is so freaking short, and I want to ask why he annihilated me two years ago, and I want to ask question after question after question, but then I open my mouth and all that comes out is "Owen." Still, that one word sends a storm of images crashing into me. Owen at seven. Owen at ten. Owen at thirteen. Owen at fifteen.

Owen at sixteen.

It's the last one that makes my chest feel like it's caving in.

I clear my throat. It sounds like an old, brittle floorboard, creaking under bare feet. "You're here," I say, which is quite possibly the stupidest thing I could've said to him. Twenty-some-odd months of dreaming about getting even, and now all I can do is state the obvious.

He opens his mouth slowly, carefully, like I'm a small animal he doesn't want to spook away, and he says, "Yeah." Just the one word, but even so, I can hear his almost-accent — like he went to Australia for an extended vacation, staying just long enough for the language to coat his tongue. When I was little, I was forever trying to get within earshot of him. He was an anomaly, after all, not just by the way he spoke, but also by his unruly hair and his quiet demeanor. So naturally, I fell for him.

And naturally, it ended in tragedy.

I can't seem to find any words. They all took a train to some-where safe. Finally I raise my chin and stare him down, doing my best to give him a smirk that tells him he didn't even hurt me the last time I saw him, and I say, "Why are you here, Owen?"

He twists the toe of his sneaker into the trunk of a palm. "Why am I here?" This is Owen, when he gets nervous. He answers questions with questions. I used to think it was ador-able. Now, though, not so much.

"Why are you here, Owen?" I say, sort of snottily, swooping my arm across the neighborhood like it's all my property or something.

He winces. Not his face but his posture, just a tiny change in the line of his shoulders and the arc of his back, something that a normal person wouldn't even notice. He folds his arms across his chest, only to unfold them and jam his hands in his pockets, only to haul them back out and gesture with his thumb to the house behind him. "I live here."

For the first time since I arrived in New Harbor, I look next door, at the unfamiliar yellow Jeep parked crookedly in the driveway, at the large potted plants dotting the front porch. "You moved in with the *Simons*?"

Owen shifts his weight. "No. I mean, the Simons moved out? And then, um, we moved in." He glances over his shoulder at his house, almost like he's checking to make sure it's still there, and then he says, "Mrs. Simon is expecting a baby, and I guess they needed more space?"

You've got to be kidding me. Owen and Janna, right here in the same cozy acre of New Harbor. My resolve implodes. "What the hell?" I basically yell, triggering a dog to start barking somewhere in the distance. "You moved *here*? Right next to my uncle?"

"We had to foreclose on the house," Owen explains quickly, his ears tinged red. "We couldn't afford it. All the medical bills from the accident —" He stops. Inhales. If he thinks he's going to make me feel sorry for him because life handed him his ass, he's mistaken. I've been holding my own ass for nearly two years, and it has never been heavier than it is at this exact moment. "We were able to rent this one cheap," he goes on finally, in a high voice, a strange voice, almost a bleat. And then he clears his throat and shifts his weight, glancing at Rusty's driveway. "Where's your dad's car? Did you come by yourself?"

I blink at him, shocked. He doesn't know about Dad? Rusty hasn't bothered to mention Dad's death to the McAllisters? I don't know why this comes as a surprise. Rusty is Rusty: a smile on his face and nobody to worry about except himself. Besides, Rusty has never been one to offer personal information, particularly when it's embarrassing or reflects badly on him. Particularly when he knows he'd have to answer the questions that would likely follow, like *Where is Grace living?* and *Why isn't she here with you?* And beyond that, it isn't as though Dad was ever close with anyone else in town besides Rusty. Dad wasn't very social, and other than casual conversation at picnics or gatherings, he didn't really spend time talking to anyone here besides us. He came here for family, and that was it.

Still.

It's sad that Rusty is the only one here who knew Dad died.

I turn toward Owen, look him in the eye and square my shoulders. "Yes, I came by myself, because after Labor Day weekend a couple of years ago? *That* weekend?" He opens his mouth to say something, but I start talking faster and faster, my words like miniature knives, aimed right at him, one after the other. "Well. A few weeks after that, Dad had a heart attack, so I ended up spending a month in the hospital at his bedside, while he barely clung to life, during which Uncle Rusty basically fell off the face of the earth, where he stayed, mind you, even after Dad died, so I ended up in the foster system until Rusty finally decided to man-up and sign the guardianship papers." I hold my arms out, like I'm on exhibit, feeling vaguely psychotic. "And so here I am."

Well. That's out there now.

It sounds a lot more pathetic when I say it out loud.

Owen just stares at me for a moment, like he's waiting for me to say *Kidding!* And when I don't, his expression slowly collapses. He opens his mouth, closes it, and then he opens it again and says, "Your dad died, and Rusty was …?"

I can feel all the loose ends in my life tangling around my ankles like seaweed, threatening to pull me under. "MIA," I supply. Something loud is roaring in my ears. I speak over it, my voice rising several octaves as I go on. "Yeah. I mean, you know Uncle Rusty: late to his own funeral." I laugh, an awkward creation that sounds more like a cough.

Owen scrubs a hand back and forth over his buzzed-off hair. The silence condenses. "Look, I'm really sorry …" he says finally, his voice trailing off. He takes in a breath, his shoulders sagging. I'm not about to make this easy for him, not after everything, so I don't speak. I just stare him down as he goes on. "About all of it. Your dad. Your uncle." He turns to look at me. "Us," he says, his eyes so green that I can almost trip and plunge right into them, and for a second I do. I feel like time has rewound and it's the summer before sophomore year, just before everything went sideways.

But then Owen takes a step in my direction, his hand reaching for me, and everything comes slamming right back. I scramble away from him, and his arm drops to his side. He says, "Grace? I'm not sure where you stand with us, but —"

"You should know exactly where I stand!" I holler. The cat slinks past me, and I scoop him up in one hasty motion. "Who *are* you, even?"

"I'm Owen," he says, and the pain in which he says it, the defeat in his posture, the sincerity of his tone, they are boulders rolling on top of my chest.

Jesus. What is wrong with me? I'm feeling sorry for him? After everything he's done, I'm *feeling sorry* for him?

All of a sudden I can't get back to Rusty's quickly enough. I take several staggering steps backward, tripping on a root and scrambling to right my balance. Then I stab an index finger at him and say, "Stay away from me." It comes out loudly, unexpectedly, like it was a ghost trapped in my vocal cords and it's finally flown to the light.

I turn and bolt away, focusing solely on the ground underneath my bare feet, my breath in the thick night air, the cat squirming in my arms, my hand on Rusty's porch railing as I glance to the side to check whether he's still there. But he's already gone.

Five

"Why didn't you tell me the McAllisters moved *next door*?"

The front door bangs shut behind me so loudly that the picture frames rattle against the walls. Lenny twists in my arms. I deposit him on the floor — just drop him in the entry with a *thwump*.

"Huh? Who?" Rusty says, blinking at me, his voice thick from sleep. He gropes around for his hat, which tumbled to the floor when he sat up, and then rubs one of his eyes with his fist.

I'm pacing, shaking my hands out. My pulse is galloping so fast that I can hardly hear. I know very well that I look unhinged, walking in anxious, barefoot lines back and forth in front of the couch, but I fear that if I stop moving, my entire life will implode. "*The McAllisters*," I basically shout at Rusty, rolling my eyes. Like there has ever been more than one McAllister family in my life. "They moved next door and you didn't bother to tell me?"

"Right," Rusty says, yawning. "Right. Well, I was gonna tell you, but I fell asleep."

I throw both hands up in the air. "You fell asleep," I say, trying to keep my voice steady but failing.

Rusty stretches and plunks his feet on the coffee table, crossing his legs at the ankles. "Why does it matter so much? You and Janna aren't friends anymore, right?"

I shrug. That's one way to put it.

"And a while back, I heard that you and Owen had called it quits," he says, putting his hat back on, "that you two haven't spoken in ages. So I figured it wouldn't matter to you where the McAllisters moved."

I stop walking and fold my arms over my chest. Rusty looks mildly confused as he waits for me to explain why I reacted so strongly. But I'm not about to tell him why Janna and I aren't friends anymore, or why I walked away from my relationship with Owen. I pinch my forehead with my thumb and index finger. "Right. It doesn't matter," I say, my words coming out screechy. "I just think you should've mentioned it, is all."

He shrugs. "Fair enough. Sorry for not telling you."

Well. I don't know what to say to that. It's difficult to argue with someone once they've apologized. We're quiet for a moment, and I stare out the window into the blue-black night. This move to New Harbor — what a complete disaster. How will I even *sleep* knowing that Owen is next door? And Rusty, he hasn't even mentioned Dad's death yet. "Why did you come for me, Rusty?" I say. I don't think the words before saying them; I just say them.

Rusty glances up at me, surprised. "I want you here." But his answer comes too quickly. There's no way he had time to think about it, no way his reply is anything but a canned response. I'm not looking for canned. I need honesty. Or else, a well-crafted lie. Anything that shows me he cares, at least a little.

I'm not going to make this easy for him, not when I've waited so long. Birthdays and Christmases and Thanksgivings and orchestra performances — all of them with no family to speak of. "It took you nearly two years to figure that out?" I say.

Rusty looks uncomfortable. "Look, G, after —" He stops. Takes a breath. Starts again. "I wasn't in a good place for a while. I couldn't have taken care of you. You deserved more than that," he says, and for a beat, he looks so broken up about Dad's death that I almost feel guilty for confronting him. Rusty was so much more than a brother to Dad. The two of them were virtually inseparable, even though they were so different — Dad with his kind, gentle personality, and Rusty with his charisma and contagious smile. Somehow they fitted together perfectly, best friends above anything else. I have no doubt that Dad's death crushed Rusty.

Still. That doesn't change anything.

I straighten my spine, steeling myself. "Don't try to flip this on me. That's not fair."

"I'm not," he says, and again, it's too quick. He wipes his palms on his pants. "I'm not."

"Rusty, I —"

"Everything's going to be okay," Rusty says, standing up and yawning like a prairie lion. Just like that, he's casual again. "Let's get some shut-eye and talk about it tomorrow?"

Tomorrow.

This is actually happening. I'm living here. With Rusty. Next to the McAllisters.

"Right. Tomorrow," I say, trying to file the terrified edge off my voice. I've gone all this time without seeing Owen, and now that I have, I can feel the ground starting to erode under my feet. It's only a matter of time before everything sweeps out from underneath me.

Six

Back when I was twelve, Owen asked Janna and me to help him carry a turtle-nest enclosure out to the beach. It was a fence-like coop built from scrap wood and chicken wire he'd found in his garage. When Janna opened her mouth to tell him we were busy, Owen said, "An animal has been eating the eggs before they can even hatch," to which I said, "Ohmygod that's so sad," to which Owen said, "I know, right?" to which Janna rolled her eyes, sighed and said, "Fine. *Fine*. We'll help."

Owen had forever been building things. It had started back in the second grade, when he'd found an injured squirrel in his backyard. That night his parents found him in the garage trying to hammer together a wooden box where the squirrel could recuperate, where it would "feel protected." His words. From the second grade.

So Janna and I helped Owen muscle the enclosure out of the McAllisters' garage and onto the beach. Once we got it in place, the three of us stood over it for several minutes. Owen smiled at nothing in particular. At the eggs he was protecting, maybe. I felt the corners of my mouth creep up as well. Finally Janna said, "Owen, are you sure there's a turtle nest in there?"

Owen shrugged. "See where the mother tried to camouflage it? And her tracks in the sand?" he said, pointing to the little perforated lines that were coming and going from the nest. As he did so, his opposite hand brushed against mine.

Something inside my chest *staggered*.

He must've felt it, too, because he turned toward me and his eyes locked on mine. He didn't break his gaze. Neither did I. At least not until Janna loudly cleared her throat and said to Owen, "Well, then, I'm going to reclaim my best friend right now and go back home, because we have an Uno game waiting for us and I have lots of stuff to talk to her about that doesn't involve turtle tracks. So you can see we have to go."

Owen and I exchanged a look, his expression fleetingly irritated, and then Janna yanked me away by the wrist. When we got back to her house, she grabbed my shoulders from behind and frog-walked us into her room, where she closed the door, whirled around toward me and said, "What was *that*?"

I wiped my hands on my jeans. "What was what?" I said, in this weird, loud voice that sounded like it had come from a little boy.

"That *look* you and Owen gave each other at the beach," she said. Her chin wobbled and she sort of deflated, collapsing on the edge of her bed. She'd always teetered on the very edge of every emotion — the highest of the highs and the lowest of the lows.

"Do you like him, or something?" she asked.

What I should have said was that I'd liked Owen since the

beginning of time, that my feelings had gone well beyond feelings and had inched into an area that could be described only in a cheesy ballad. But what I said was "Kind of."

She examined me closely, one eyebrow arched so high that it disappeared into her bangs. I furrowed my brows at her, staring her down until her facial muscles relaxed. Janna and I had probably five eyebrow conversations a day. This was one of the reasons why I loved her. "Kind of," she repeated finally. She looked vaguely relieved. "Well. The thing is that he's my *brother*. And if you two got together it would make our friendship so awkward. So just —" Massive sigh. "Just don't, okay?"

"Okay."

In my defense, I *did* try to avoid Owen. Honestly, I did. Last thing I wanted was to hurt Janna. I loved her like a sister. Sure, I had friends back in Tampa, but Janna was the one I called to whisper my secrets to in the middle of the night. The first person I'd texted when I'd gotten my period. She was the friend I'd always felt closest to, the friend who understood me best.

So I managed to steer clear of Owen during the next couple of years — simply giving him a hello when we passed each other in the hallway or a smile when our eyes caught at the dinner table. I figured Janna must've lectured Owen about it, too, because he made himself scarce whenever I was around, either hanging out with friends or holing up in the garage with his projects, which, I discovered, had morphed from animal enclosures and birdhouses to … well, actual works of art.

It was during Christmas vacation, freshman year, which would've been Owen's sophomore year, when Owen and I were thrown together again. Janna and I had planned a *Harry Potter* marathon, and I was in charge of snacks. Dad had just dropped me off in the McAllisters' driveway, my arms loaded with bags of chips and candy and sodas, and I was walking past the garage, where a sleepy indie-rock tune slipped out of a wireless speaker on the workbench.

I lurched to a stop.

There he was, facing away from me, bent over a short stretch of driftwood, a mallet in one hand and a chisel in the other.

"What are you making, Owen?" I asked.

He jerked around, leaped up and exclaimed, "Oh, hey, Grace! Nothing." And then he crossed his arms, tapping his thumb on his biceps. "I mean — I was just goofing around. Like, with some wood?" His face turned an adorable version of crimson.

I tipped my head sideways in an attempt to see what he'd been working on. No dice. My eyes trailed back to his. "Were you … chiseling?"

Clapping his hands together and still blocking my view of his project, he barked a laugh and said, "I guess?"

He looked so charmingly flustered, so uncomfortable, that I dropped the subject. "Cool," I said, giving him a quick wave and slipping inside. Later that night, though, after Janna had fallen asleep and the house was silent, my curiosity got the better of me. So I slid quietly out of bed, down the hallway, through the kitchen and out the back door to the garage. Sawdust and tiny chips of wood stuck to my bare feet as I waved my hands around in search of the light switch. I slammed my pinkie toe into what I assumed was a workbench, producing a noise like I'd just stepped on a couple Fritos. Balancing on one foot and swearing creatively, I slapped my hands at the wall until I found the switch. Flipping it up, I was momentarily blinded by the fluorescence, and then I turned toward the workbench.

And I sucked in my breath.

It was gorgeous, if a piece of driftwood could be gorgeous. An old man's face, worn and creased, climbed out of the wood as though it were trying to escape, so real and so lifelike that I half expected it to open its mouth and speak. Was it Owen's grandfather? His teacher? A man he'd seen on the beach? With Owen, you had no way of knowing. With Owen, an explanation for something like this had to be earned, not blurted out while I was walking past with an armload of snacks. I ran a slow hand over the wood. His style was impulsive, totally charming. The lines were meticulous, uncovering how much he paid attention to the smallest of details.

Guilt gnawing at me for intruding on Owen's privacy, I clicked off the light and turned to head back into the house. I'd just stepped out of the garage when I saw Owen, lit up by the full moon, standing at the side door just off the kitchen, wearing nothing but a pair of low-slung jeans and a look of confusion.

Um.

"Owen!" I basically yelled. "Holy shit, you scared me!" I tried to say this rather casually, but the words exited my mouth decked out fully in Christian Dior.

I mean, I was busted. No way around it.

Owen ran a hand over his hair — which, back then, was a few inches longer and messy on top — and then his eyes drifted down a little, from my neck to my T-shirt to my legs. Then they shot right back to my face.

And that was when I realized I was wearing exactly what I'd gone to bed in: gigantic flowered underwear and a white T-shirt barely long enough to cover my butt.

Lovely.

I crossed my hands high over my chest, suddenly all too aware of just how disastrously white the white in my white T-shirt actually was. He shifted away, his stance awkward. Clearing his throat, he said, "My room is across from the garage, so I saw the light come on. What are you doing out here?"

"I was —" My words caught in my throat, because what if he hated me for invading his privacy? What if he never spoke to me again? What if he told Janna? What if she screamed at me about it? What if I ended up losing both Owen and Janna because I couldn't keep my big fat nose out of Owen's business?

But Owen already knew what I was doing, so there was no sense in lying. Looking at my feet, I sighed and said, "I just wanted to see what you were making." I swallowed so loudly I was certain he heard it. "I mean — you're interesting, and I thought whatever project you were working on must be interesting, too."

Why did I just say that?

A beat of silence, then: "I'm interesting," he repeated slowly.

"Uh-huh," I said, and then I immediately decided to staple my lips together first thing in the morning. And then secure them with duct tape for good measure. Pretty sure I could live a full life without saying another word.

Owen stared at me.

On the plus side, he seemed to have forgotten about my current clothing ensemble.

"I'm sorry for invading your privacy," I said. "It was a jackass move. Can we just … forget this ever happened?"

He stood there and looked at me, statuesque, biting his lower lip. "Did you hate the sculpture that much?"

My eyes jerked up to his. "No! It's — God, it's brilliant. I mean, where did you even learn to do that?"

He shoved his hands into his pockets, which inadvertently tugged his jeans down a millimeter lower.

That area of skin just beneath his hipbones.

Oh my sweet holy lord.

Someone dial 911.

Owen said, "So I'm taking this art class in school and we're spending a semester on sculpting? I was just, like, practicing on wood. Seemed like the obvious choice for me." He shuffled his bare feet on the concrete and looked at me from under his lashes.

Wiping my hands on my T-shirt, I said, "Who is it? The man in the sculpture?"

He shrugged. "It's the cook at Voodoo Pastries. The place out by the interstate, where they serve bacon donuts? Oh, don't go making faces until you've actually tried them," he said, bumping me with his shoulder.

Was he flirting with me? Pretty sure he was flirting with me.

There was an alarm going off somewhere in my brain, telling me that if I stayed out here any longer, tomorrow I might regret it. This was my opportunity to end the conversation. Just laugh the whole thing off and head back to bed before I screwed up my friendship with Janna. I didn't, though. What I did was bump him right back. "I wasn't making a face," I said.

Here I was, half naked, flirting with the one guy who was clearly off-limits.

What the hell was wrong with me?

All right, this: my crush on Owen was unbearable, stretching almost as long as my entire fourteen years, and I honestly felt as though I had no choice in the matter.

At least that was what I told myself.

Owen smiled at me. "You squinched up your nose. Which is what you do when something grosses you out. And you wouldn't have made that face if you'd actually tried a bacon donut."

"I wouldn't wager a bet on that," I said.

He cocked an eyebrow at me. A challenge. "Actually, I totally would. Ten bucks says that when you try a bacon donut, you'll melt into a useless puddle of carbohydrates."

"You're on."

The next day, I told myself I was just settling a bet when Owen picked me up at Rusty's. But I hadn't told Janna about the outing, and neither had Owen. And it wasn't Janna who was on my mind as I sat across from Owen in a booth at Voodoo Pastries, Owen watching intently as I took a bite of a bacon donut, closed my eyes and, yes, melted into a useless puddle of carbohydrates.

Victorious, Owen toasted me with his own half-eaten pastry and then threw the entire thing in his mouth, crashing back in the booth as he chewed. After he swallowed, he leaned across the table toward me, his knees brushing against mine and his forearm grazing my hand. I could feel his breath feathering my face as he said, "If you think this place is good, you should check out Sweetbrew in Sarasota."

I blinked at him. He was still touching me in multiple places and making no effort to pull away.

I was so dead.

No time to dwell on it, though, because the next clandestine excursion happened the following night, at Sweetbrew, where they served — no shit — jalapeño-and-coconut-flavored coffee. Also delicious.

Christmas vacation freight-trained on, each day more excruciating and amazing than the last. At night, Owen and I snuck off to sample lobster ice cream and spicy egg pizza, inching closer and closer to each other. During the day, I was with Janna, pretending not to notice her brother.

But then it all caught up to me one night at the McAllisters', a couple of days before I left to go back home. While Janna was in the shower, I walked into the living room and found Owen on the couch, bent over his laptop, completely enthralled. And I just couldn't take it anymore.

"Whatcha looking at?" I asked.

He glanced up, momentarily surprised, and then he smiled and motioned for me to sit beside him. Looking back now, I should've shaken my head no. And if I'd known what would happen to me months later, I would have done that.

Convinced Janna was still in the shower, I took a chance and sat down, sliding close enough to see the screen, where there were pictures of carvings — wooden arms and faces and flowers, climbing out of blocks of wood and logs. They were people and nature and expression, life in motion, yet somehow perfectly still. "Wow. Those are gorgeous," I said.

"I knew you'd appreciate them," Owen said.

"Wait. Say that again, please?"

"Say what again?"

"Appreciate," I said, smirking.

Owen jabbed me in the side with his elbow. "Are you giving me shit about my accent?"

"Not at all," I said. Owen's first three years of life had been spent in Australia. It had been just long enough for some of the accent to stick. His father, who was full-on Australian, met his American mother in Melbourne while she was there on vacation.

She'd canceled her flight home and married Owen's father two weeks later. Owen had come along immediately, and Janna, a year later. Shortly after Janna had been born, they moved to the United States. But Owen's trace of an accent had stuck around all these years. And while I'd teased him about it for most of our lives, I'd always found it so charming and so fascinating and so knee-buckling that it unplugged me from rational thought.

Which was exactly why I opened my mouth again and said, "I've always loved your accent, actually." *Shut up, Grace. Shut up.* But my clown car of words just kept tumbling on out. "I used to stand on the other side of your bedroom door and listen while you were on the phone with your friends. Or else hover outside the garage while you mumbled to whatever project you were working on." I laughed once, a semi-hysterical bark. I'd never been in less control of my words. "Probably this sounds an awful lot like stalking. Like, one small step away from 'Does this washrag smell like chloroform to you?' But the fact is, I like the way your words rumble in your chest. I like the way they sound."

He turned toward me, and our eyes met.

My heart buckled.

Neither of us moved. We were maybe a couple of inches apart, too close, and his breath was mixing with mine.

Reaching up, he traced a finger along my jaw to my cheek, and then behind my ear, finally cupping his hand around the back of my neck. I closed my eyes, feeling him cross the short distance between us. And he kissed me, just barely. Unsure, feathering his lips on mine. Then his other hand snaked around to my back and he said my name, pulling me closer and kissing me in a feverish way that bordered on panicked.

We didn't even hear Janna step into the room.

When I first realized she was speaking, her voice seemed far away, like sound filtering its way around a mountain.

"What the hell?"

Owen and I flew apart. My hands gripped the couch cushion. I was too terrified to look at Janna, so I kept my eyes on the ceiling fan, trying to imagine it drying the sweat off my forehead. I'd always hated confrontation.

"What the hell?" Janna said again, louder this time. "Don't sit there and pretend that I didn't just see you two totally hooking up. You promised me, Grace."

Owen stood up. "Janna —"

Janna whirled toward him. "Shut up, Owen."

I was still avoiding eye contact with her, but I knew she was staring at me now, because I could feel her eyes burning holes into the side of my face. So I let my gaze slide down to her, and I met her stare.

Which was terrifying, for the record.

She had toweled her flaming-red hair partially dry, and it was sticking up in curly tufts all over her head. Her cheeks were covered in angry ruddy patches.

"Look," I said, trying to keep my voice even, trying to keep myself from sounding as hysterical as I felt, "Owen and I are —" I stopped abruptly, because what was I going to say, even? I had no idea what Owen and I were right now. I cleared my throat. This was the moment I should tell Janna the truth about my feelings for Owen. I knew that. But there was no way I'd do it with Owen listening. So instead I said, "I like hanging out with Owen."

She just stared at me for a heartbeat. A drop of water dangled off one of her curls and then fell to the carpet, producing a round, dark blotch. "You like hanging out with Owen," she repeated.

I folded my arms over my chest. "Yeah. I mean — yeah."

"Fine," she said evenly.

"Fine?"

"Fine. Hang out with him, then."

It wasn't fine, though. She didn't like sharing me with Owen. And even though I tried to divide my time equally between them, and even though I did my best to make Janna feel at ease, she turned reserved, polite, as though I were a parent or a teacher rather than a best friend. She never turned her full-force animosity or jealousy on me, not exactly. Our friendship just fizzled, like I'd thrown a bucket of water on a fire: the coals were still there, but they'd stopped glowing. They were cold.

Seven

I've cracked a little the past couple of years. From the stress, I'm guessing.

Like, refusing to speak to my new foster parents for weeks on end, and playing my violin till my fingers bled, and — best sit down for this one — hiding three stolen wallets in the bottom of my suitcase.

Yeah.

I've developed some interesting tics.

Okay, so mostly one particular tic. Pickpocketing.

Probably a clever, self-respecting criminal would've just pocketed the cash and ditched the wallets in a Dumpster. But then a clever, self-respecting criminal wouldn't gift all the money to a particular Tampa business on the corner of Second and Twentieth, either, so I suppose I'm neither clever nor self-respecting.

In foster care, I always hid the wallets under my mattress. Not possible at Rusty's, where my futon mattress rests on a wooden rack that would be best described as a barbecue grill. So that morning I transfer all my clothes to my bedroom desk — the closest thing I have to a dresser — tucking the wallets underneath a stack of T-shirts.

I stand in the shower until the water runs cold, and then quietly towel off and dress, wholly unnerved by the too-silent house. Memories are like land mines that I step on everywhere I turn. Outside the bathroom window is the old, dilapidated swing set that I had totally forgotten about, both swings still wound tightly around the poles on each side, where they've been ever since the sixth grade when Janna became obsessed with whether she could swing high enough to flip herself clear over the top.

Furthermore, it's nearly impossible to walk down the hallway without a quick glance at the other spare room, where I always used to sleep. It's still covered floor to ceiling in posters of Europe, from back when I went through one of those I-want-to-travel phases and Rusty permitted me to tweak the decor. The nightstand is still peppered with the lucky sand dollars Dad gave me, the dresser is still home to an off-white lamp, and the bed, well, it still dons a familiar blue quilt.

Those things mean nothing, I tell myself every time I walk past. Still, my hands clench into fists, nails biting into my palms, as blurry images crowd my mind, packed so tightly it seems like they might split my skull. Old wounds, for sure, but they still stab as sharply as ever, so I spend a good hour wandering from the living room to the kitchen, and then back to the living room. The place feels flimsy and rickety, like it might topple into a heap if I lean the wrong way. When I was younger, Rusty and I used to pile into his truck practically every summer morning, making the ten-mile trek to a roadside diner, where we'd eat waffles topped with whipped cream and strawberries. Or else he'd sneak me into the bar during his shift at work, and I'd sit in the unused back office in front of a boxy, old-school TV, eating microwave popcorn and watching the sort of R-rated movies that Dad would never approve of.

Now, though, Rusty is nowhere to be found.

In the kitchen, I throw some grounds into the coffeemaker. Slouching against the counter while the coffee brews, I drum my fingers on the Formica and stare at the pictures that adorn the fridge. Some of the photos are familiar; they've been there since before I can remember. They are Rusty and Dad and me, all in different configurations and ages. But others are new, totally foreign — fishing trips, cookouts, football games. All the stuff I've missed.

The message is clear: life has gone on for Rusty.

Suddenly something enormous and barbed is swelling in my throat, and I'm finding it painful to swallow.

Sometimes, I really feel like I was abandoned.

This happens to be one of those sometimes.

Doing my best to ignore the thick, sour shot of resentment, I spin away from the fridge. And just as I do, the front door flies open and I jump like crazy, sucking in my breath and banging my elbow on one of the cabinets. I whirl around and find Rusty's mother, Eleanor, thumping her way into the house, a massive black purse looped on one forearm and a duffel bag on the other. She stops short, blinking at me for several moments, surprised.

So Rusty didn't tell her I was coming.

Fine. Whatever. I wasn't expecting a parade.

Eleanor bumps the door shut with her hip and drops her duffel bag at her feet. "Hey, slick," she says. Her standard greeting.

I take a couple of steps in her direction, wondering whether I should hug her. While she's lived with Rusty for years, we've never actually been close. She makes no move toward me, so I hitch to a stop, cross my arms and lean nonchalantly against the wall, directly underneath a stuffed marlin. Though I'm fairly certain that there's no way to lean nonchalantly underneath a stuffed marlin. "Hey, Eleanor," I say.

She stares at me for a moment — longer than necessary, to be perfectly honest — and then, with a sideways smile, she says, "Nice to see you, kid." And she hobbles her way to the counter to unload her purse. In her early twenties, she was an army nurse. Not a big deal these days, but back then it was sort of badass to be a woman working right in the middle of a combat zone. She didn't last long, though; she was discharged because a bomb dropped on her barracks, causing a beam to effectively squash her lower right leg. As a result, she moves like she's made of bulky, mismatched factory parts. "How've you been?" she asks, shifting her weight from foot to foot.

"Okay, I guess," I say, watching her. I'd forgotten how she's always in motion. A bundle of clunky, kinetic energy.

She jerks open the fridge door and peers inside, like maybe she thinks some elves dropped by in the middle of the night and brought some real food. I've already discovered that the fridge contains one Styrofoam takeout container, a dozen or so Michelobs and something that appears to have been derived from Spam. Eleanor closes the door, turns around to face me and says, "Sorry about your dad."

And there it is.

This marks the first time Dad has been mentioned inside these walls since I arrived, and the air seems heavier because of it. To her credit, Eleanor does appear sorry. But the fact remains — she wasn't sorry enough to attend Dad's funeral.

"Thanks," I say. For some stupid reason, I think maybe she'll explain Rusty's actions — or nonactions, rather — over the past couple of years. But she just stands there and stares at me. Clearing my throat, I turn away and busy myself by finding a few stray packets of coffee creamer. When I turn back around, she's still gawking at me like I'm a painting at a museum — *Pathetic Orphan*, circa 2018. The buttery morning sun shines through the window, backlighting her springy gray hair and making her look as though she has a halo.

A total sham.

"So," I say. I'm such an artist with the English language. I should be writing Broadway plays or penning catchphrases for condom commercials.

"So," she says pleasantly, rocking back on her heels.

A long moment passes when I hear nothing but the distant caw of a seagull. I glance at the clock on the microwave. Ten thirty-five. It's going to be a long day. Clearing my throat, I pour two cups of coffee and slide one down the counter in her direction. She squints at it for a second and then hobbles her way over to pick it up, making a sour face at the steam as she takes a noisy sip. I follow suit, the coffee burning a trail all the way down to my stomach.

She smells like cigarettes. Or else, cigarettes smell like her. I've never known which. She's smoked since before I knew her, and has been racking up heart attacks for almost as long. In point of fact, under the skin in her upper chest she has a rect-angular device that serves to shock her heart into working if it craps out on her. By interesting coincidence, it's exactly the same size as her cigarette packs.

I'm not technically related to Eleanor — Dad and Rusty shared only the same father — but I've known her for so long that I feel as though I am. Which is exactly why I'm certain that she's about to say something that would be best kept to herself.

"Looks like maybe you've put on a little weight around the middle," she says, all matter-of-factly.

Here my self-esteem has been hovering around normal, and I've been waiting for a senior citizen to knock it down to nega-tive twenty thousand.

"Maybe a couple of pounds? I'm not really sure." I say this warily, a red flag that she's sticking a toe over an invisible line, if she's actually paying attention.

She isn't.

She gives me a wide, hospitable smile and then kicks off her shoes in the middle of the floor, curling her toes under till her joints crack.

Changing the subject, I tip my head toward her duffel bag and say, "Were you on a trip?"

She shrugs, plucks a magazine from a stack of mail strewn across the counter, studies it vaguely and then tosses it back in the pile. She's been talking to me for all of two minutes, and she's already fidgety. She hobbles her way out of the kitchen. "Was at the casino for a few days," she says over her shoulder, grabbing her duffel bag and stabbing a thumb over her shoulder, toward her bedroom. "Well, I'm just gonna —"

"I was just leaving to go for a walk," I blurt. And before she can reply, I'm grabbing my purse. I'm shoving on my sunglasses. I'm hustling out the front door. Because if anyone in this house is going to walk away this time around, it's going to be me.

Eight

I regret this decision immediately. First thing I see after I scramble down the porch steps is Janna, standing at the window in front of the McAllisters' kitchen sink, filling a glass with water. I feel — suddenly and with mounting anxiety — like I'm about to burst into tears.

I don't, though. I don't do anything, actually. I don't call out to her. I don't wave or try to get her attention. I just freeze right where I am, open-mouthed and idiotic, for I don't know how long, my feet slowly sinking into Rusty's front lawn, the sticky, humid air like a wet blanket shoved into my lungs.

Janna looks the same, only slightly skewed in some obscure way that I can't quite put a finger on — her hair a bit longer or her chin more angular — as though she were a supporting character in a dream I was having. Other than that, she's still all tangly red curls and gingham dresses and quirkiness, still unconventional and adorable. Just seeing her feels throbbing and slow and painful, like a toothache.

This is the girl whose secrets and juice boxes I used to share, the girl who talked loudly and obnoxiously through every Netflix series we ever watched. For most of our lives, we orbited together inside the same tiny universe, and yet today we are virtually strangers. I wonder whether she's missed me like I've missed her. Whether she's missed *us*.

Swallowing once, I duck my head and pretty much run across the road to the beach, the shortest route to town. Everything in New Harbor that isn't a beach is old and quaint, and what isn't old and quaint is some version of pink. The beachfront is lined with just a handful of shops and restaurants: a general store, one of those touristy shops that sells puka necklaces and beach towels, a couple of antique stores, an ice-cream parlor, a burger joint, a pizza place and a bar.

And that's it.

In other words, if you want to get to downtown New Harbor, walk straight down the beach and then turn left — into 1958.

Even so, the stores I've wandered into year after year, the buses that transport tourists back and forth from hotels and beaches and outlet malls in neighboring cities, the boardwalk benches where I've sat and eaten ice cream with my family, the sand I've dug my feet into since before I could walk — all of it, everything, is as much a part of me as my own skin.

Before I can stop it, a sort of peace settles in my chest.

This.

This feeling.

Right here, right now. This sense of familiarity and history and belonging — I want to clutch it to my chest and never let it go.

I finally feel like I'm home. Or I'm remembering what home

feels like. I'm not sure which. All I know is that I can breathe again. In front of me is a long sprawl of white sand, and beyond that, the Gulf of Mexico. I stare at the ocean but don't go any farther, not even tempted to walk down to the shore and stick a toe in the water. Because, historically, a lot of terrible things have happened in the ocean. Shark attacks, for one. Also, jellyfish stings. Drownings. Rip currents. Bacterial diseases.

Etcetera.

Shielding my eyes with my hand, I watch a fishing catamaran whiz by offshore. Back when I was in elementary school, Dad bought a cheap, broken-down fishing boat, and he and Rusty spent an entire week coaxing the motor into running. I had no idea how either of them learned to fix it, and I was pretty amazed when they put it in the river and it actually ran. When I questioned Dad about it, he told me that it was in a man's genetic code, mending broken things, and by the time I got into high school I almost believed him. By then he'd fixed our dishwasher and changed the timing belt in his car and nursed our water heater back to health and tweaked the gears in my bicycle.

Just then, the hum of an engine catches my attention. I turn my head to find a small, skinny boy driving down the beach in one of those lifeguard four-wheelers. I recognize him immediately as Andy Simon.

Simon, as in: the family that used to live next to Rusty.

Simon, as in: the family that packed up and moved across town, allowing my worst nightmare to move in.

While the Simons lived next to Rusty for years, I've mostly known Andy through Janna. Andy was Janna's Other Best Friend, the one she hung out with when I was at home in Tampa.

Over the years, there was an awful lot of competitiveness between Andy and me, even though (1) he always joked about the best-friend-competition thing, and (2) he refrained from calling, texting and pestering Janna whenever I was in town, so I imagine that (3) it was probably pretty annoying when I called/texted/pestered Janna three hundred times an hour whenever they were hanging out, so I guess that (4) I was the only one competing.

Anyhow, when I see Andy, I'm not sure whether to wave or to run in the other direction. No time to figure it out, though, because he turns and looks right at me. He gives me a bit of a shocked look and then a weird little salute, and in doing so, his passenger-side wheel grazes one of those NO DOGS, NO ALCOHOL, NO MOTORIZED VEHICLES beach signs, bending it over cockeyed. He kills the motor and leaps off, his head jerking around in all directions. His gaze finally lands on me. Every part of his face is bright red. He says, "If my boss saw me hit that sign, I'm dead." He draws a finger across his neck, just in case there's any question as to the meaning.

I say, "I doubt that —"

"No. Seriously. He goes by the three-strikes-you're-out rule, and I got to the third strike, like, several strikes ago. I'm on borrowed time. Tell me, the guy at the lifeguard station? The one over my left shoulder — don't look *now*, for Christ's sake — is he looking at me? Just pretend to pick something up and glance over there, please."

I'm an actress in my own life.

Andy gives me a hurry-up gesture.

I clear my throat. "Right," I say. "Okay." I bend down to the sand, and as I come back up, I glance toward the lifeguard stand, where a boy probably a few years older than me is staring at us, wearing a bright yellow lifeguard T-shirt and a scowl. I say, "Um."

"Shit." Andy turns around and waves to his boss, thoroughly casual. "I'm totally getting fired today," he says through his smile, without even moving his lips. "Pretend that you twisted your ankle and I jumped off the four-wheeler to help you, tragically hitting the sign in the process." He prompts me with his eyes. "Do it, please."

And here's the thing: I do. As strange as it is, this feels like the most normal exchange I've had since I set foot in New Harbor. I hobble toward a nearby bench and grip my leg, feigning pain as Andy kneels down and pretends to tend to it. "So you're a lifeguard now?" I ask, glancing at his ear. The thing about Andy is that he has only about fifty percent of his left ear. Back when he was four, a dog bit off the entire bottom portion. Consequently, all of his profile pictures have literally been taken in profile.

The two of us have always had an unspoken pact: I don't stare at his ear and he doesn't stare at my nose. So my eyes dart away as Andy, poking around on my ankle, says, "Yeah. But probably not for long. I've already been reassigned to" — he glances up and makes finger quotes — "ground duty."

His boss shakes his head a couple of times, spins around and then climbs back up on his tower. I say, "Your boss isn't watching anymore."

Andy's eyebrows shoot up. "Yeah?"

I nod, and Andy tosses a quick look over his shoulder. Convinced he's in the clear, he walks to the fallen sign and tries to jam it back into position, an action that he lacks either the strength or the cunning to accomplish. Possibly both. Leaving it sloping and crooked, he collapses next to me on the bench. "So, Grace Cochran," he says, grinning idiotically at me for a moment, like he's mulling over my last name's endless dick-joke possibilities, "you're back in town."

"Yup," I say.

"Cool. For how long?"

"Indefinitely."

"No shit?"

"I shit you not," I say.

I wait a couple of ticks for Andy to ask why I'm living here. Or else mention Janna. But he doesn't. All he says is, "So you'll be going to New Harbor High this year?"

I wince mentally. The thought of walking up and down the hallways in Janna's school makes me slightly nauseated. "Yup."

He rubs his palms together. "Need a date for homecoming? Happy to oblige."

His question seems so abrupt, so odd, that I almost laugh. Is he joking? He doesn't seem to be. He's looking at me intently, awaiting my answer. "I'm not much for school dances," I say finally.

Not exactly a no, but he shrugs good-naturedly, appearing to understand the subtext. "So. Senior year," he says, crashing back against the bench, a small smile on his face. "Can't wait to graduate and get out of New Harbor."

I raise my brows at him but don't comment, because all I want to do is stay. All I want is to find a way to be comfortable here. New Harbor — it's home to so many happy and horrific moments. It's the happy ones, though, that have the most pull. Family has magnetic properties, it seems, and foster kids know this attraction more than anyone else.

Exhibit A: Mia, who lived with the Marios for a short time and whose mother was a train wreck — drugs and violent boyfriends and God knows what else — yet Mia always yearned to go back home.

Exhibit B: Me.

Andy and I are silent for a moment or two, and then he reaches down to brush a bit of sand from his leg. The motion causes his wallet to slide out of his pocket and slip through the slats in the bench. It lands soundlessly in the sand beneath him.

I jab him with my elbow and gesture to it. Because I have strict rules when it comes to thievery. The first one is nonnegotiable. The victims have to be assholes. Not just run-of-the-mill assholes, either — they have to be the infuriating, exasperating, greasy sort of asshole who looks down your shirt or up your dress or otherwise makes you feel completely naked. Second, the victims cannot be wealthy. Also unconditional. Stealing a hundred dollars or more is considered a felony, and while, admittedly, I'm a lot of things, I'm not a felon. Third, there has to be zero risk of getting caught. If I can't get away with it clean, it's not going to happen. I would not survive two seconds with the sort of kids who populate juvenile hall. I know this without a doubt, because I've lived with those types of kids in foster care, and the only thing that stopped them from kicking my ass on a daily basis was the fact that there were too many supervising eyes. And lastly, all of the money I take, every last cent, must be donated to my charity of choice.

There are other conditions as well. I have to be wearing my pink sundress, because it makes me appear roughly twelve. The innocence of youth is important when it comes to these things.

And the lucky agate necklace Dad gave me — I need to have that on, as well. Baseball players aren't the only ones who clutch their superstitions like life preservers. Thieves are as superstitious as they come.

So honestly, it takes a lot for all these things to line up. The perfect storm rolls in, say, probably only once or twice a year, which is exactly why I've acquired only three wallets to date, netting a grand total of — *wait for it* — twenty-three dollars.

The first wallet came to me on its own. It was Owen's. I didn't steal it. Not really. It slipped out of Owen's pocket without his knowledge and he left it behind. Initially, I kept it with the intention of using it as a projectile — you know, hurling it at his head right before kicking him in the balls — but that moment never came. Instead, a couple of months later, I calmly took the eight dollars out of his wallet, sealed the cash up in an envelope and sent it to the Hillsborough County Women's Crisis Center. Which, at the time, was the only thing that made sense.

Nine

The time I spent with the Marios was fairly painless.

I mean, "painless" is a relative term — and my expectations were low after the Nose Fiasco. So the correct statement here would probably be: I was pleasantly surprised that I didn't have to hide in the corner of my room with a paper bag over my head.

The first several weeks with foster families are a bit awkward — or at least they were for me. I was that stray puzzle piece that had been left out on a porch for a few days. The humidity and sun had warped me, and I couldn't quite slide into place. I combated this by saying absolutely nothing. This is not a gross exaggeration. For a good three weeks, I did not speak at all. Mrs. Mario found this colossally sad, and — a fan of clichés — she'd pat me on the hand, her eyes a duet of sorrow and worry, and say, "Just take it one day at a time, dear."

Which is probably the most nonsensical saying in existence. Know who else is taking things one day at a time? Everyone. Because that's how time works.

I started talking right around the time that Mia arrived. Mia, who was also temporarily without a family, stayed with the Marios for roughly four months. At the tender age of thirteen, she had more street cred than most professional gangsters, so naturally she found me about as remarkable as Minute Rice.

Mia used to always call me The Mathlete. Only problem with this was that my school didn't even have a math team. Nor was I particularly good at math, for that matter. Fact is, I just *looked* like a mathlete.

Here, in New Harbor, though, I've mostly been known as Janna's Friend, because Janna's personality is so large that it eclipses everything else. Which isn't necessarily a bad thing, but it's a thing, and now, as I walk back to Rusty's without Janna by my side, I feel strangely exposed, particularly when New Harbor High's track team jogs past me on the beach, led by their coach, Janna's dad.

Mr. McAllister's eyes snag on me, his gait hitching a little and his mouth falling open in shock. After a beat, his lips curve up in a tentative smile and he cuts over toward me, signaling the team to continue running.

For the record, I've always adored Mr. McAllister. I'd likely donate my right lung to him if he needed it. So even though Janna and I are shitty, and Owen and I are even shittier, I'm not about to project any of it onto their parents, particularly their father.

"Grace June!" Mr. McAllister hollers, calling me by both my first and middle names, something only he could ever get away with. Not just because he always makes me laugh, and not just because he's a complete pushover, but because he's awesome without even trying to be awesome — with his horn-rimmed glasses and messy hair and gangly limbs. Built like a Pez dispenser, he's tall and straight from neck to foot, so when he wraps me in a hug, lifting me up and squeezing me hard, he has to really bend over to set me back down. "You're back in town!" he says, tipping his head toward me as he waits for my reply. Because of a firecracker incident when he was a kid, he's nearly deaf in one ear, so he has this habit of tilting his good ear toward you during conversation, giving him the appearance of a puppy that's just heard an interesting sound.

"Yup, here I am," I say, holding both arms out as if to present myself. "What are you doing, holding a practice in the middle of summer?"

He wipes the sweat off his forehead with the sleeve of his T-shirt, which is adorned with a large seven-pointed star — his way of broadcasting to the world that he used to be a world-class sprinter in Australia but now leads a mundane existence here on the Gulf Coast of Florida, teaching kids how to hurdle and sprint and throw the javelin and whatever. He says, "Gearing up for a big tournament. The track world does not sleep, m'dear." He pauses for a moment, just smiling at me. "God, it's been forever, hasn't it? How've you been? Do Janna and Owen know you're here?"

"Not sure about Janna, but Owen does," I say, leaving it at that.

"How long are you in town?" he asks.

Here we go.

"Indefinitely, I guess?" He gives me a strange look, so I gesture down the beach, toward Rusty's house, and say, "I moved in with my uncle yesterday." I try to swallow. The motion is incomplete. The rest of my words work their way up my throat slowly and painfully, like they're physical things, almost too heavy to move. "Because my dad died a couple of years ago. From a heart attack? Rusty's actually my only living relative. So, you know …"

His face blanches a little. "I had no idea. I'm sincerely sorry." I can see all the dots connecting in his head — forming the *Where have you been living?* and the *Why did it take you so long to move in with Rusty?* questions — but Mr. McAllister is nice, and nice people don't ask those sorts of questions. So instead he reaches an arm around me and gives me a squeeze. "I'm sure Rusty is honored to take care of you," he says, which is funny, in an unfunny sort of way, because in truth, Rusty doesn't take care of anybody but himself. And he doesn't even do that very well. Mr. McAllister's arm springs free from my shoulder, and he says, "Let me know if you need anything, all right?"

I nod, even though I know that I won't. I've been dealing with Dad's death for nearly two years. The therapist thing? I've done it. I took all my loss and all my guilt and all my sadness, and I handed it to my therapist in a little box. We opened it together and examined everything inside. The five stages of grief? I've gone through them. I denied and blamed and cried and screamed and punched pillows. This isn't to say that I've gotten over Dad's death. You don't ever get over losing someone you love. Grief isn't something you can hurdle. It's something you carry on your back. You just find a way to cart it around without letting the weight of it fold you in half. You learn to live with it, because you don't have a choice.

What Owen did — I shoved that into a box as well. But then I sealed it up with duct tape and hurled it into the deepest, darkest ocean. Problem is, the tide brought it right back to me.

Ten

"Relationships are like yard sales. They look good from a distance, but once you get up close, you realize that all they offer is a bunch of crap you don't need."

The quote is stuck in my head like lyrics from a song.

I can't remember who wrote it, only that Eleanor read it out loud several years ago, from either a magazine or a book, and then she crowed like it was genius. At the time, I rolled my eyes. Now, though, I might nominate the author for a Pulitzer.

So I'm in the kitchen the next morning, waiting for the coffee to brew, counting the relationships in my life where the yard-sale quote applies and also spraying Lysol all over Rusty's grimy counter, when an unfamiliar blonde woman pads into the kitchen, wearing nothing but Rusty's oversized pajama top, which screams *last night's hookup.*

Ew.

She's right up Rusty's alley — early thirties and pretty, with a waterfall of shiny long hair and a quick, breezy smile.

"You must be Grace!" she says, wholeheartedly friendly, which is sort of alarming. "Wow. I feel like I know you already. I'm Faith." She says her name as though I'm supposed to be familiar with it. When she realizes I'm not, she clarifies easily, "Rusty's girlfriend?"

Ah. A girlfriend.

Rusty has forever been looking for The One, and forever finding her.

"We're practically family," she says, beaming widely, closing the distance between us and throwing her arms around me in a hug, all skinny arms and boobs and hair. Almost as soon as I realize I'm in the hug, I'm out of it, both without any contribution on my part. "Is it nice to be back in New Harbor?"

After a considerable pause, I say, "Um. Yeah. I guess so."

She nods, unaware of my lack of enthusiasm, and then leans against the counter, barefoot and casual, like she's hung out in this particular spot every day of her life. She says, "I'd love to grab lunch with you sometime. Just to get to know each other?"

I hold back a sigh. This is Rusty's doing, no doubt. He's always pushed his women on me, probably because he thinks I'd benefit from a female role model, given that my mom died so early in my life. I glance up at Faith, who's waiting for me to reply. Suddenly I feel as though my mouth has been packed full of thumbtacks. "Okay."

Her face breaks into yet another spontaneous, carefree grin.

I smile back.

Jesus God. This is exhausting.

"Rusty will be out in a minute," Faith says with a quick glance down the hall. "You know your uncle — he's weird about getting dressed and combing his hair before he sees anyone in the morning." Is she actually talking about Rusty? The guy who wanders around the house in underwear that resembles a baggy gray sail ripped off an old pirate ship? Evidently she is, because she leans toward me and whispers, "Rusty's just thrilled to have you here, you know. Between you and me, he can't stop talking about you."

Which is sort of interesting, because at that exact moment, Rusty shuffles into the kitchen, stopping short when he sees me. For a couple of ticks, he looks surprised — like he forgot I moved in. Suddenly my stomach feels uncomfortable, as though someone just inflated a blimp inside it. And then Rusty recovers. "Mornin', G," he trumpets.

He picks up a banana and sniffs it, like it's a foreign object or something. Rusty's steady diet of junk food used to concern Dad to no end. Back when I was five, Dad bought Rusty a Salad Shooter for his birthday, hoping to prompt Rusty into eating healthier. Later that year, Rusty took the very same Salad Shooter, wrapped it in bright red paper and gifted it back to Dad for Christmas. I don't know whether Rusty considered this a joke, his regifting it to Dad, or whether he'd simply forgotten who'd given it to him. Either way, it turned into a joke, because the Salad Shooter was passed back and forth between Dad and Rusty every Christmas from then on, clear till Dad died.

Rusty tosses the banana on the counter, crams his hand into the front pocket of his shorts, pulls out a wad of bills and says, "Been meaning to give you this since you arrived."

I look at the money and then back at him.

Rusty says, "That caseworker lady — Sandra? Sally?"

"Sarah."

"Right. Sarah said you need clothes somethin' awful. Go

buy yourself a few things, on me." He puts his free hand on my shoulder and squeezes.

My vision blurs, and I blink several times.

Why is he doing this? Out of guilt? Probably. He's never given me money in all my life. If he thinks he can just buy me a couple of outfits to erase what he's done, he's delusional. "My clothes aren't that bad," I say. An all-out lie. My wardrobe consists of a handful of smallish sundresses, a pair of shorts, a few state-issued T-shirts and a frayed pair of jeans.

Rusty says softly, "Yeah, they sort of are."

Humiliation burns on my face. "I can buy my own clothes."

Rusty stares at me for a long moment. The kitchen is so quiet that I can hear the refrigerator humming. "Look," he says gently, his hand still on my shoulder, "I'm just looking to do something nice."

My chest constricts, almost like I'm afraid of Rusty, but not quite. I'm afraid of him hurting me again. Afraid of him seeing what I've become. He's so much like himself, so unaffected by everything that has happened, so charmed by the idea that we can somehow become a family now.

I mumble something about having to use the bathroom, and then I spin around and walk out, turning my back on both him and his money. And as I hustle down the hallway, I feel strangely as though I just drove another wedge between us, faster than I knew we were standing close enough to be split back apart.

Eleven

They're too young to be on the bus by themselves, and I'm half tempted to ask their names so I can alert social services. This is exactly the sort of thing that would infuriate Sarah — two unsupervised elementary-aged kids on a bus at nearly ten o'clock at night. While the older boy is taller and has shaggier hair than the younger one, both of them are scrawny and towheaded and freckled. You could draw a slanted, downward line between their two blond heads. They're clearly brothers.

Now, I generally like to mind my own business. But they're sitting directly in front of me, so I can't help but see the older one repeatedly whacking the younger one in the leg, the younger one saying, "Ow," and the older one saying, "Give me your arcade money," and the younger one saying, "No," while the older one smacks him yet again. Then the younger boy finally digs around in his pocket, pulls out a few bills and hands them over to his brother.

And I can't take it anymore.

I lean forward, right next to the older kid's ear. "Give him back his money," I say in a low voice, "or I will sell your kidneys to the devil."

It's sort of hypocritical of me to threaten somebody for hijacking someone else's money. But here's the thing: I've never taken to be an asshole. I've never taken just to take.

This makes me feel rather superior to the kid.

The older boy turns around and glares at me over the top of his seat, surveying my short stature and my mathlete appearance and my bright pink shopping bag.

I stare him down. "*Now*," I say. I'm cranky and exhausted and emotional, frankly miserable from walking around the mall in a neighboring town, trying to find clothing that doesn't make me look ... well, cranky and exhausted and emotional. In the end, I bought a ten-dollar sundress from the clearance rack, just to prove to Rusty that I don't need his charity.

The older boy raises his chin a little, but I can see a tiny spark of fear in his eyes as he digs around in his pocket and fishes out a handful of crinkled one-dollar bills. His eyes still locked on me, he chucks them at his brother. I dismiss him with a bored expression and settle back in my seat. I don't know whether there's such a thing as karma, but if there is, I have to wonder if this particular event will help or hurt mine.

There's only a handful of passengers on the bus tonight. The kids in front of me, a harried-looking lady in hospital scrubs and a couple of men, both wearing dark suits and dark hats and dark frowns, like maybe they're heading to the 1920s to stage a bank robbery.

The bus crosses the causeway and turns right. Outside my window, a familiar pine blinks in and out of view. It comes over me all at once, the feeling I always get when I see that tree. Though I wasn't with Owen at the time, I can see everything inside my head in full Technicolor and surround sound, from the one time he described it to me.

Dan Webb was having an exhibit at some gallery in Orlando, a rare gift for art fans in Florida. Owen was in his Toyota, pulling out of town. In his passenger seat was a small segment of a two-by-four that he intended to use for the artist's autograph. *Lame*, Owen told me, but he'd thought it was fitting.

He said he hadn't even seen the little girl who ran out in front of him.

He said the girl hadn't seen him, either.

Her injuries landed her in the hospital, paralyzed from the waist down. It paralyzed Owen as well. He spent half the summer holed up in his room, avoiding everyone, leaving unfinished projects to gather dust in the garage, ignoring my texts and calls and knocks on his door. I didn't see him for weeks on end, until the very end of summer, on Labor Day weekend. It was probably nine o'clock at night when I heard a tapping on my bedroom door. Figuring it was Dad, I didn't even sit up in bed or open my eyes. I flopped my forearm over my face and croaked, "I just barely took it, so it hasn't started working yet. The world is safe."

The door opened. "What hasn't started working yet?"

Owen.

In one jerky motion, I sat up. Yup, an Owen-shaped shadow was framed by the light in the hallway. I swallowed, suddenly thankful that the room was dark. I'd had the flu for a week straight and hadn't slept in almost as long. Hadn't taken a shower in days. So while, yes, Owen was probably suffering from secondhand BO right now, at least he couldn't see me.

"Dad's Ambien," I explained slowly, because I didn't know what else to do but answer Owen's question. I coughed a little and waited a moment for Owen to reply, and when he didn't, I went on, just filling the space with words. "Evidently, I have the sort of flu that makes sleep impossible, because I've barely slept all week. Which is unfortunate because school starts in two days, which means orchestra tryouts start in three days, which means if I'm going to make it past fourth chair, I need to sleep. So: Ambien, even though it did super-weird things to me last time I took it. I actually got out of bed and showered and got dressed and made an Oreo sandwich. Like, two pieces of bread and Oreos inside? Bizarre, right? And I had no memory of it whatsoever. Dad teased me about it for a month." I paused for a beat. Still no reply. I said, "So."

"So."

Awkward silence.

I filled it with another round of coughing.

Owen still hadn't moved from the doorway.

Finally I couldn't take it anymore. "Are you okay?" I blurted. "What are you doing here?" The end of my sentence was swallowed up in a loud explosion of boos and shouts that came from the living room, where Dad and Rusty and what sounded like a hundred of Rusty's friends were watching the Gators' season opener. Pretty sure they were all drunk.

Owen shut the door, muffling the commotion a little, and then he walked across the room with painful slowness, shoulders hunched. He sat on the very edge of the bed. Fumbling around for a moment, he turned on the reading light beside the bed. I blinked a couple of times and stared at him. He looked terrible. Pale skin. Hair everywhere. Dark smudges under his eyes. Slowly, carefully, he said, "I heard you were sick, so I came to check on you. I was worried."

It was the concern in his voice that killed me. Visceral stab, right in my chest. Because here he was, trying to machete his way through a forest of guilt, and yet he was still worried about me. "Who told you I'm sick?" I said.

He shrugged. "It's a small town."

This was true. Nothing happened in New Harbor without someone leaning over, listening with one ear and then gossiping about it to the entire universe. Lately, most of the gossip had been about Owen. Things like *I heard he's been going to a shrink*, and *The McAllisters are paying the girl's medical bills*, and so on. I didn't know how much of it was true. I was afraid to ask. So I asked the simplest of questions. "How are you holding up?"

His voice sounded defeated as he said, "I've been better."

"I'm sorry, Owen. I'm so, so sorry. I know you think it was your fault, but that girl ran across the street without even looking."

In an exhale, he said, "She'll live her life in a wheelchair because of me."

"I'm sorry," I repeated in a whisper, tucking a stray hair behind my ear. I was starting to feel the effects of the Ambien. My arm felt floppy, like someone had snuck into the room when I wasn't looking and stolen all my bones.

I turned toward Owen. The room tipped on end.

Whoa.

It's strange that, even though my recollection of what happened next has never been clear, I remember the fuzziness of it like it's a dream I've been trapped inside for the past couple of years.

I went into another coughing fit.

Owen stood up. "I should let you sleep."

Jerking to my feet I said, "Please don't leave yet." Even to my own ears, my voice sounded a little weird, like I was speaking underwater. So I got really close to him and spoke loudly, making sure he could hear me. "I've missed you."

A firestorm of emotions filtered through his expression, pain and relief and guilt and longing, and he said, "I think the Ambien is making you loopy."

I held up a finger. It wobbled in the air. "Quite possibly," I said, smiling for what felt like the first time in weeks. I felt euphoric, strangely optimistic, all my problems just melting away. "But I *have* missed you, and I can't stop thinking about you."

Evidently Ambien Grace was a rather Honest Grace.

Didn't matter. It seemed right, telling him how I felt.

He hung one hand on the back of his neck and looked at me. This was good. *This was good!* One hand clamped behind his neck meant he was happy or pleased. Two hands laced together behind his neck — that was a bad sign. I didn't know when I'd learned the meaning of his gestures, but I had.

Seizing the opportunity, I sort of staggered toward him and grabbed his free hand, collapsing on the bed and pulling him down with me. "Staaaaay," I said.

God, it felt good to be near him again.

I scooched close to him. He looked surprised, but he didn't protest or move away. We stared at each other. I felt so weird. Invincible. Like I could do almost anything. Take first-chair violin. Get an A in geometry.

Make out with Owen.

I closed the distance between us and kissed him with all I had in that moment, with a stampede of emotions, with everything I'd felt before we'd gotten together and everything I'd felt since.

Except that I was the only one doing the kissing. Owen was dead still.

I backed away. "Sorry! I'm sorry! You're still messed up from everything. I totally understand. I just —"

He cut off my words when his lips crashed back on mine. His breathing was shallow, rapid, and my hand snaked along the waistband of his shorts.

The sound he made.

It wasn't innocent.

None of my thoughts were innocent. They were a lifetime of watching Owen and thinking about Owen and wishing for Owen. I started to float away. It was the best sensation I'd ever had, spiraling into nonexistence as I melted against Owen. All I knew was his body pressing up against mine and his palm sliding behind my back to draw me even closer. All I knew was his shirt, fisted in my hand, as I inhaled the scent of laundry detergent and soap and Owen Owen Owen.

I was somewhere beautiful.

I was somewhere perfect.

I was kissing Owen.

I was soaring inside my own body.

I was thinking that we were getting carried away.

I was trying to concentrate on my words:

Owen, I'm not ready for this.

I was telling Owen.

I was telling him.
I was saying
Owen
we
need
to
stop.

Twelve

And then everything went black.

Thirteen

When you're a virgin for fifteen years of your life, it's pretty easy to tell when you suddenly aren't. And even if you don't remember it when you wake up the next morning, and even if the boy has long since gone, the tale is crystal clear.

Girl gets loaded on Ambien.

Boy takes advantage of girl.

Girl hates him forever.

The end.

Fourteen

There's this pizza place downtown that Janna and I used to haunt on the weekends, holing up in a corner booth to eat and laugh and tell stories about anything and everything. I'd always bring home leftovers, a slice for Dad and three for Rusty, and also an order of breadsticks, just because I liked the way they made the house smell.

The woman who worked behind the counter used to eye Janna and me suspiciously over her glasses, because during the summer of our eleventh year, the two of us had come here three nights in a row, each time sliding a handful of quarters into the ancient jukebox in the corner of the room, entering "I'm Too Sexy" exactly twelve times, and then sitting down and watching the customers slowly decompose to the tune of Right Said Fred, twelve times in a row.

Today, though, as I wait at the counter for several minutes, the woman — or any employee, for that matter — is nowhere to be found. In front of me, next to the register, is an abandoned cup of soda and an order of breadsticks, and behind me, a growing line of tourists and locals. A man wearing a Red Sox cap and a scowl steps up beside me, rolls his eyes and grumbles, "Five minutes. I've been waiting for a full five minutes, and I haven't seen a single employee."

"I'm sure someone will be right out," I say, glancing behind him. I recognize a couple of the people in line — Logan Davis and Sawyer Simon. I've always liked Logan. He's one of those people who look happy all the time, even while he's talking. It's hard to dislike someone who appears cheerful every living, breathing second of the day. Also, he has one of the most beautiful skull-and-crossbones tattoos I've ever seen, if a skull-and-crossbones tattoo can actually be beautiful. The first time I saw it, I went directly to Dad and spent months persuading him to let me get a small tattoo on my foot, only to chicken out the second I stepped into the tattoo parlor.

Standing next to Logan is Sawyer Simon, Andy's twin brother. While the Simon brothers were technically in utero at the same time, Andy and Sawyer are polar opposites, in both appearance and demeanor. Andy is ... well, *Andy* — a half-missing ear and a bumbling grin. But Sawyer, he's the shining star of New Harbor High's track team, Coach McAllister's protégé and record holder for the 400-meter sprint and, of course, one of the best-looking guys in all of Florida. However, he's fully aware of these things, which makes him wildly unappealing to me. Today, Sawyer's wearing low-slung shorts and a tank top, a pair of aviators parked on top of his head. He's leaning to the side, flashing an unlucky female tourist one of his practiced heart-lurching smiles.

Seeing Sawyer in action is like watching a shocking sports

replay on TV, the sort of replay that shows a player getting a nasty injury — taking a hit that leaves a bone jutting out of his leg or whatever. You don't want to look at something like that, but you just can't help yourself.

That's Sawyer: the sort of guy you watch through parted fingers, half disgusted yet half curious.

He glances up, notices me there and mashes his lips together. After a few ticks, he gives me a nod and a grin that doesn't quite reach his eyes. Pretty sure it's always bothered him that he has zero effect on me.

Still.

He makes me uncomfortable.

And so when I awkwardly turn back around, I knock over the soda on the counter with a fantastic clatter. Like, sticky brown liquid everywhere, dripping off the Formica and splashing onto the floor. I'm grabbing some napkins, attempting to mop up the mess when Janna comes bursting through the double doors that lead to the kitchen, wearing an Island Pizza apron and a harried expression, a stack of pizza boxes teetering precariously in her arms.

Oh shit.

Shit shit shit.

Janna doesn't see me at first. Only the mess I've made. "Great. Just what I need right now," she mutters under her breath, surveying the spilled soda as she deposits the boxes on the counter. Then her eyes trail up to meet mine. Recognition shoots across her features, and then something else — something I can't quite put a finger on. Regret, possibly. Or disappointment. Whatever it is, it causes her to freeze.

Several seconds tick past.

"You work here?" I blurt, and then I groan inwardly. Obviously she works here.

Red Sox Guy clears his throat impatiently. I glance toward him and give him a quick apologetic look. When I turn back to Janna, she's still staring at me. The thing about Janna is that she concentrates on only one thing at a time, and she concentrates all the way.

Currently, she's concentrating on wishing I wasn't here.

"I've been working here for a couple of weeks now," Janna says finally. She's wearing a silver ring on every one of her fingers, thumbs included. Her explosion of curly auburn hair is held into a bun by a pair of chopsticks. It's all very *Janna*, and it makes me miss her, even though she's standing right in front of me. "So you're back," she says.

"Yeah," I say, without as much conviction as I would've preferred. "I mean — yeah." My voice is shaky, totally off-balance, and it hitches in my throat.

Janna flashes a frown that lasts about as long as a movie frame. "Sorry about your dad," she says, her eyes shooting away from me, a talent she's perfected over the past two-plus years.

I start to ask who told her, but then I realize that the information probably came from Owen or her father. It bothers me that I've become a conversation piece in their house. "Thanks," I mutter.

Silence prevails.

Feeling the need to shove words into the empty space, I say, "So how've you been?"

Janna shrugs. "Busy. We've been short-staffed here for the past few days because the lady who works the counter is sick," she says, and then she presses her lips together like she's told me too much.

I nod, cross my arms and then uncross them, and then cross them again. I want to apologize. I want to tell her what her brother did to me. I want to explain how horrible the past couple of years have been. I want to admit that I've been here for almost three full days and I'm still terrified and alone and confused, but before I can say anything at all, Red Sox Guy grumbles, "While this reunion is lovely, the rest of us might want to eat."

Janna's eyes meet mine, and we share the smallest of looks — a tiny glimpse of us the way we used to be — but then it evaporates. She grabs the top pizza box, all business, and says to me, "Meatball?"

I did, in fact, order a meatball pizza, because the meatball pizza here is absolutely, unequivocally my favorite meal ever. In fact, if you sprinkle the meatball pizza on top of the meatball pizza, I'm pretty sure you can travel back in time. "Of course," I say, my tone matching hers.

After I pay her, and after she hands me my pizza, she gives me a small, courteous wave. And I realize: the past two years, with all their tragedy and pain, haven't changed us one bit. We're still just acquaintances.

Fifteen

Sometimes I think that Dad knew what had happened to me Labor Day weekend, and that was why he had a heart attack.

That it literally broke his heart.

He knew something had gone horribly wrong with Owen and me that weekend. This much was true. I was a zombie the entire hour and fifteen minutes home, refusing to speak, staring blank-faced out the passenger-side window of Dad's car as he drove through Bradenton and over the Skyway Bridge. When we got home, I walked straight to my room, locked my door, turned on my computer and typed *Ambien* and *sex* into a search engine, looking for answers. Looking for anything, really, because I couldn't remember any of it. Not a single, solitary moment.

Online, I found dozens of stories resembling mine.

Owen texted me around noon — just a *Hey, is your flu on the mend?* sort of text — not even acknowledging what he'd done. It was a slap in the face, really, and it proved to me that his accident had completely changed him. That I didn't even know who he was anymore. So I blocked his number. I threw away all of his pictures. I cried into my pillow.

My sorrow was so loud.

It was a bass speaker, pounding in the house, shaking the windows, crashing open the front door.

Dad must have heard it.

I kept telling myself that I'd confront Owen. But then school started, so I promised myself I'd do it after I got situated in my classes, and then after I tried out for orchestra, and then after my biology test, and then after the weekend, and then after the end of the month. After. After. After.

But I didn't.

I didn't.

Mostly, I was ashamed. It's a corrosive thing, being ashamed.

And maybe Dad felt it and maybe he didn't, but the fact is, he'd been perfectly healthy all of his life, and then right in the checkout line at Publix, he just collapsed. And when I found myself next to his hospital bed, pleading to God — tubes snaking out of Dad's body and a machine breathing for him — I found that Owen was the easiest thing to forget.

Sixteen

"Hey."

Faith jerks around toward me, surprised. Or at least I think it's Faith. She looks completely different than she did a week ago, when she padded into the kitchen wearing Rusty's pajamas. Her blond hair, which hung halfway down her back that morning, is now cut into a bouncy, shoulder-length bob.

I've been outside for probably thirty minutes now. I come out here sometimes, right before sunup, just to sit on the steps, arms wrapped around my pulled-up legs, listening to the cicadas and the quiet lapping of the Gulf, the heavy, humid air pressing down on me like a paperweight. It's consistency I'm after, I think, some sort of evidence that certain things are constant. This morning is the first time I've caught Faith slipping out of the house, though.

"Hi!" she says, sort of loudly, shifting her weight and blinking her doe eyes a couple times. She points with her thumb to her car. "I was just leaving. It's not like I stay overnight a lot."

Glancing at her bare feet, she laughs once, just a quick *ha*, grinning with a friendliness that makes me feel horrible for the things I thought about her the first time we met. "Okay, so I kind of stay here a lot. But I won't anymore if it bothers you."

I shrug. "It's fine." At this, she collapses down beside me on the steps and starts putting on her sandals. She smells like dryer sheets and daisies and clothes you find at Target. Her face is smooth and makeup-free, and she looks probably a decade younger than her actual age. Glancing sideways at her, I say, "You cut your hair."

"Oh. Right." Her hand shoots up to her head, like she forgot. "I had this gut feeling I was due for a change. That's something I do — go with my gut. Rusty finds it rather terrifying."

I do my best to fend off the huge smile that I feel migrating to my face. Because what am I thinking? Smiling enthusiastically at Rusty's girlfriend is practically the same thing as smiling enthusiastically at Rusty.

Faith roots around in her purse for a second. "Oh, for Pete's sake," she mutters, pulling out her car keys, which are shellacked together with a melted lollipop.

I raise an eyebrow. "You have kids?"

"I have *twenty* kids." She must see the shock in my expression because she goes on to clarify. "I'm a preschool teacher."

"Ah. Phew," I say, and there I go, starting to smile again. This time, I don't fight it. "Do you like being around kids all day?"

She looks wistful for a moment. "Yeah. I do," she says. Then she pries the lollipop off her keys. Making a face, she wraps the candy in a jumble of tissues she finds in her purse. "Before that, I worked as a secretary for an accounting firm."

"What? Really?" I can't picture Faith in a blazer and sensible heels. Actually, I can't picture her wearing anything that isn't casual or cotton. Which is odd because I hardly even know her. "So why'd you start teaching preschool?"

She stands up and brushes off her backside, shouldering her purse. And then she grins, spontaneous and bright. "I went with my gut."

#

My conversation with Faith blasts some sort of fresh air into my head, and by afternoon I feel like I might actually be capable of a little female bonding. So I stride out of the house like I'm wearing heels and lipstick, like I'm heading to a women's rights protest or something. Suddenly I have a purpose, even though it's only to try to sort a few things out with my former best friend. I have to believe that while my relationship with Janna is fractured, it isn't broken beyond repair. In fact, it's quite possibly the only connection here that I might be able to salvage, and I need that desperately right now.

There's no way on God's green earth I'm knocking on the McAllisters' front door, so I head to Island Pizza on the off chance that Janna's working again. By the time I step into the restaurant, I've almost convinced myself that I won't find her there, so I'm mildly surprised to see her leaning casually against the counter, bright red apron tied around her waist, hair twisted into knots all over her head, talking to Andy. I pause for a moment just inside the doorway, my heart thrumming in my ears. Suddenly I feel like I'm doing something vaguely dangerous or criminal, like scaling over a fence onto private property.

It's midafternoon, so the only customer is an old guy in a

corner booth, sipping soda and penning answers into a cross-word puzzle. Neither Janna nor Andy notice me right away. Andy is leaning across the counter, laughing, saying something to Janna as she beams back at him, sunrise bright. I look sharply away. I think about all the mistakes in my past — some Janna knows about, and some she doesn't. No way could I tell her about what happened with her brother. Sharing that particular secret would create a whole new sort of misery between us. Just thinking about it now thrusts me back in time — all of a sudden I'm waking up in that bed again, groggy and confused and dehumanized, every trust I've ever had in the world slipping away like sand through my fingers.

I swallow. I'm still alive, though.

I'm okay.

I can do this.

I don't walk straight up to her. Instead, I make a beeline for the old-school jukebox in the corner of the room. The place is suddenly dead quiet. I'm very aware that my little ambush has caught Janna's attention. My whole body goes prickly and warm as I run a shaky index finger down the glass in search of one particular song. When I find it, I root around in my purse for a quarter, pop it into the machine, key in the song number and press the play button. Then, trying to look much calmer than I feel, I walk up to the counter to the tune of "I'm Too Sexy."

Like old times.

Janna arches an eyebrow as I come to a stop in front of her. I can't tell whether she's annoyed or impressed. Andy shifts his weight and tugs down on his faded black T-shirt that says *I was into Civil War reenactments before it was cool*, which may or may not be ironic. He props his hands on his hips and then drops them to his sides. "Hey, Grace. How are you? Calzones are on special today. I was just leaving." And he practically runs out the door.

I chew on my thumbnail.

Here's the thing: I've always had a very clear sense of the rules of friendship. And I know without a doubt that I'm the one breaking them. Or that I *had* broken them — same difference, seeing as how I've let this awkwardness drag on so long. Fact is that I never actually apologized to Janna; I flushed eleven years of friendship down the toilet and then didn't even bother to say I was sorry. What sort of person *does* that?

I steady myself with a hand on the counter, where Janna is busying herself by wiping down the already gleaming Formica. "So I was never good at this, you know," I say.

Janna raises both brows. A light coat of mascara is the only makeup she's wearing, so her freckles are out in full force. "This?"

Suddenly I'm exhausted, like I haven't slept for two years. "Confrontation."

Janna just stares at me, and then she rolls her eyes. A renegade curl has escaped one of her knots and is springing straight up in the air. "That's a bullshit excuse and you know it," she says. Yet she doesn't appear *mad* mad. Her expression is annoyed, like she's been waiting for this moment for God knows how long, and now that it's come, it's a total letdown.

I draw in a breath, and in my exhale, I say, "Look, I'm sorry. About Owen. About everything. I should have — I should have stayed away from him."

Understatement of the century.

Unblinking, Janna says, "My appendix burst last year. I've

never felt pain like that. Dad had to actually carry me into the hospital, and I ended up having emergency surgery. It was terrifying. And Owen" — I flinch before I can stop myself — "he was a mess for months after the accident. Total disaster. And that's not even to mention what Mom and Dad have been through. The girl from the accident? My parents felt obligated to pay for her medical bills. *All* of them. So, yeah, we ended up totally broke. It would've really helped to have my best friend the past couple of years, Grace. But you disappeared off the face of the earth."

"But you were mad at me," I say. It comes out in a whine.

"I was *hurt*, actually," Janna says. Her eyes are leveled on mine, but her lower lip is trembling the smallest bit.

I fold my arms over my stomach. "I'm so sorry." My voice is just a whisper. "I just — I just wanted to make sure you knew that. What I did was stupid and careless and I'm so, so sorry for hurting you."

I wait for a moment for her to say something, but she doesn't, so I turn and walk slowly toward the door. The song hasn't even ended yet. Pathetic. But Janna's eyes snag on mine right before I walk out, and she gives me a small nod.

Seventeen

"Because it's bigger," I explain to Rusty late the next morning
when he asks, for probably the fifth time since I moved in, why
I'm sleeping in this particular room instead of the one I've slept
in since I was born. He's hovering in my doorway, shirtless and
unshaven, eating powdered donuts out of one of those boxes
you get two-for-three-dollars. "And there's better light in here,"
I go on, gesturing toward the window. Never mind that my
curtains are closed, because it seems like every time I glance
out the window I see Owen.

I mean, *honestly.*

First thing in the morning, there he is, standing on the
McAllisters' front porch, drinking a cup of coffee and gazing
out at the ocean like he's trying to stare a new truth into it.
And there he goes in the afternoon, heading to the garage,
where he works past dark on whatever project has been holding
him captive. And there he is every Saturday night — just like
freaking clockwork — stepping out of the house in crisply

ironed clothes, climbing into a Jeep and disappearing for hours.

On the other hand, I've lived here for two and a half weeks now, and this is probably the third time I've seen Rusty. He's always hanging out with Faith or working at the bar or fishing or sleeping. I don't know what I was expecting from him when I moved in, but it wasn't quick, informal conversations in front of the coffeepot, all of them variations of "Hey, how's it going?" or "Sure is hot today."

Now, as he hovers in the doorway, he repositions his hat, leaving powdered-sugar fingerprints on the brim. "Well, at least let me buy you a bedspread," he says, gesturing to the old, crumpled-up blanket thrown over my sheets. I don't know whether he's remembering how I reacted when he offered to buy me clothes, but he shifts his weight, looking nervous all of a sudden, like maybe he's afraid he crossed some sort of line again. It isn't an expression I remember from all those years growing up. He's always been so confident.

"I don't need a bedspread," I tell him.

He peers into the room, the corners of his mouth slightly downturned. "Seems weird, your sleeping in here."

I understand the implication. This room was where Dad always slept. And if I look out of the corner of my eye, I can almost see Dad in here, leaning against the wall, one leg kicked out casually, watching Rusty and me like he used to, back when our relationship wasn't painful.

"But if you want to call it your own, I s'pose that's your deci-sion," Rusty says, snapping my attention back to him. Just like that, Dad's gone.

I stare at Rusty for a moment, thinking maybe he'll actually mention Dad. Which is beyond misguided. It's clear that Rusty and I will never really discuss Dad's death, that my feet will remain stuck in this quicksand of confusion and sadness.

True to form, Rusty takes a step back, reminds me that I have an appointment coming up with my therapist, nods a goodbye and ambles away.

#

Literally every horizontal surface in the house is dirty, so that afternoon I grab a rag and a spray bottle and start cleaning. Keeping busy is the best way to ignore Eleanor, who seems constantly underfoot, hanging out in the living room or wandering the hallways or burning something in the kitchen. Even when she isn't home, I feel as though she is, with her ashtrays and half-empty soda cans dotting the house and her glops of makeup in the bathroom sink.

This afternoon, she's sitting on the couch, my violin in one hand and a glass of booze in the other, wearing a white robe with a huge, dignified-looking family crest embroidered on the front. Which is noteworthy only because (1) she's been wearing it for two days straight, and (2) we don't have a family crest, and if we did, it sure as hell wouldn't be dignified. More likely than not, it would consist of a pair of rolling eyes, a prescription for Zoloft and the word *goddammit.*

She strums a chord on my violin, not even bothering to use the bow. Rusty used to do the same thing, except he'd sing along in a loud, twangy baritone, which I always thought was the funniest thing ever. But here, now, with Eleanor plucking at the strings, it feels a little patronizing. "Do you like playing this thing?" she says pleasantly.

I blink at her. "Do I like playing that *thing*?"

"That's what I'm asking." She plays a new chord. The violin buzzes disagreeably at her, and she makes a surprised face and goes back to the original chord, humming a tune I don't recognize.

"What sort of question is that?" I say. Eleanor doesn't reply, just props one of her ankles on her opposite knee and jiggles her foot, awaiting my answer. It isn't a condescending gesture, but it sort of feels that way. I wonder whether it's a gift of hers — making me feel idiotic without even trying. I dismiss her with a wave of my hand, sliding out of the room to find some more paper towels. When I come back, she looks at me as though she's still waiting for my answer. So I sigh and say, "Of course I like playing it."

With the violin, there's no bluffing your way over a twisty spot, like you can with the guitar. There's no lying, because it will call you out, expose all your weaknesses. And I have a lot of weaknesses. Still, I love playing the violin. I love listening to it. I love humming along with it. I love the way the bow feels in my hand. I even love the way my neck aches after I spend hours practicing.

Nobody else in our family is musically inclined. In fact, Dad and Rusty burst out laughing when I informed them that I wanted a violin for my birthday. I was nine years old, and back then the world seemed huge and endless and full of possibility. So I stood there, hands on my hips, and stared them down till they stopped. When they realized I was serious, they swallowed their laughter and did their best to humor me. Figuring it was just a whim, Dad bought me the cheapest violin, an old Stentor that I practiced on till my fingers chafed. Through the years,

I've gone through three more before settling on a Mendini that seems more like a friend than anything else. I never took lessons. Instead, I taught myself how to play — just the internet, my stubbornness and me. Money was always tight for us, and I never gathered enough nerve to ask Dad if we could afford lessons. I have to wonder how much better I'd be right now if I'd been taught by a proper teacher.

Eleanor's ice jingles as she takes a long pull of her drink, yanking me back to the present. There's probably nothing wrong with drinking alcohol in the middle of the afternoon. But then, there isn't much right about it, either. And since my mom died from alcohol abuse when I was two, I have strong opinions on the matter.

I crouch down to wipe the dust off the entertainment center. "I mean, I've played for a long time." Eleanor leans back on the couch and nods at me, her overly pleasant expression indicating she's indulging me. I fold the paper towels in half and clean behind the television. "I guess there's something calming about it," I go on, doing my best to keep from sounding defensive. "Over the past couple of years, it's been … I don't know — helpful, I guess?"

It's an honest thing to say to her — more honest than I intended, really — and once I say it, I half expect her to laugh. That doesn't happen, though. She has a strange set to her mouth, like maybe she's getting ready to say something serious. She must decide against it, though, because she swoops one arm dramatically at the front window and changes the subject. "Hang out on the beach much since you've been back?" she asks.

"Nope," I say. Eleanor cocks a questioning eyebrow at me, so I clarify. "It's too hot."

She shrugs. "This is Florida. It's always too hot. You can get in the water to cool off."

I move Dad's lucky bamboo, dust underneath it and then set it back down. Turning toward Eleanor, I say, "I don't really like swimming in the ocean, remember?"

She guffaws like she's never once heard me say this, though I know for a fact that I've told her, time and time again.

I mash my lips together. I will not respond to her. I will not respond to her. I will not respond —

"It's just not my thing," I say, sort of loudly, and then I smile at her. I don't feel like smiling, but I conceal this by scooping up a pile of fast-food bags, walking out the front door and stalking down the driveway to the trash can.

I don't see Owen right away. Not until I've stuffed the bags in the trash and turned to make my way back to the house.

He's standing in front of his garage, watching me.

I feel a familiar stab in my chest, a missile finding its target. I hate how my body reacts to his presence. Also, I hate how I can't walk out of Rusty's house without seeing him, without feeling as though I should wear a disguise. Because why am I ducking around when I haven't done anything wrong? Why am I the one who always feels guilty?

He's the one who took advantage of *me*.

I march toward Rusty's, back straight, chin in the air, not looking in Owen's direction or altering my course or showing any sign that I've seen him.

"Hey," he says.

I whirl around to face him. He's walking toward me, smiling at me. *Smiling.*

God.

It's just like him to disappear when he makes a horrific mistake, and then — *poof* — materialize after the smoke has cleared, acting like everything is perfectly normal.

My voice low and guttural, I say, "Don't you dare smile at me. Not anymore. Not after everything."

Owen's brows furrow.

I roll my eyes. "Oh, my God. Don't give me that innocent look. You know exactly what I'm talking about. You took *advantage* of me, Owen." Which is one way to put it.

It's my stomach that feels the accusation first. Like I just missed a step at the bottom of the stairs. Owen opens his mouth and then shuts it. Shoving both hands in his pockets, he stares at me carefully. Owen has never said anything unsubstantial in all his life, and clearly he isn't going to start now.

The most insane thing? I want to forgive him. He was my friend — no, my childhood crush — and he took something away from me that I'll never get back. I was fifteen and my virginity was stolen and I can't even remember it.

I wait for Owen to acknowledge it out loud. But instead he closes his eyes for a tick and says, "What are you talking about, Grace?"

So he's going to deny it.

"Really?" I basically yell. "You really want me to explain it to you?"

He shakes his head no, but says, "Yes."

"Remember that Labor Day weekend a couple of years back, when I was loaded on Ambien?" He nods. He has this weird look on his face. I keep going. "Last thing I remember, we were in my bed, and I was telling you that things were getting out of control. That we needed to stop. When I woke up, hours later, my pajamas were — I was bleeding and —" I look down because my lower lip is starting to tremble. "You —"

His eyes widen and he takes an unsteady step backward. "What are you saying, Grace?" he whispers. His hand drifts up and covers his mouth. He speaks through it as he says, "You think I ..." He looks at me with unfocused eyes, shaking his head back and forth, like, *no no no no no.*

God, he's good.

I wonder whether he's spent the past couple of years practicing this.

I throw my arms up in the air. "You're denying it. Perfect." My heart is pounding so fast that my toes are starting to prick. Taking a step toward him, I say in a low voice, "Look, you sonofabitch, if I was going to rat you out, I would've done it a long time ago."

"Grace, I don't — that night —" He laces his fingers behind his neck and looks up at the sky for a second. "I mean, things got really out of hand, but I would never do that. We stopped," he says, his voice pleading. "You told me we were getting carried away, and I agreed with you. We just — we talked until you went to sleep, and then I left."

"Come on, Owen. Don't insult me. I'm not an idiot."

"Why would I do that?" he says, his expression earnest. "Why would I do that to you?"

"That's something I've been asking myself for nearly two years," I fire back. I'm close to tears. "Maybe because you were a complete mess at the time? Totally not yourself? Absolutely *unhinged*?"

He presses a closed fist against his forehead. His voice is muffled as he says, "I did not touch you without your consent."

"And why should I believe that?"

His hand falls to his side. "How about because you've known me since you were *four*?" he says, and his eyes are the biggest, deepest pools of sadness.

And for an instant, for a fraction of a second, I believe him. His sincere expression, the tears in his eyes, the long thread of history we've shared. And I'm filled with too many emotions at once — longing and hope and doubt and confusion and anger. But the negative emotions are the ones that elbow their way to the surface first. I wedge both hands on my hips and say, sort of sharply, "And afterward, you thought I wasn't answering your phone calls and texts because …?"

"I thought you were just blowing me off," he says. "That you decided that we weren't worth the hassle. I was a mess, like you just pointed out. You and Janna were all screwed up —"

"Bullshit," I say.

"It's true. And I knew that the only reason you were even kissing me that night was the Ambien. Otherwise you probably would've thrown me out of the room the second you saw me."

I can't do this anymore. Can't look at him. Can't listen to his lies. I spin on one heel and walk away.

Eighteen

I didn't plan on stealing the man's wallet.

My intention was to speed walk down the beach until my feet fell off, in order to get as far away from Owen McAllister as possible. Half of me wanted to keep walking for the rest of my life, and half of me wanted to go back and shake the truth out of him.

It was the last one I was trying to avoid.

I never thought he'd deny it. And every time I remembered that innocent look he'd had, confusion came crashing into my lungs, dark and unending.

Because what if he'd been telling the truth?

I knew Owen. I'd known him for almost as many years as I'd been alive, and he'd looked so *genuine* this afternoon.

And so I walked. I walked until the air felt thin enough to breathe again, and until I had blisters on my feet, and until I finally broke down and hopped onto a bus that was headed toward Rusty's. But then there was this guy standing right next to me in the aisle of the bus. He looked like a burnout twenty-something surfer or a long-lost member of the Beatles. Shaggy, mop-top hair. Slouchy posture. A gaze that landed on my boobs one too many times. Suddenly I felt like a desperate animal with its leg caught in the sharp teeth of a metal trap. Fury and vehemence and panic flashed in my chest, and I had a split second to make a choice: punch him in the face or steal his wallet.

I chose to steal his wallet, obviously.

And now I'm regretting it for several reasons, the most pressing being that after I relocated his wallet and made my exit off the bus, my dress got caught in the bus's closing doors.

The thing about running alongside a bus is that you can't do it for very long. I mean, inside my own mind, I'm quite a runner. My brain understands perfectly how to canter along in quick, graceful strides until the bus gets to the next stop and the doors open. Problem is that my mind has to subcontract the job to my flabby and uncoordinated legs, which aren't graceful at anything. So I stumble as the bus rounds the first corner, my dress rips and, as they say in NASA, I'm launched.

I would've surely face-planted on the asphalt if it wasn't for the rather tan hand that snatched my arm and reestablished my balance. I don't know who I was expecting to have come to my rescue, but it sure as hell wasn't the guy whose wallet is currently residing in my purse.

Um.

I blink at him. "Hiya. Hey," I say finally. *Hiya. Hey?* What am I saying, even? Doesn't matter, I suppose, because it's already come out of my mouth. I glance at the bus as it rumbles away, wishing I could teleport myself back on it. Because what if he knows I have his wallet? What if he followed me off the bus?

What if he calls the cops? What if his sleazy, creepy hand hasn't been washed in months and he's giving me a rare and incurable skin disease?

I shut my eyes and pray to God.

And then to Jehovah.

To Jesus.

To Allah.

To Tom Cruise's god.

I can't tell from the quick peek I had at him whether he's concerned about my safety or concerned about how to kill me without witnesses, so I look down at the asphalt, and my words just start tumbling out of my mouth: "Thanks for that. It would've hurt like hell to fall face-first on this road." I pull down what's left of my dress. "I mean, at best, I would've been banged up pretty badly, and at worst, I'd be suffering from a subdural hematoma. Also, I faint at the sight of blood. Not, like, the Victorian way — by just sort of sinking to the ground — but the hardcore way," I say, illustrating a hard fall with my free hand, adding a sound effect for good measure. This is me when I'm nervous: an entire *Game of Thrones* novel out of my mouth in about two seconds flat. In my defense, his hand is still death-gripping my arm, and panic is starting to set in. "I mean, it's not like I'm *afraid* of blood, per se," I go on. "Not like I'm afraid of snakes or brain cancer. It's just that blood kind of short-circuits my mind into self-preservation mode, and the fainting occurs." I try to straighten up a little in an effort to dignify myself, but I find out quickly that I've tweaked my back somehow, because — *holy crap* — I get this tear-inducing jolt of pain in my lower back. I yelp and my knees start to buckle.

He supports me by the arm. "You okay?" he says, and he

doesn't seem enraged or spiteful or ready to pin a criminal record on me. But here's the thing: he's looking down the top of my dress.

Like, at my boobs.

Which — to repeat — is exactly why I took his wallet in the first place. I mean, I look maybe twelve in this sundress. What sort of disgusting perv is he, anyway?

Rage boils under my skin.

I open my mouth to ask him whether he's on the child predator list and/or whether he's ever been sucker punched in the junk, but then I stop because I remember that his wallet is still in my purse. Best not to press my luck. Wrenching my arm free from his grasp, I take a painful step backward and say, kind of forcefully, "I'm fine."

Keep in mind that I'm still stooped over like the guy who rings the bell in *The Hunchback of Notre Dame.*

"Fact is, you look sorta pale," he says, a toothpick bobbing around in the side of his mouth. His voice is too breathy, and he smells like sweat, and he puts his damp, disgusting palm on my arm again.

I need to run.

I think this so loudly that I wonder whether he hears it. Only he doesn't. I can tell that he doesn't. He's still looking at me like he's alphabetizing my body parts. And maybe I'm just paranoid, and maybe I'm deranged, but all I can feel is his clammy hand on my arm and the sun gluing my hair to my head, and it's like this massive tidal wave has crashed into me and I'm getting sucked underwater, unable to breathe. I keep thinking *It's all right It's all right It's all right,* but it isn't.

IT ISN'T.

"Get the hell away from me," I say through my teeth.

A couple of tourists stop on the sidewalk, watching us.

He looks at them and shrugs like I'm a lunatic, his hand springing free from my arm. Holding his palm up to face me, he smiles, that damn toothpick still bobbing in his damn mouth. "No need to be like that, miss," he says. Then he turns and saunters away.

Nineteen

I get exactly three seconds of sleep that night.

All right, so that's probably an exaggeration. But the thing is, your back makes up a large percentage of your body, so when it hurts, your entire life sucks. I finally out-fatigue my pain around five in the morning, but then I awake what feels like seconds later to a tapping on my forehead. I wrench my eyes open, and my first coherent thought is, *Has Eleanor always had such furry eyebrows?* Which is stupid because I really couldn't care less about Eleanor or her eyebrows. Probably I was dreaming about eyebrows. Or else, silver-colored fur coats. My eyes drift shut again. I'm exhausted, heavy-limbed —

Another rapid-fire tapping on my forehead. *What the …?* I sit straight up, forcing Eleanor, who, yes, is the tapper, to jerk backward in alarm. But I'm even more alarmed because — holymotherofgod — my back is absolutely killing me. How has it gotten so much worse overnight? *How?* I lower down to the futon a centimeter at a time and then, slowly and carefully, turn toward my bedside clock, which is completely blank. Like, off. No numbers whatsoever. I blink a couple of times and then look at Eleanor. "What's going on?" I say, my voice thick from sleep, kicking my feet out of the covers because it's probably a thousand degrees in my room.

Eleanor says, "Don't you have an appointment with your shrink this morning?"

I sink into my pillow. "My *therapist*," I correct. "And the appointment isn't till eleven."

"It's five of."

"Five of *eleven*?" I say. Stupidly, I squint at my blank alarm clock again. It must have died at some point overnight.

Shit.

I fly out of bed. By *fly* I mean that, inch by inch, I gingerly roll out of bed and stand upright. Well, not exactly upright. I cannot straighten my back. Pretty sure that someone snuck into my room overnight, stole my spine, flung it into the road, rolled over it with a tractor and then backed up and rolled over it again for good measure. It's bent to a permanent fifty degrees.

Also: Why is it so hot in here?

Eleanor rubs her chin and smiles. "Grace Cochran has overslept and will be late for an appointment for the first time in the history of the world."

I stop moving because I need my entire body to dislike her.

"You," I say, slowly, "are a child." She shrugs in innocence.

I pull on a pair of shorts and a clean T-shirt. "I did not oversleep," I say, digging a pair of socks out of my drawer. "Not technically. I mean, I set my alarm last night." I make my way toward the light switch and flip it up. Nothing happens. No light. No nothing. I crank it up and down a couple more times, like maybe that will make a difference. "Is our electricity out?"

"Appears that way."

I want to throw something at her. This is in no way a physical possibility, so I roll my eyes. I don't have the mental capacity to come up with anything better. I can't come up with anything at all, actually, so I just hobble out of the room. "Where's Rusty?" I ask over my shoulder.

"Not sure," Eleanor says.

Naturally, Rusty's gone. There's a crisis in my life right now, and Rusty's gone. Again. Suddenly I feel rather old and weary.

Eleanor, who's following me down the hall, says, "What happened to you, anyway? Why are you stooped over?"

I sigh and knuckle-rub my forehead.

I need to go back to bed so I can sleep off her personality.

"I hurt my back."

"You going to be able to drive?" she asks. "I could be your — what's it called? Porter. No, chauffeur. I could be your chauffeur. Where's the appointment?"

"In the medical building by Sarasota Memorial," I say with a sinking feeling. Even with Eleanor's help, I'll be late. "Mind if I borrow your cell?" Eleanor glances toward me, one of her eyebrows almost meeting her hairline. "What?" I say, sort of loudly. "The power is out, so the landline will be dead. And I don't have a cell phone."

"You don't have a cell phone?"

I exhale in a loud gust. "I lived in foster care for the past two years," I say, by way of explanation.

She looks at me, struck dumb, and tips her head toward her purse. "Have at it."

I cancel my appointment first. Then I punch in Rusty's

number, not even giving him time to say hello. "The power is out in the house," I tell him.

Long pause, then: "Right." Rusty's voice is scratchy, like he's recently woken up. I can hear Faith murmuring in the background. Evidently he slept at her house last night. I wait while he clears his throat. "Right," he says again. "The electric company called about a half hour ago. Said they shut it off. Seems I forgot to pay the bill."

I blink. "You *what*?"

His voice a little clearer now, Rusty says, "It's all good. Just an oversight. They were real nice about it. Said they reckon the power'll be back on in about an hour or so."

I unload on the couch, not even trying to stop the colorful four-letter word that comes out of my mouth. Unlike Dad, Rusty has never cared if I curse. Back in middle school, I accidentally slipped and told Rusty he was "the biggest bullshitter I've ever known." When I realized what I'd said, I clamped my lips together and took a step backward, preparing for trouble. But all he did was chuckle. This morning, though, he sounds more sleepy than amused as he says, "Sorry, G. If it gets too hot, just open a couple windows or turn on a fan till the power comes back on."

I hit the END button without another word. Placing Eleanor's phone on the coffee table, I start peeling off my nail polish, just for something to do. Eleanor collapses down beside me and says, "So how'd you hurt your back?"

The question is innocent enough. Some might even consider it polite. Still, though. I don't have an innocent, polite answer, so I keep it simple. "I fell, trying to catch a bus." Which isn't a lie.

"Why?"

"Why what?"

Eleanor crams a cigarette into her mouth and lights it. "Why were you trying to catch the bus?"

"I went for a really long walk, and then I was too tired to make it back home." Again, not a lie. But I hear the slightest bit of defensiveness in my tone, and I'm sure Eleanor has as well.

She knows she's starting to get to the bottom of this.

Taking a hit off her cigarette and pulling one of those rubber-faced maneuvers that smokers do, where they blow smoke off to the side so they don't wallop you with it right in the face, she says, "Did you go for a walk because you had that fight with Owen? Oh, don't get your panties in a wad. It wasn't like I was spying. You were in the driveway, right in front of God and everyone."

"My panties are not in a wad," I say, rubbing my temple. "My private life is none of your business."

She flicks her ashes into her cupped hand, and then glances at me. "So were you? Fighting?"

Oh my lord.

"We were chatting," I say. Then I grimace, because never in my life have I said the word *chatting*.

"Huh."

"Huh, what?"

"Looked like more than that, is all."

"Well, it wasn't," I say. If I could shut down this conversation right here and now without opening myself up to future mockery, I would. Since I cannot, I say, "He's just —" I stop and sigh, and then I begin again. "He's not exactly my favorite person anymore."

Eleanor gives me a strange look. I immediately worry that

she overheard some of my conversation with Owen in the driveway. That she's starting to put it all together. That it's only a matter of time before she figures it all out.

Twenty

When Faith calls the landline the next morning, I'm lying on the couch reading, all tanked up on Diet Coke and ibuprofen, my back feeling quite a bit better. Faith starts speaking as soon as I pick up, steamrolling right over my hello. "Grace! Thank God. I thought nobody was home," she says, presumably because I let the phone ring about fifteen thousand times before I bothered to answer. "Is Rusty home? He isn't picking up his cell."

"That's because he's asleep," I point out. I know this not because I actually saw him sleeping but because I know Rusty. If he has the chance to sleep in — like, say, if nobody bangs a cymbal in his ear — he'll do it.

"Of course he is," Faith says. She has a smile in her voice, as though she thinks Rusty's laziness is totally charming. "Anyway, I hate to bother you but I have sort of an emergency. I think I left my work keys in Rusty's bedroom. Which I did not realize until I got to work and couldn't find them in my purse. And currently I have a dozen very young children standing behind me, and half of them have to pee. If you could just check for me, I would owe you big."

Phone in hand, I make my way to Rusty's room, where I stand in the doorway and look around, remembering why I've always avoided it. The place is a dump. There's a landslide of moldering clothes spilling from hamper to floor, a thick layer of dust over everything, and what appears to be an old abandoned sandwich on the dresser. In some quiet corner, cockroaches are probably hanging themselves.

And yet Rusty is sleeping soundly in the middle of it, star-fished on the bed, snoring like a bear. Curled up next to him is Lenny, whose expression translates roughly to *Get the hell out of here.*

Keeping one eye on the cat and propping the phone between my shoulder and ear, I step carefully into the room. I skirt a pair of tighty-whities — which, for the record, appear as though they've been neither tight nor white for quite some time — and, yes, yes, find Faith's keys on the nightstand. I snatch them up and yell-whisper, "I found them!"

At which time two things happen simultaneously: Rusty lets out a loud snore, and the cat jumps up, arches his back and hisses at me.

Whoa. This cat.

He's half O. J. Simpson and half O. J. Simpson.

I jerk backward, knocking a stack of papers off Rusty's dresser. They're a mess of to-go menus and expired fishing licenses. I've picked up probably half of them when I see it.

The pamphlet for Dad's funeral.

I squeeze my eyes shut and try to breathe. It's strange how just a simple sheet of paper can hit you with enough force to hurl you back in time. How all of a sudden there I am, devastated and alone and broken, sitting on that pew, staring at the box that holds my father.

Dad's death — it's still so fresh sometimes.

And I don't think I'll ever get all the way past that. Because grief isn't something you can walk through and come out on the other side. You can make it maybe seventy percent of the way, and the other thirty percent, well, that's the portion you have to live with.

This. Right here. Right now. This is part of my thirty percent.

Rusty didn't go to Dad's funeral, so I don't know how he got this pamphlet. Did someone give it to him?

If so, who?

I let the question hang in the air for a moment. The room is desperately quiet. Finally I swallow and open my eyes.

"How did you get this, Rusty?" I whisper.

It isn't Rusty who answers, though. It's Faith. Her voice comes through the phone, which I completely forgot I'm holding: "What did you say, Grace?"

"Nothing," I say, and I walk out of Rusty's room, quietly closing the door behind me.

#

There was this thing Dad and I used to do in New Harbor, and it was usually combined with a trip to the grocery store. We'd take the long way home to Rusty's and stop at the river to feed the ducks. Dad never lasted more than a day here without asking me to go or, else, cleverly trying to slide it past me on our way out of the grocery store ("Didn't know what I was thinking, buying all this bread for a weekend trip!"). He did it so many times it became a running joke. "Dad," I'd say in a fake-serious tone as we were walking down the bread aisle, "we're in New Harbor for two days. We probably should pick up five loaves of bread." It wasn't that Dad particularly liked ducks; he'd just heard they were good luck. And while I was fairly certain that he'd confused superstition with the term "lucky duck," I never called him out on it. I always just humored him and went along, grabbing a couple loaves of bread and stretching out on the riverbank with him, talking about everything and nothing, or just sitting in companionable silence and tossing chunks of bread to the ducks, hypnotized by the circular swirls they made in the water.

After my little meltdown in Rusty's room, I figure that maybe I can balance out a crappy memory of Dad with a good one, that I can restore some sense of family, that I'd just feel better if I could get to the river. Which goes to show you how delusional I am. I pictured this quiet, serene evening, tossing bits of bread to the ducks and feeling close to my father. Instead, I find myself caught in the middle of a thunderstorm, huddled under a tree on the riverbank with a bag of soggy day-old bread, not a duck to be seen.

It isn't unusual, this sort of weather. Summer is Florida's rainy season, and I used to carry an umbrella in my purse, back when I had half a brain. And despite the fact that I'm basically hugging the tree trunk, the rain is starting to soak me, so I dart across a neighboring parking lot and find shelter under the eaves of a restaurant. I'm there for probably five minutes before I see Owen's mom.

Or else, Janna's mom.

Mrs. McAllister?

She's hustling in my direction, her purse over her head in an effort to keep her hair dry. When her eyes snag on me, she smiles and waggles an index finger at me. "So this is where you've been hiding since you pulled into town," she says, and the familiarity of her voice makes my chest clench up like a fist. I can barely conjure up an image of my own mom — just a cascade of auburn curls and a voice like syrup — so, growing up, Mrs. McAllister was the closest thing I had to a mother. She was the one who sat Janna and me down on the couch and explained periods when we were eight, the one who taught me how to cook, the one who helped me pick out a dress for my first school dance. It's both calming and distressing, seeing her now. She gives me a fierce hug and says in my ear, "If I knew that all I had to do to see you was go out to eat, I would've done it ages ago." And then she pulls away and gives me an amiable, relaxed grin. Mrs. McAllister conceals a sharp eye underneath her pleasant, friendly demeanor, so for a few uncomfortable seconds I feel like she's looking clear through my skin, into the very darkest parts of me. Finally she says, "I haven't seen you once since you've been back in town, and you're living right next door."

I usually like to present a happy face to the world, so I force a smile, not surprised in the slightest when I see her eyes drift down to my teeth. A dentist, Mrs. McAllister is obsessed with teeth in a way that would be annoying if I didn't like her so much. I can see her standard question — "Have you been flossing religiously?" — hovering somewhere in her expression. It's a question that has always made me snort, because I don't even go to church religiously.

Finally I say, "Sorry, I've been busy getting settled."

She waves a hand at me, unconcerned. "I've been basically

living at work, anyway." Then she straps her purse over her shoulder and says, "Have you seen Janna yet?"

I feel a pang somewhere in my stomach, an agonizing twist of all my problems, braided together as one. "Yeah," I say.

Mrs. McAllister has been trying to repair my friendship with Janna ever since it unraveled, so she waits a moment, hoping I will elaborate. When I don't, she changes the subject, her tone somber. "Owen told me that your dad passed away. Honey, I'm so sorry."

I give her a weak smile. "Thank you."

"I had no idea," she goes on. "We've been so busy that we haven't had a proper conversation with Rusty in years. If we'd come over to chat instead of just waving at him from our driveway, I'm sure he would have told us."

"It's okay," I say.

But she just keeps on going. "I'd just figured that you were steering clear of town because of your misunderstandings with Janna, and of course whatever happened between you and Owen. I had no clue that your dad —"

"It's okay," I repeat. But then I feel awful, so I soften my voice and go on. "I totally understand. I know you've been busy. I'm sure Owen's accident has been rough on you guys."

She nods once, kicking back into mom mode. "Things were touch-and-go for a while. But Owen's doing better now. He's even been going to —"

"There's my bride!"

Mr. McAllister is loping toward us, smiling broadly. He picks up his wife and swings her in a circle, like something you'd see in the movies, and then he whispers something in her ear that makes her blush and swat him away.

"It's our anniversary, so we're going out to dinner," she explains to me, although she isn't looking at me while she speaks. She's smiling up at her husband.

I feel like I'm standing there by myself until Mr. McAllister turns toward me. "I heard you playing your violin the other day," he says, a ghost of a smirk on his face. He used to tease me incessantly about the violin, in much the same way that he teased Janna about drama club and Owen about art. He's an athlete, after all, and he feels as though everyone should be an athlete.

"Surprised he heard anything at all," his wife mutters.

He leans toward her with his good ear. "Huh?"

She waves him off and arches an eyebrow at me, which then leads to him teasing her about the fact that one of her hands is slightly bigger than the other ("like a fiddler crab"), which then leads to her giving him crap about his back hair ("You could probably knit a scarf out of it"), which then leads to all of us just laughing and laughing and laughing. And by the time I leave to go back to Rusty's, I realize just how much those two have always felt like family to me. And so, strangely enough, I found what I came for after all.

Twenty-One

Everything in my room is pink.

Like, the curtains, the throw rugs, the blinds, the shams, the comforter, all of it impossibly, horrifically pink — as though a bottle of Pepto-Bismol had hauled off and sneezed in there and then blown its nose on the throw pillows.

I jerk to a stop just inside my room, stunned to silence. My purse, still damp from the thunderstorm, slips off my shoulder and onto the floor. Faith is bent over my bed — wearing cropped leggings, a matching shirt and a pair of sneakers — tossing a new comforter over the sheets. When she sees me, she straightens up and grins. "Rusty sent me to find you a few things for your room." She pauses for a moment, presumably waiting for me to reply. When I don't, she says, "What do you think?"

"Um, it's —" I break off suddenly as I catch sight of Owen through my bedroom window. He's walking out of his house, dressed in khakis and a crisply ironed shirt. I glance at my watch. Six forty-five. Just like clockwork. Where does he go every Saturday night? To see a girl? That's it. He must have a girlfriend.

"It's …?" Faith prompts.

"Oh!" I say, my eyes shooting back to her. "It's, um … really pink."

She smiles, wrinkling her nose a little. "I know. When I was your age, I always wanted a pink room. They say it's calming. Though Rusty will probably have a stroke when he sees it." She shoots me a conspiratorial grin. "Once we transfer your old posters in here, it'll balance things out a little."

"My old posters?"

"The ones in the spare room?" she says offhandedly, struggling to stuff my pillow into a sham. "Why don't you go grab them?"

My breath halts abruptly, as though she just slapped a hand over my nose and mouth. I can feel my heart slamming in the back of my throat, loud and manic. "Sure," I finally manage, panicky sweat gathering at the base of my neck as my wobbly legs lurch into the hallway. I take maybe three steps and then jerk to a stop, heels digging painfully into the wooden planks of the floor. Terror, cold and wet, slides up my spine as I stare into the spare room.

I've walked past this room every day since I moved in several weeks ago. Even glanced at it as I've made my way down the hallway. I've become reasonably adept at keeping myself together each time. But I haven't stood in the entry. Haven't really looked at it till right now. Haven't stared at the tiny nightstand scattered with Dad's lucky sand dollars or the whitewashed dresser or — *Oh God* — the blue quilt on the bed. Seeing it now feels sharp and shocking and severe, a bone unexpectedly snapping in half.

I take a staggering step backward.

I turn toward Faith.

I try to look very, very calm.

So calm.

And then I tell her that I'll be right back, that I need to run outside for something, and I rush out the back door and into the yard. I don't inhale until my feet hit the grass, and then I bend over and suck air into my lungs as though I've been trapped underwater.

I'm not having a breakdown.

That's not what this is.

I just don't know how to move beyond what happened that night.

Wrapping my arms around myself, I walk slowly across the lawn. The seats of the swing set are still damp from the rain as I free them from the poles that have held them captive for so long. Collapsing into one of the swings, I try to figure out what to do. Because I can't live like this.

I can't.

I think about Owen's shocked expression when I confronted him in the driveway. Would he lie to me about something like that? What if he *wasn't* lying? What if —

"Hey."

I look up. Janna is crossing the space between her house and Rusty's, her bare feet silent on the damp grass. Her hesitant smile is a white flag of surrender, a clear indication that she's thought about my apology and decided to accept it. I feel something warm and grateful crack open inside my chest. "Hey," I say, as casually as I can muster, as she sits down in the swing next to me, her fingers curling around the rusty metal chain and her feet kicking out in front of her.

"What're you doing out here?" she asks.

I root around in my head for a reasonable lie but can't find one. I can't find anything at all, actually, which is probably why I'm sitting out here to begin with. I tell her the truth. "Escaping."

Janna arches an eyebrow at me, an unspoken question: *From what?*

Life, actually. But I don't say that. Instead, I say, "Rusty has a new girlfriend. I just had to get away from her for a minute."

Not a lie. Not really.

Janna looks at me dubiously for a second. But in the end, she lets it go, as though we have an unspoken agreement to keep things simple as we try to navigate through our first real, honest-to-God conversation in two years. "Ah," she says. "I guess Rusty hasn't changed much."

I laugh before I can stop myself, just one maniacal bark. I've been trying not to feel betrayed by Rusty. It doesn't always work. "No. He hasn't changed a bit." I pause for a moment, glancing at Rusty's house and then back at her. "Which is probably why it took him so long to sign my guardianship papers."

Janna stares at me, long and hard. "I don't get that."

I feel my cheeks flush with embarrassment. I hide it by bending down and waving off a mosquito. "He told me he was too upset to take care of me. Dad was his only brother. Rusty took it pretty hard. I guess he was drinking all the time, a mess. It's — whatever. It happened," I say with a shrug.

She frowns. We sit there in silence for another minute. I know that she wants to ask me about foster care, and what it was like. That she wants to know exactly what happened to Dad and what happened to me after he died. That she won't stop till she knows it all, because that's how Janna operates. But when she finally opens her mouth, "I landed the lead in *Grease*," is what she says. It's as though she can still read me after all this time, and she knows how badly I need a change of subject.

Relief spreads through my body. "That's great," I say. Janna has been a drama diva forever. I've spent more afternoons than I can count lying on her bed, a thick script in my hands and her cold feet in my lap, helping her practice her lines.

Community theater, Janna goes on to tell me, leaning back in the swing so far that the ends of her coppery storm of hair skim the grass. Her costar is a college guy — a dark-eyed, dark-haired Greek god.

"How *very*," I say, grinning. Janna has always had a thing for guys with dark hair. Actually — scratch that — Janna has always had a thing for guys in general. By middle school she already had a list of boyfriends as long as my arm.

"Yeah," she says. She sits back up, flushed and smiling. "He's my costar, so it's not like I'm going to date him. Okay, I'm totally going to date him. God. Why do I get myself in situations like these?" she says, her voice like fresh-squeezed orange juice, sweet and tart and totally organic. I feel the rest of the world evaporate, and all at once I'm a regular girl and we are regular friends. "Enough about me," Janna says. "How's it going with Eleanor?"

I groan. "Do you really want to know?"

She snorts. "Probably not."

I tell her anyway.

Twenty-Two

I wake with a start the next evening, overcome with the distinct impression that I was disturbed by something, yet I don't know what it was. I blink, slightly confused, as my eyes adjust to my reading light. Above me, the curtains dance in the current of the ceiling fan. A book is on my lap, still open, the words on the pages sloped away from me. My clock reads 11:00 p.m.

That's when I hear a crashing sound.

Panicking, I jerk upright, swing my feet to the floor and creep across my room, skirting a squeaky floorboard as I reach into my closet to grab an umbrella. Holding it like a police baton, I ease open my door.

Across the hallway is the doorway to the spare room, a looming, shadowy rectangle. I swallow once.

Ignore it.

Turning resolutely away from it, I glance down the hallway. It's empty.

I freeze, silent, waiting.

Another sound. It isn't exactly a crash this time — more like a scuffling, coming from … outside? Both hands gripping the umbrella, I tiptoe down the hallway, tentatively parting the curtains and peering into the side yard. Nothing out of the ordinary. The light in the McAllisters' garage is on. Owen is bent over a chunk of wood, carving away.

He must've just dropped something.

And I'm totally paranoid.

I collapse against the wall, grumbling under my breath. Back at the Marios', there were sounds everywhere. They were part of the hum of the city, totally familiar. But in New Harbor, where it's so quiet, a squirrel scurrying up a tree sounds like an assassin wading through the sawgrass with a hatchet.

I've just turned to go back to my room when I hear another scuffle-thump.

The front porch.

The hairs on the back of my neck prickle. Gripping the umbrella, I creep to the phone and dial 911. "Someone's breaking into our house," I hiss as soon as the operator answers. She asks me a couple of cursory questions — "Are you the only one home?" and "What's your address?" and "What sort of sounds are you hearing?" — while I sidle to the front window and slowly pull a gap into the curtains. And there is —

Rusty.

Kissing Faith.

Actually, scratch that. He isn't just kissing her. He's sticking his tongue down her throat like he's marooned on an island, and her tonsils are the only ship that will take him home. And she's waving one arm around to the side, unbalanced, trying to get purchase of the railing so she doesn't fall off the porch. Beside her feet is a plant, the pot shattered.

Striding to the door, I yank it open. "What the heck, you guys?" I basically yell. "You scared the crap out of me!"

Nothing. Not even a glance. Rusty and Faith are still swallowing each other's faces. The operator, though — she speaks up: "Miss? Are you okay?"

"Sorry. It was my uncle, making out with his girlfriend," I tell her, because *False alarm* doesn't quite do it justice. Regardless, the operator is nice about it, since she works for New Harbor 911. If I dialed 911 in the city, only to tell the operator that my intruder was, in fact, my uncle sucking the face off his girlfriend, the operator would've probably sent an officer right over, just to tell me how stupid I was.

I apologize one last time and hang up, and that's when Rusty and Faith come up for air. Rusty turns toward me and barks a laugh, adjusting his cockeyed hat. "Hey there, G," he says, smiling widely, without even the good sense to look embarrassed. This is the first time I've spoken to Rusty in days. The first time since our power was turned off, actually. There's no mention of this as he hoists up a screeching Faith and yeti-tromps over the threshold with her in his arms. "Holy shit, woman! What did you eat for dinner?" he asks with a snort, and then he just stops right there and looks at me.

"What?" I say.

"So we have some good news, kid." He tips his head to the side a little, like he thinks I'm going to guess. When I don't, he smiles like a lunatic and says, "We got married today."

Well.

Faith squeals, grinning at me, easy and carefree. "It was totally spur of the moment! Can you believe it?"

I blink. I shift my weight. Finally a handful of words work their way up my throat. "Um. It's actually" — I glance at Rusty — "yeah … pretty unbelievable."

Let me just point out that Rusty has already been married five times. Six, if you count his annulment in the early nineties. His last marriage? It took place in Vegas, by way of a Cher impersonator.

Whom he hit on.

Rusty grins broadly at me, and then he plants a loud kiss on Faith's forehead and carries her down the hallway.

I collapse on the couch. The sudden quiet in the living room leaves me feeling exhausted and wrung out — supernaturally heavy, like I might sink clear to Russia if I so much as exhale. It shouldn't matter to me that Rusty is a complete child, and in some ways, it doesn't. In some ways, it's sort of endearing. One of the finest weapons in Rusty's arsenal is his irresponsibility. But I'm not in the mood for irresponsibility. I'm not even in the mood for conversation, unless it involves an apology, and that clearly isn't going to happen. Part of me wants to yell at him about it, but another part of me knows that yelling at Rusty would be a huge waste of time. And anyway, I don't feel angry. My anger is still sleeping or it has been knocked out with ibuprofen and is sprawled out in a dark corner of the house, waiting for me to stumble over it. I'm too tired to be angry. Tired of waiting for Rusty to act like he cares. Tired of dodging the ghosts in this house.

Tired of avoiding that room.

The thought hits me sharp and fast, like a rubber band snapping against bare skin. I squeeze my eyes shut for a second, wishing I could stuff it back to wherever it came from.

Maybe I need a self-intervention.

Maybe if I were to walk into that room once a day or even a few times a week, I could be desensitized.

In a shining moment of idiocy, I jerk to my feet and struggle down the hallway, using trembling muscles that have not yet learned to walk. Not into that particular room, they haven't. Not willingly. Not in the past couple of years. My legs shake and halt as I step into the room and slap on the light switch.

For a quick second, for a single gasp of time, I see it for what it is: just a room. Furniture and curtains. Throw rugs and lamps. But then my eyes slide toward the bed, across the familiar bumpy hexagonal patterns of the quilt, the dark blue pillows scattered against the headboard.

And I nearly go to my knees.

I'm crushed underneath a mass of darkness.

I'm going to be sick.

I'm unable to

I'm

Reeling backward, I scramble down the hallway and out the front door, bursting onto the porch and leaning over the railing, nauseated and gasping.

I can't live like this.

Every time I walk down that hallway, every time I glance at that room, every time I see Owen, every time I breathe or walk or sleep or move, all I will ever think is: What really happened that night?

The evening is nearly silent, the only noise coming from Owen in the garage — a tap of chisel on wood, a shuffling of sneakers over sawdust.

What really happened that night?

Before I can second-guess myself, I'm lurching off the porch, careening to the McAllisters' garage, jerking to a stop in front of Owen and yelling, "Did you do it?!"

"Grace?" Owen is gaping at me. He's wearing a Gators' T-shirt and a frown, staring at me like he doesn't recognize me.

I'm shaking almost too badly to stand. I clutch the workbench, trying to keep myself upright. "I need to know the truth, Owen. I need to know if it was you."

His eyes are the deepest oceans of sadness. "Grace …"

"Owen. *Did you?!*"

He dips down to meet my gaze. He holds my stare. His expression is fierce. "I would never take advantage of you like that," he says, and his honesty is everywhere, in the slopes of his eyebrows and in the earnest tilt to his mouth and in the green-green of his irises.

He's innocent.

My mind gallops in circles, trying to reshuffle the facts of that night, trying to shift around the beliefs I've had all this time. Trying to switch everything: How I pinned the blame on Owen without even considering other options. How I didn't give him the chance to explain.

How I was wrong.

I keep my voice steady, but it takes every bit of determination that I have. "Can we go somewhere to talk?"

Twenty-Three

We're sitting at a table in Anthony's, this kitschy little burger joint downtown. The place is tiny and too fluorescently lit for this time of night, but it's clean, and it's open till one in the morning. Owen drove us here in that Jeep I've seen in front of the McAllisters'. As he backed out of the driveway, I noticed that the steering wheel was covered in pink fur and a very tiny, very gaudy, very feathery stuffed pelican dangled from the rearview mirror. Owen saw me looking and grumbled, "I really need to get my own car."

"Janna's stuff, I take it?"

A nod for a reply, and then: "I think she figures that if she puts enough girly shit in here, I'll be too embarrassed to drive it." This sounded so over the top, so ridiculous, so *Janna*, that for the first time since I'd been back in New Harbor, I burst out laughing.

"Exactly," Owen said as he slid to a creeping stop at the intersection of Ocean and Main, pausing longer than necessary before slowly accelerating. The cautious way he drove, the way his hands clamped down on the steering wheel — I could tell how much he hated it.

We didn't say anything else for the rest of the drive. I knew that Owen was sorting things out in his mind before he spoke. That's the way he operates. There are no empty words. Everything that comes out of his mouth has meaning, or else he doesn't say it at all. It's one of the things about him that I always loved.

Liked.

One of the things about him that I always *liked*.

And now, as we sit across from each other in a booth at Anthony's, Owen is still silent. Only his fingers make noise as they tap the table. I busy myself by staring intensely at a table-sized advertisement for a burger — "A full pound of meat!" — beside his left elbow. The coffee aroma rising from my cup and our looming conversation has me slightly woozy. I push the cup around, just for something to do with my hands. Finally I glance up at him. Bad idea. He's searching my face with those eyes.

They're excruciating, those eyes.

They're reaching into my chest, turning an invisible key. Opening something that needs to stay shut.

"Is that where you're going to college?" I blurt, pointing to his T-shirt. "University of Florida?"

He nods once. "They have an amazing art program," he says, and then he leans toward me. "Grace —"

"How's everything at home?" I say.

He half smiles at me. "Fine. Everything's fine."

"I sense a *but*."

Humoring me, he tells me that his dad has been busy getting the track team ready for a big summer tournament, and that his mom has been slammed at work, and that Janna has gone mental preparing for *Grease*. But all of his words seem so far away, like they're muttered from across the room. Across the world.

And then he's silent again. It isn't an awkward silence. It's the sort of silence that's ready to implode. I don't look at him. I can't. I know exactly what he's about to say. My heart thrums in my chest. I wipe my palms on my clothes. *Don't say it, Owen. Please don't say it.*

He leans toward me, ducking down and forcing me to look at him. "Grace?"

I meet his eyes and swallow.

"Someone raped you," he whispers.

My heart feels as though it's been stuffed full of rocks and then tossed into the ocean. It's sinking, dragging my chest and lungs with it. I can't breathe. I can't move.

I'm drowning.

For the past couple of years, I've considered myself *used* or *taken advantage of.* But *raped.* That term — I can feel it physically. It thrashes in my stomach, harsh and barbed and relentless, clawing it to shreds.

Was I raped?

Yes.

Yes, I was.

But I don't know how I'm supposed to feel about it now.

You'd think that twenty-two months would be enough time for me to sort through my feelings on the subject. But I've been so busy dealing with Dad's death, so preoccupied by Rusty's absence, so overcome with adjusting to life in the foster system, that my feelings about what happened on Labor Day weekend were packaged up and put away. Now that I'm finally facing them, they've grown too big to consider.

I don't think I'm strong enough to do this.

At some point, I'll have to be. But right now, everything is too raw and too abrasive. Right now, Owen is sitting across from me, waiting for me to speak.

I don't, though. I just close my eyes and nod — *yes, I was raped*. With this confirmation comes rolling guilt and shame, like I made some sort of horrible tactical error that caused the rape, like I was an awful person for letting it happen, like confessing the truth is an admission of my own wrongdoing.

Like I'm so filthy I could scrub myself for days on end and still be dirty.

Deep down, I'm aware that I shouldn't feel this way.

But I do.

I keep my eyes shut. I don't want to see Owen's expression. I keep waiting for him to bolt, like he has in the past when things got difficult, but when I open my eyes, he's still there.

I blink at him for a moment.

He's not the one who raped me.

I don't know whether I'm supposed to feel relieved by this, but I am. Maybe there is still some hope left in the world. Maybe some things can be trusted.

I can't help it: a tear skitters down my cheek.

Before, when I thought he'd done it, I was angry. At him, mostly, but also at myself, for trusting him so implicitly. Now, though, I don't know what I feel. I think of all those voices in the living room that night. I don't even know who was there, besides Dad and Rusty. Maybe the rest of them were strangers. Maybe the rest of them were friends. Familiar faces. I have no clue. All I know is that at some point after Owen left my room, one of them came in and —

I don't realize how badly my hand is trembling until Owen reaches for it. Sucking in my breath, I flinch away. It's an awful thing to do. I know this. But it's a reflex. My distrust in him has been part of me for so long that it lives in my cells. I look away so I won't have to see the hurt in his face, and then I whisper, "Who was there, Owen?"

Long pause.

His voice strained, Owen finally says, "A bunch of Rusty's friends from work. Your dad and my dad. Andy and Sawyer came over when I was leaving. I guess they'd heard all the noise from next door and figured they'd join the party."

"How many?" I croak. "How many all together?"

"Probably twenty-five people."

Twenty-five people.

I clear my throat. I'm trying so hard not to lose it right now. "Did anyone seem …?"

Did anyone seem like a rapist? Did anyone seem like the sort of person looking to annihilate my life? Did anyone seem like a monster?

"No," Owen says in a sigh. "I mean, a bunch of the adults were pretty drunk, Rusty included." He pauses for a beat, just looking at me. I can tell he's waiting for me to tell him everything I remember about that night. He's thinking about suspects. Timelines. Clues. But I'm not going there with him. Not right now. Maybe not ever.

We're silent for several moments. I stare blankly at the

blackness out the window, my frowning reflection blinking back at me.

"Grace," Owen says, "what are you going to do?"

I sigh. "I don't know. I mean, it's not like I can walk into a police station and just *tell them*."

"Why not?"

I picture myself sitting in an interrogation room while some random cop asks me to give him all the details about what happened, while he asks me why I didn't come forward sooner. I think about how humiliating it would be to recount it all, to tell the police everything. "It was almost *two years* ago," I say.

I don't add that there was physical evidence.

I don't add that I was bleeding, or that I had stabbing pain for days.

I don't add that there was mental damage, and it's still tracking its dirty feet all over my life.

Owen leans toward me and whispers, "Grace, I know this is probably painful to consider, but your uncle —" He stops and draws in a breath, and then begins again. "You blacked out at his house. His strange behavior after your dad died, his absence from your life the past couple years ... it could've been guilt. He might've —"

"*No*. Rusty is — no. He's not a rapist. He's a screwup, yes. But not a rapist." Owen stares at me, unconvinced, as I go on. "And neither was my dad. Or your dad. Or Andy or Sawyer, for that matter."

Owen leans toward me. "But Sawyer. He's —"

"A complete ass, but rape isn't his style. Which leaves Rusty's work buddies. Did you ... recognize any of them that night?"

Owen shakes his head no. "They all looked like transients — college kids, making a few extra bucks over the summer."

So it was a complete stranger.

I don't know how I feel about that. I close my eyes, wishing for problems like unexpected quizzes or hangnails or frizzy hair. Those are the problems I want. Owen says softly, "Have you told anyone else about what happened to you that night?"

"No." I've never even considered telling anyone. The stupid truth of it all? I didn't want to get Owen into trouble. His family has been important to me for so, so long.

"I think you should talk to Janna about it," Owen says. "It might help to have a girl's perspective on this."

I collapse against the back of the booth. "Janna has just barely come back into my life."

Owen smiles, just a little. "Janna never really left."

That's probably true. But I don't know whether I want to tell Janna. I don't know anything right now. My brain is heavy, overloaded. I can feel exhaustion starting to take over, and I cover my mouth and yawn. Without a word, Owen finishes the last of his coffee, throws down a few dollars and tips his head to the door.

As I climb into the Jeep, I do my best to forget about all those male voices I heard in the living room that night. I do my best to forget about the expression on Owen's face when he told me I'd been raped. I do my best to forget about Rusty's unexplained absence from my life.

I do my best.

Twenty-Four

There's never been a lack of people available to assess my mental state over the past couple of years. Caseworkers, counselors, therapists, doctors ... you name it, they've stood over me with a pen and a folder, recording my progress or lack thereof. A week or two after Dad died, my therapist tried to give me a prescription for Paxil, claiming that it would alleviate my anxiety when I was out in public. Which was a bad idea in countless ways, the most prominent being that one of the side effects of Paxil is diarrhea. Pretty sure diarrhea would cause anxiety when I was out in public. And the thought of taking a prescription drug made me hyperventilate, so I played my violin instead. Like, excessively.

When I wake up the next morning, feeling as though the Gulf of Mexico has taken up residence in my stomach, I roll over, grab my violin, sit on the edge of my bed, close my eyes and rip into my favorite reel.

It doesn't help.

With my eyes closed, all I can see is Owen's concerned expression from the night before — the way his mouth turned down when he asked me about Rusty.

Words like *probability* and *likelihood* wedge themselves into my brain.

I pull on some clothes, grab my purse and hustle to the nearest bus stop. I don't know where I'm going, only that I'm going.

Climbing on the bus, I take a seat in the back row, staring out the window and watching houses and businesses and palm trees zip past. I rub the area on the back of my neck that always gets stiff when I spend too much time practicing without using a stand to hold my sheet music. Long ago, Dad gave me a music stand for Christmas. It was a gorgeous contraption of knotty walnut that smelled like varnish and stain and absolute devotion. We were pretty broke, so I knew that he'd virtually emptied his bank account to buy it. And the way he placed it in front of me, the light in his eyes as he watched me peel off the wrapping paper, I burst out crying.

I was just … gone.

And now, so is the music stand. Gone, that is. Like most of the things that were in the house when I was taken into foster care. Who knows what happened to everything? Social workers rummaged through the house and brought me some of my clothes, a few books. The things they deemed important to me. Everything else, though — it was all taken away.

The bus jerks to a stop in front of the library, nudging me back to the present. I jump up and hustle off, feeling oddly as though this is where I was heading all along. Janna has always been big on the library, forever dragging me here. She never read any of the library's books, though. She always brought her own, proclaiming that she just liked to sit and read with words whispering all around her.

I've just curled up on a soft chair by the window, and I'm flipping through a book I found on Vanessa Mae, and I'm thinking about my bow skills and whether my elbow was dropping this morning, thereby contributing to my crappy playing. The library's air-conditioning is set at a perfect temperature, and the chair is the sort of soft that feels almost like a giant baseball glove, holding me exactly where I need to be. I've almost forgotten about my problems when a loud clatter yanks me out of my book, my comfort zone and my chair, all at the same time.

I yelp — like, literally yelp, as though I've just discovered a three-inch spider on my foot — and jerk my head toward the noise. I find Andy Simon behind me, stooped over a pile of books, an expression of complete and utter dismay on his face. "Oh my God, Andy," I say, my palm on my chest, "you scared the absolute living crap out of me."

He turns toward me, his face cycling through about eighty shades of red. "Grace! Hey. Hi. Hello. I didn't even see you there." He folds his arms over his chest, then squats down and starts picking up the mess.

Awkward silence.

I look down at the books. "Did you drop those?"

"Um," he says. He doesn't look up. "Yes?"

More silence.

"Do you … want some help picking them up?" I ask.

"No!" he practically yells, and one of the librarians gives us a thin-lipped stare. He tosses her an apologetic wave and scoops up the books, holding them tightly to his chest as he stands. The book on the bottom is facing me, the title beside his forearm: *How to Convince Her to Love You*. Can't say I'm surprised. Not sure whether Andy has even had a girlfriend before.

"So," I say, pointing to the book, "some light reading?"

Andy shifts his weight and says, "It's not what you think." He blows out a loud exhale and pinches his eyes closed with his free hand. I tip my head sideways to read a couple of the other spines. *The Nerd's Guide to Romance. Attracting the Love of Your Life, 101*. After a second, he says, very quietly, "Okay, so it's exactly what you think. I can totally forget you saw these books, if you can totally forget you saw these books."

"What books?" I say. "I didn't see any books."

He sighs, opens his eyes and winces. There's a bead of sweat rolling down his brow. "Yeah, you totally did."

"I kind of did."

"You can't tell Janna," Andy blurts, "because everything will get awkward and weird, and she'll never want to speak to me again. Our friendship will be ruined."

My eyes feel like they're boinging out of my head. "Wait. Hold up. Janna? You're reading those for Janna?"

He grimaces. "Yeah. I mean, yeah. Not that she'd ever fall for someone like me. But the thing is — no offense — Janna and I have been closer than ever since you've been out of the picture. Sorry! I'm sorry. That sounded a lot better in my head. It's just that Janna and I, we're, like" — he holds up his free hand, twisting his middle finger around his index finger — "tight. And sometimes I think that she might feel the same way, but she doesn't even know it? And maybe all I have to do is, um, trip a switch in her head, or something."

"Trip a switch in her head."

He swallows and nods, absentmindedly tugging on the rough edge of his half ear. Then, realizing he's drawn my attention to it, he lets his hand drop. "Yeah. Like, Janna doesn't think of me that way. Not sure *anyone* thinks of me that way, really. I mean — it's not easy being Sawyer's brother."

I make a face. "Not all girls find your brother attractive, you know."

"Most of them do. Have you seen him lately? All he does is work out. His thighs are the same circumference as my waist. If he wasn't my brother, *I'd* have a crush on him." When I snort and roll my eyes, he says, "No, I'm serious. He's a freaking golden boy. He's been breaking speed record after speed record the past several years, and he's only getting faster. Clemson's already recruited him for track."

I wave a dismissing hand at him. "Whatever. I'm not impressed." Looking to steer the conversation away from Sawyer, I say, "If you're so interested in Janna, why did you ask me to homecoming the other day?"

The red in Andy's cheeks deepens. He rubs his forehead with the heel of his hand and mutters, "I thought maybe if I made her jealous? I mean, she was kind of miffed at you anyway, so ..." He must see exasperation in my face, because all of a sudden he looks panicked. "I know! I'm sorry! It was a dick move. It's just — I'm at a loss here, and I've tried everything. I even became a lifeguard because of her, hoping she'd — I don't know ... see me differently, or whatever? Please promise me that you won't tell her about all of this."

"Andy, Janna and I just barely started talking again. I can't imagine bringing all this up to her."

"*Promise me*, Grace."

I sigh. "Okay. Fine. I promise."

He clears his throat and shifts his feet, his face still basically purple, and then he says, "So what're you doing here, anyway?"

I'm trying to distract myself.

I'm running away from life.

What I should be doing right now is asking Andy if he noticed anything strange the night I was assaulted. If he saw anyone go into my room. I swallow down the thickness in my throat. *Ask him, Grace. Ask him if he saw anything unusual that night.*

ASK HIM IF HE SAW ANYTHING.

I open my mouth, but "Um, Andy?" is all that comes out. Because I know that once I start asking questions, I'll be pushing some huge boulder into motion. And I'm not sure whether I'm ready for that yet. I'm not sure whether I'll ever be ready. Andy is staring at me, waiting for me to continue. I swallow. "Good luck with Janna."

Twenty-Five

The first thing I see when I step into the house that evening is Faith, standing at the kitchen counter, the head of a fish in one hand and a knife in the other, her hair sectioned off into a dozen of those old-school pink foam curlers.

She holds up the fish. "Dinner preps," she says, by way of greeting. "Rusty is actually working a day shift today, so I thought we could all eat together. Well, everyone except Eleanor, who has some sort of thing going at the senior center? I'm not exactly sure. Didn't want to pry." She hustles to the far end of the kitchen to deposit the fish head in the trash can, and then heads to the sink, brushing past a large, stain-blotched cookbook, one of the countless things she's already moved here from her old apartment.

Using her elbow to flip up the lever on the faucet, Faith washes her hands. She says, "When Rusty said we had fresh fish in the fridge, I had no idea I'd have to *dismember it*. I'm a vegetarian, so it was kind of gross. I mean, it still had eyeballs."

I wrinkle my nose in solidarity and unload into a kitchen chair. My eyes find the Salad Shooter — the one gifted and regifted between Dad and Rusty — sitting atop the counter, a pile of sliced cucumber beside it, and I smile, just a little, because it sort of feels to me like Dad got the last word. "So you're going to start eating meat?" I ask.

"I'll be eating fish. For my fertility diet."

I blink at her. "Fertility diet?"

She spins around to face me. The motion causes her curlers to rock back and forth on her head. She grins, spontaneous and bright. "I'm not getting any younger. I want to have babies right away."

Well. That surprises me. Though it probably shouldn't. Lightning-fast decisions seem to be a particular talent of Faith's — suddenly chopping off six inches of hair, switching careers, changing her diet, jumping headlong into marriage. Maybe impulsive change works well for her, but I have a hard time believing it will for Rusty. "How does Rusty feel about having kids? He's *forty-four*."

Faith pops a couple of cucumber slices in her mouth. "He's excited," she says with her mouth full, and then she shoots me an apologetic look. "Sorry, I was raised without proper manners." Swallowing and tossing a handful of cucumber slices into a bowl, she goes on, "Rusty wants kids as much as I do. Which is to say that he really, really wants kids."

A sudden ache blooms under my rib cage, almost like I'm jealous of a baby that hasn't even been conceived yet, but not quite. It's more like … hurt. I feel like I could disappear for days and Rusty wouldn't even notice I was gone. I wonder whether he remembers I'm here half the time, whether he remembers I exist. Granted, I wondered the same thing while I was in foster care, but it's almost worse being ignored by him here, now, in his house, where my clothes are swinging on the backyard clothesline and my shoes are lined up next to the front door. I'm everywhere here, yet he hardly seems to notice.

Almost on cue, Rusty barrels through the front door, a gigantic stack of mail in his arms.

I stare at him for a moment, my heart crashing in my throat. *Did you do it?*

His only answer is an easy smile. "Ladies," he trumpets. His gaze falls on Faith. He kisses her once on the nose and then backs up, patting her affectionately on the top of the head. "Whatever those things are? They're adorable."

She claps a hand over her mouth. "Oh, my God. I totally forgot about the curlers." And with that, she scurries off to the bathroom.

Rusty unloads the mail on the table. It's an avalanche of envelopes and magazines and bills. Pretty much explains why he was late paying the electric bill. Gesturing at me with a sweep of his hand, he says, "Guess some things never change, huh?"

"Excuse me?"

He flips through the mail, not looking up. "Sundresses. You still wear 'em. When you were little, it used to drive your dad crazy."

I look down at my dress and swallow. I wasn't prepared for Rusty to mention my clothing. Or Dad. You'd think I'd feel angry, listening to him talk about my father so nonchalantly after all this time. But all I feel is a mass of tears building just behind my eyes. It's been so long since I've heard Dad mentioned in casual conversation that I want to hold on to the moment a little longer. So I wait a little while before I say, "It did?"

He glances up from the mail, a soft smile on his face. "It did. When you were three, you wanted a leopard-print sundress for your birthday. Went on and on about it for days."

"I don't remember that," I say quietly.

He laughs. "I sure do. Your dad had to drive all around the damn county lookin' for one. Know how hard it is to find a leopard-print sundress in a toddler size? Damn near impossible. But your father — he'd've done just about anything for you." A shadow passes over his expression and his words fall away, and for the first time since I arrived, I feel like I'm with one of the few people in the world who really understands what it's like to miss my dad. Then Rusty clears his throat and hands me a letter from social services. "I guess Sarah's coming for a visit in a couple of days?"

"Ah," I say. Visits and/or inspections are standard procedure for kids like me. Social workers feel the need to poke their heads into the house to make sure that we don't have a meth lab in the bathroom. Or, say, stolen wallets hidden under our T-shirts. The most important things are that the house is in order and everyone is present for the visit. "Just make sure you're here for it, okay?" I say.

He nods. "'Course."

Silence drops between us, and I chew on my thumbnail for a moment, wanting to thank Rusty for sharing that story about Dad. Instead, I spring to my feet and stride to the cupboard. As I pull down some plates for dinner, I can almost swear I hear him sigh.

#

I'm quiet all through dinner, thinking about tragedies and swallowed feelings and the things people do to cope. So after everyone goes to bed that night I walk decisively into the living room, to the desk where Rusty keeps his old computer. After pressing the power button, I pace back and forth while the desktop fires up. Once the screen blinks to life, I collapse into the chair and do something I've wanted to do for years: I type *Owen McAllister* and *motor vehicle accident* into a search engine. A couple of short articles pop up, dated back to the summer that everything went crooked. I read the first one.

Owen McAllister, 16, a rising junior at New Harbor High and a member of the student council, struck 7-year-old Zoey Barnes with his 2009 Toyota in the intersection of Main and Seventieth. Miss Barnes was flown to St. Joseph's Children's for treatment, her spinal injuries leading to paralysis.

The other article is basically the same, but it has a picture of a tiny blonde girl lying in a hospital bed. Her skin is pale and sunken, her body covered in bruises and scrapes and bandages. She's smiling but the gesture is miserable and thin, full of effort.

All the air whooshes out of my lungs. I cup my forehead in my hands and stare at the desk. Has Owen seen this picture? I know the answer immediately. Of course he has. And he probably beat himself up over it for months. Owen's built cages around turtle eggs and nursed baby owls back to health. Hurting this little girl must've been unbearable for him, and I left him to deal with it on his own. I shake my head, ashamed and embarrassed. Ever since our conversation at the restaurant, Owen's been coming over, knocking on the door, trying to talk to me, and I've been hiding in my room.

More than ever, I'm aware that I underestimated him, that

he doesn't just bail when things get rough. In fact, he's better at talking through problems than I ever imagined.

Still, though.

I suspect he'll press me about going to the authorities. I suspect he'll confront me with his suspicions about Rusty.

I suspect I still have feelings for him.

But avoiding him after all he's done for me, after everything I *haven't* done for him —

God.

How can I keep doing that?

So when he knocks on Rusty's front door the next day, I'm there to open it, immediately stepping out and joining him on the porch. Resolved as I am, I still feel a little startled and uneasy as I come to a halt beside him, a thick tangle of anxiety lodged deep in my chest.

At the sight of me, Owen unloads a sigh of relief that makes him appear forty instead of eighteen. It's strange how both of our childhoods ended so abruptly. Now we're big, clunky adults shoved into teenagers' bodies, not sure how to think or what to say or which way to act. "How're you holding up?" he says, his Australian accent more prominent than usual.

I turn toward him. Our gazes collide for a nanosecond before we both glance away. "I'm — I'm here," I say.

I feel … guilty. Why do I feel so guilty? For mistakenly blaming Owen for something he didn't do? For not being there for him after his accident? Yeah, but it's more than that. I feel guilty for the sexual assault, which is ridiculous. It wasn't my fault.

Even so, I feel like I should've done something to stop it.

I lean against the banister. I can feel Owen watching me.

"I've tried to check on you a couple of times," he says carefully, "but you weren't home."

I don't want to lie to Owen. Not now. And I shouldn't have to. He'll understand. "I've been … processing everything," I say, and he nods.

Both of us are silent, then Owen opens his mouth to speak, taking a step toward me. I jerk backward. He sighs and kicks the railing with the toe of his shoe. "Sorry," he mutters. "Didn't mean to startle you."

Here he is, the guy I falsely accused of rape, apologizing to me. I'm such an asshole.

"You don't need to apologize." I sigh. "I'm just jumpy, you know?"

"Yeah. I know," he says, sitting on the top step of the porch. He doesn't speak, but like with all of his silences, his words are hiding in his posture, in the expectant slope of his shoulders, in the way his brows tilt as he stares up at me. His body is saying, *Please sit down beside me* and *Please talk to me* and *I want to be part of your life again* and *Let me help you.*

I don't know whether I can do any of those things.

Owen has been nothing but a gentleman to me. I know that. But every time I look at him, I'm reminded that someone else *wasn't*. And how do you explain something like that? I can't. Not now. Not to Owen. But I can sit and talk to him. It isn't as though he doesn't already know the ugly truth. So I carefully lower myself down to the step, putting a good foot of distance between us.

Owen rests his elbows on his knees and whispers, "I'm concerned about you staying here. At Rusty's."

My gaze fixed on a tangle of sea grapes between Rusty's and

the McAllisters', I try to keep it together. The porch feels sinister and threatening all of a sudden, a snake in the grass. Turning to Owen, I say, "It wasn't Rusty."

Owen is clearly skeptical, but he doesn't press. "Have you gone to the police?"

"I need more time to think this through," I say, which is stupid, because I've already had almost two years. But it doesn't feel like it's been that long. It seems recent, scratching around in my chest, bone on flesh, trying to claw its way out.

It will wreck me.

I'm not ready for that.

"But Grace —"

"Don't push me on this, Owen. I need time. Telling you was one thing. That was private. But telling the police —" I blink several times and look away until my vision clears. Then I take a couple of breaths and continue. "Telling a bunch of strangers about the most humiliating thing that ever happened to me, watching them gut my life and spread the mess all over town for everyone to see? I can't do it right now, Owen. I *can't*."

He mashes his lips together. We don't speak for a moment. "I need to know exactly what you remember," he says finally, each word coming out slow, like he's thinking every syllable before speaking it. "About that night."

Well, that gets my attention, if he didn't have it already. I shake my head side to side, because I'm not having that particular conversation with him right now, not when I'm already feeling panicky and threatened and bare. "No. I don't — no."

"Why?"

Because I don't want to relive it. Because it's too embarrassing. Because talking about it makes it more real.

For the second time since I moved to New Harbor, I remember Dad's words, from back when he and Rusty fixed that old fishing boat: *It's in a man's genetic code, mending broken things.* I wonder if that's all I am to Owen, a broken thing, and he's just predisposed to fix me.

Or whether he's just worried that part of me still blames him.

"Why do you care?" I say, my tone just this side of suspicious. "Are you worried that I still think you did it? Are you just trying to clear your name?"

As soon as it's out of my mouth, I regret it. The expression on his face — it's as though I've hauled off and punched him in the stomach. "I care about you, Grace. Don't you get that? I've always cared about you."

Maybe he did, way back when. But everything is different now. And anyway, I know very well that he's dating someone, the way he walks out of his house every Saturday night all dressed up. "Are you this protective over your girlfriend?" I blurt, and then I snap my mouth shut, blushing and embarrassed, not even sure why I'm bringing her up.

Owen blinks. "What are you talking about? I don't have a girlfriend."

Why is he lying? "Tell me the truth, Owen," I say.

Owen shakes his head. "I am. Why are you even asking me this? Where is this coming from?"

I don't trust you anymore.

I don't say this, though, because it won't make sense to him. It doesn't even make sense to me. And I'm not about to admit that I've been watching his every freaking move since I came back to New Harbor, either, so I turn toward the flower bed and mutter, "Forget it."

"You know what I think?" he says softly. "I think you're just trying to change the subject so you don't have to talk about that night."

"Well, you're wrong."

"Then tell me what happened."

I open my mouth and then let it drift shut.

He closes his eyes. "*Please*, Grace."

I try some words out in my head, but everything is too humiliating and honest to say out loud. Finally, my voice a rasp, I tell him what I remember. "I was in bed before anyone even arrived that night. I heard people ringing the doorbell and walking in, but I was so exhausted that I wasn't really paying attention." I stop, do my best to catch my breath and then start up again. "You arrived just a few minutes after I took Dad's Ambien. I remember talking to you. I remember —" I break again, the crooks of my knees slick with sweat and my face flaming. Suddenly I can't look at him. All I want to do is shrink into something small. A dust mote. A fleck. "I remember kissing you, and you weren't really into it, and then you suddenly were. Things start getting fuzzy from there. Your hand was up my shirt. I started panicking. I couldn't — I remember telling you we needed to stop, but I don't remember you replying." I swallow down the phlegmy stiffness in my throat and glance up at him. His face is pale, and he's as still as death, eyes pinned on me. "Everything went black then, like I fell into a dark hole, like I —" Owen is bowing his head now, squeezing his eyes closed, like he's filling in all the blanks, seeing everything as it's happening, like every word and thought has physical force — knives twisting in his chest. "When I woke up, I didn't even know where I was." I slap the tears off my face, suddenly angry.

"I went to move and I got this horrible pain. I had bruises on my thighs. I was bleeding."

Owen bolts to his feet and paces the length of the lawn. I think maybe he's going to keep on walking, but he turns and strides back, his green eyes flashing some complex emotion that's vengeance and rage and protectiveness, all knotted up in one. "Did you find anything out of place that morning, notice any sort of clue?"

"Just one thing," I whisper, remembering the excruciating pain when I rolled over in bed that morning. Remembering how my heart sank when my eyes fell upon something achingly familiar on my sheets. "Your wallet."

Twenty-Six

I've always included a note with the money. Nothing crazy, just a little something along the lines of *Thank you for what you do.* Like the smooth, discriminating criminal that I am, I don't sign it. I just wrap the note around the cash, stuff it into an envelope and send it off to Hillsborough County Women's Crisis Center. No return address.

In this case, the money amounts to a whopping two dollars. I was dragged and/or catapulted by a bus — with enough force to throw out my back, mind you — for two freaking dollars. You can hardly buy a Chia Pet on Craigslist for two dollars.

Still, though, I feel guilty, semi-hysterical, like I'm pushing at my skin from the inside, trying to shove my way out, while I stand in line at People's Market to buy a stamp.

In front of me are two firefighters, both in uniform and both reminding me of Dad so much that for a single, helpless moment, I actually consider hugging them. Dad was a volunteer firefighter since before I can remember. I have at least a dozen sacred memories of climbing, wide-eyed and awed, into Engine 13 for a parade or an event. It made such an impression on me that by the time I turned six, I declared to Dad that I wanted to follow in his footsteps. Dad laughed like this was the funniest thing ever. He apologized about it later, telling me that he thought I was kidding, seeing as how I was afraid of basically everything, fire and natural catastrophes included. But his reaction still stung a little, mostly because I knew he was right. I'm not the type to run toward danger. I'm the type to sprint away from it.

First thing I notice when I step out of the store is Andy, singing a Kenny Chesney song. Or else, a Luke Bryan song. I don't have much of an ear for country music, so I'm not exactly sure. All I know is that Andy is sitting on a bench that faces the ocean, a guitar in his lap, crooning. I stop right beside him. "Hey," I say, checking my watch. Sarah is due to show up for her visit in T-minus sixty minutes, and I need to get back to Rusty's to tidy up the place. "I didn't know you played the guitar."

"Cochran!" Andy flattens a palm over the strings to stop the sound. For a split second, he gives me that same guilty look he had in the library the other day, when I saw him with all those books. And then he smiles. "I don't actually play the guitar. That's the only song I know. Learned it from YouTube." He waggles his eyebrows. "To woo the ladies."

Woo the ladies?

Honestly.

"Andy," I say, "George Washington called. He wants his words back."

Andy holds up his finger. "It's quite possible that I missed my intended birth year by a century or two." Propping the guitar against the bench, he glances at the yellow plastic bag in my hand. "Shopping at The Store?"

"Yup." Officially, New Harbor's only supermarket is called People's Market, but everyone in town, cleverly, calls it The Store. Because that's what you get in a small town — things are kept simple. And anyway, People's Market is more of a store than a market. It carries everything from sweatpants to booze to homemade fudge. In my case, I needed shampoo, ant traps for the kitchen and a postage stamp. I lower my voice and say, "So. Both of us know that the only person you'd try to impress with the guitar is Janna. Where is she?"

"Green bikini," he says, pointing toward the beach with a tip of his head. And there, about twenty yards away, is Janna, hair exploding all over her beach towel, eyes closed and mouth slightly parted.

"I see it's working for you."

He shrugs good-naturedly. Putting both arms over his head and stretching, he says, "It's a five-step process, as per my book. Wooing is the first step. So that's what I'm doing. Wooing."

"Oh my God, please stop saying *wooing*."

"Sorry," he says. He does not appear sorry.

I snort and stare at the shoreline, where Sawyer is standing waist-deep in the water, throwing a football back and forth with a guy from his track team. His overly muscled body and overly perfect hair make him look like he's starring in a commercial for something — a suntan lotion or a hair product or a protein bar. Whatever it is, I'm not buying it.

My eyes trail back to Janna. Things have been better between us, for sure. We've exchanged several easy, friendly waves as we've come and gone from our respective houses, but that's about it. I'm not quite sure where to go from here. In the past, Janna's always been the one who's assumed the lead in our friendship. Now, though, I have the distinct impression that she's passing me the reins, but I'm too strung out to know what to do with them.

I'm so lost in thought that I don't notice Logan walking in our direction until he's standing right beside me, wearing mirrored sunglasses and a blue T-shirt with sleeves just short enough to show off the bottom edge of his skull-and-crossbones tattoo. In his hand is an energy drink. I hear it sloshing around as he bumps me with his elbow. "Damn, girl," he says. "It really *is* you. I thought I was hallucinating when I saw you at Island Pizza the other day."

"Yup, it's me," I say, my eyes lingering on his tattoo. Every time I see it, I kick myself a little for not having had the guts to get one when I had the chance. "How've you been?"

Logan grins. "Great. You know — busy with track. Coach McAllister has been calling extra practices, getting us primed for a tournament in August. Not sure what the athletic department was thinking when they gave the green light to two-a-days in the middle of the summer." He pauses for a minute, assessing me. Not in a creepy way, but like he's checking to see whether I've grown any taller over the past couple of years. "What about you? It's been forever, right? I don't think I've talked to you since that Gators' game at your uncle's place."

Something dark skitters across the back of my neck. Something like panic. I have to fight to keep my voice even as I say, "You were there that night?"

Logan chugs the rest of his drink and then knocks his chest with his fist, stifling a burp. "Yup. Just for an hour or so. I was supposed to hang with Sawyer, but when I got to his house, his parents told me he'd walked over to your uncle's house to watch the game."

I wrap my arms around myself and glance at Andy, who's thumbing around on his phone. "Oh," I say finally. "I don't remember because I —"

"Was loaded on Ambien," Logan supplies, chuckling. "Oh, I know."

My pulse hisses in my ears. "So I talked to you that night?"

"Yeah," he says, grinning.

"When?"

"I don't know," he says, "like, eleven, maybe? I'd left my phone over at Sawyer's, so I was outside on my way to —"

"I was *outside*?" I almost yell.

"I know, right? I didn't even see you walk out of your room. You must've gone out the back door, or something? You were standing on the lawn, trying to stay upright, talking to one of Rusty's friends — college guy? Dark hair? Crazy-tall?" Logan waits for me to comment, or to insert the guy's name. When I don't, he says, "He told me he was going to walk you back to your room."

Twenty-Seven

I go to the police station.

It's only a five-minute walk from the beach, right between the courthouse and the senior center.

A loud buzz signals my entrance. The place is refrigerator bright. A bald middle-aged man in a dark uniform sits behind a glass wall, tapping a pen on a pad of papers, staring at me. The place smells like someone's greasy lunch. And also, bleach — as though the crime scene weren't back at Rusty's, as though it were right here, where the most degrading part of my life will become news and gossip. Where I will sit under these fluorescent lights with this nauseating smell all around me, and talk about evidence and suspects.

The officer is still staring at me with interest. I close my eyes so I won't have to look at him. But then all I see is Logan's expression as he spoke, as he pulled on some invisible string, unwinding the truth.

"Miss? May I help you?"

I flinch and my eyes fly open. The officer is standing up now, leaning toward the glass, wary, waiting for me to reply.

I hover there for several heartbeats, trying to answer, but my lips are sewn shut with a thin, toxic thread of humiliation and embarrassment.

I can't do this.

"No, sir," I blurt. "I thought this was the courthouse. Sorry."

And I spin around and leave.

They say you never know what you'll do when you have to face something terrifying. We'd all like to believe that we'd be brave, stand up tall and march in and speak up for ourselves, that we know what's right, what's just, and we'd stand by it, knowing that the catastrophe that awaits can't be worse than the catastrophe that's already occurred. But the fact is, you just never know what you'll do when your nightmare arrives. What's right and just — well, sometimes that's the last thing on your mind. And all you want to do is survive.

Twenty-Eight

When I get back to Rusty's, I find the kitchen swallowed up in smoke. Eleanor is sitting at the table, wholly unconcerned, eating a rather large plate of charred pizza rolls. A smoke alarm dangles from the ceiling, half-disassembled, a knot of wires holding the casing like a dislodged eyeball.

I look pointedly at it and say, "You need to put that back together. My caseworker will be here in exactly twenty-three minutes."

After I do my best to disperse the smoke, and after I help reassemble the smoke detector, and after I grumble for the requisite amount of time, I look around the house and realize it's clean. I don't mean this figuratively. I mean that the house, with all its dusty corners and cat hair and clutter and germs, is actually, truly clean. Like, floors swept, dishes washed, counters wiped, laundry put away. And I wasn't the one to do it. It's sort of shocking, to tell you the truth.

I walk back into the kitchen, where Eleanor is now flipping through a magazine. "Did you do this?"

"Do what?"

"Clean the house. Pick up. Make the place look presentable for Sarah. Did you do it?"

She raises an eyebrow at me and turns the page in her magazine. Her nonanswer is her answer. Yes, she cleaned it. I open my mouth, only to shut it again.

Eleanor has done something … *nice*.

I don't even know how to process this information.

Rusty shows up forty-five minutes late. By the time he arrives, I've gone through about twenty mock-up mind-conversations with him, where I ask him about a tall, dark-haired college kid who used to work with him, without actually asking him about a tall, dark-haired college kid who used to work with him. And Sarah and I have exchanged a half hour's worth of vague pleasantries about the weather and about New Harbor and about my upcoming school year. And then Sarah taps her fingers on her briefcase, I brush a bit of imaginary lint off my clothes, and the room falls silent.

Now, though, as Rusty comes tromping into the house, Sarah is speaking rather loudly. "You're late," she says. No *Hello.* No *Nice to see you.* Just *You're late.* That's how I know she's angry. I've never seen Sarah angry, and I find it extremely disconcerting. Even Eleanor, who's been banging around in the kitchen cabinets, grows strangely quiet.

I try to imagine my sunflowers.

Rusty smiles at Sarah as though his grin is all it will take to defuse the situation, as though he's a celebrity arriving a couple of minutes late to a movie premiere. "Right," he says. "Well, I met my wife for lunch, and then —"

"Your wife," Sarah says, her lips tight. She yanks a file folder out of her briefcase, scratching quick, furious notes inside, sticking one forceful index finger up in the air when Rusty opens his mouth to speak. Surprisingly, Rusty's lips drift back together, and he sits beside us on the couch.

He looks profoundly uncomfortable.

That makes two of us.

After several long seconds, Sarah stops writing and looks up at him. "What is going on here, Mr. Cochran? Grace has been living here for a month. *A month*. I've left you a dozen unanswered voicemails, you're nearly an hour late for this meeting, I assigned Grace a new therapist here in New Harbor and she has yet to even see him, and now you're telling me you're married? Don't you think that a change in your marital status would be something we'd need to know?"

Rusty removes his hat, spinning it in slow circles in his hands. I'm suddenly terrified that Sarah is going to make me pack up my things. That she's going to order me to get into her car and leave. "Right," Rusty says. He clears his throat. "Right. Well, I can explain all of that."

Sarah holds up her index finger again.

I put a tall fence around my sunflowers.

The kitchen is still freakishly silent. For some reason, it bothers me that Eleanor is listening.

"This relationship," Sarah begins finally, waving that same finger, which now feels vaguely like a weapon, between Rusty and me, "is being overseen by the state of Florida, and there are *rules*, Mr. Cochran." She sighs and then glances at me. Her expression softens, like she knows that Rusty is all I have, maybe even like she feels sorry for me, and then she places her hand on top of mine and squeezes.

Something about the gesture blows my fence apart.

In a softer voice, Sarah says, "I know it's been quite an adjustment for all of you. I've given you a wide berth the past several weeks, so you two can get into a routine. But the state runs a tight ship." She pauses for a moment, staring out the window before letting her gaze trail back to Rusty. "We have a system to follow, Mr. Cochran. This is serious business, and if you can't take it seriously — well, maybe this isn't the best place for Grace."

I didn't realize how much I've feared this happening until today. My entire body feels brittle, like if I move as much as a pinkie finger, I'll shatter all over the floor.

The only sound is the ticking of my watch.

I close my eyes. Sarah is still gripping my hand, the pressure getting tighter and tighter.

"I've got this," Rusty says finally. I've never heard Rusty speak so quietly in all my life. I can't bear to look at him now. A searing wall of tears collects behind my eyes, threating to spill out.

Sarah exhales and lets go of my hand. "I'll be sending you the required paperwork for your wife. If and when you bother to check your voicemail, you'll find that I took the liberty of scheduling a therapy appointment for Grace. Please see to it that she doesn't miss it." She stands and strides toward the door, pausing for a moment with her hand on the doorknob. "Taking care of your niece is a privilege, Mr. Cochran. Don't ever forget that."

#

The room is dead quiet after Sarah walks out, and then Rusty bolts to his feet and says, "Sorry! I'm sorry, G. That was —"

"You," I supply in a whisper, closing my eyes. "That was *you*, Rusty."

"Grace —"

"It's true, though, isn't it?" I say, the words coming out before I can even think them through. "Whenever I've needed you, whenever you should've been there for me, you've been nowhere to be found, only to show up late with a smile and an excuse." It's sort of shocking, being so honest with him, but what I'm saying is true, and both of us know it. For as long as I've known Rusty, he's gone through the motions of being an adult without actually being one. I open my eyes, blinking several times to clear my vision and staring at Rusty, who's standing with his back to me, hands crammed in his pockets and head low. "What you did when Dad died," I go on, twisting my hands in my lap, "disappearing on me like that, leaving me alone for so long … it was wrong."

Rusty turns around and meets my stare. His face looks droopy and old, lined with wrinkles that I've never noticed before. He says, "He was my brother, I loved him and it hurt like hell when he died. I wasn't in any shape to take care of you."

"He was my father," I say, sort of loudly, my voice shaking, "I was fifteen, and I wasn't in any shape to be alone."

Rusty stares out the window for several moments, silent. And then he says, "Even so, you were stronger than me. I spent a damn year in a bottle of jack. Was so drunk at the funeral that I barely made it past the front door before they kicked me out."

I look down, running a finger along the frayed hem of my shorts, remembering the funeral pamphlet I saw in his room. So Rusty was there, briefly. I wonder what would've happened if I'd seen him that day — if we'd be in a better place than we are right now.

"It's just," Rusty goes on, his tone elusive, like he isn't giving me the whole story, like maybe he never would, "I knew you'd be okay. You were always so strong-willed. What could I have done for you? Nothing." He squeezes his eyes shut with his palm. "And I know — *I know* — that I should've been there for you, but I couldn't even be there for myself. Sounds like an excuse, but it's true. This is me, Gracie. I'm not perfect. I've made mistakes in my life, made mistakes with you, and I'm real sorry."

I've waited so long for an apology, and now that I have one, I don't know how I'm supposed to feel about it. Does it matter to me? Yes. Does it make everything all right? Not really. I will myself not to blurt out *It's okay* or *I understand*, because neither of those things is true, and I don't want to shove empty words between us right now.

Knotting my hands together to keep them from shaking, I watch Rusty as he walks back to the couch, sits down beside me and puts a weighty palm on my back. Clearing his throat and straightening up, he says, "I want to make it up to you, if you can find it in your heart to give me another chance."

Thing is, I feel like I've already given him another chance. And another. And another. Time and time again, he's wedged a lit stick of dynamite inside me, blowing me apart. I wonder if there's enough of me left to do it again. I wipe my hands on the couch and meet his stare. His eyes are hopeful but despairing. They're devastated yet eager. They're my family's eyes, and they're begging me for another chance. I take in a breath, and in my exhale, I say, "Okay."

Twenty-Nine

It was the Marios who taught me how to parallel park. They had two college-aged kids — the oldest would probably become a lawyer, and the youngest would probably *need* a lawyer — and had hosted dozens of foster kids, so by the time I arrived at their house, they were pretty easygoing about the whole driver's ed thing. We'd go out every Sunday to practice parallel parking in their dented-up Chevy Impala, so old it was practically biblical, not at all unlike Eleanor's three-bedroom Cadillac, which I'm currently parking in front of my therapist's office building.

I arrive as planned, at exactly two forty-five in the afternoon, sliding the car into park and just sitting there for several minutes, tapping my fingers on the steering wheel and watching people walk into the medical building next to the hospital. Eleanor's air conditioner doesn't work for crap, and her car smells like a wet ashtray, but I'll be damned if I'm going to sit around in a therapist's waiting room for longer than absolutely necessary. At exactly two fifty-five, I turn off the car, grab my purse and slog inside, trudging my way into the elevator.

To be clear, I'm not a fan of elevators. Never have been. Something about being in a box that dangles several stories above the ground, supported by only a metal cable, is mildly terrifying to me. But the alternative here is to hike up ten stories of steps.

So I'm standing inside the elevator, sweating despite the air-conditioning and my flip-flops and my breathable clothes. The woman leaning on the opposite wall nods hi, and I nod hi, and then the elevator comes to a stop at the third floor and the doors slide open, admitting a half-dozen or so men. Now, I don't know any of these guys from Adam. And I doubt they even notice me. But when they wedge their way into the elevator, squashing up against me and bumping into my shoulders and sucking up all the oxygen, my heart starts banging out of my chest.

There are too many of them. The elevator reeks of aftershave and sweat and men men *men*.

I can't breathe.

Time upends, and I start thinking about all the things I've been trying to forget. Suddenly I'm sick with the flu, head spinning from Ambien, listening to a living room full of men shout at the TV.

I need to get out of here.

"You okay, miss?" one of them asks.

Valid question. Probably looks like I'm having a heart attack. I nod yes.

The elevator slows to another stop and the doors open. A tall, dark-haired man squeezes in.

A scream starts working its way up my throat.

I mash my lips together as the elevator inches its way up. I can't seem to draw any air into my lungs. My chest is starting to burn. Seemingly in slow motion, the elevator doors slide open on the tenth floor. "Excuse me!" I basically yell, squeezing my way out. I stand in the hallway for a moment, dizzy and manic, and then I make my way to the restroom to splash some water on my face. By the time I'm sitting across from my new therapist, I've erased all traces of my panic attack or mental breakdown or whatever it was.

My therapist, Dr. Monkton, is short and wide, and he has this gigantic mustache that tends to twitch whenever I speak. Which isn't a lot, mind you. I'm working on a need-to-know basis right now, and as far as I can tell, this guy doesn't need to know anything at all.

Apparently Sarah has given him the gory details of my orphanhood. He already knows that my dad died, it wrecked me, and my only living relative took a long time to step forward and claim me. So I spend a half hour answering his questions about Dad and Rusty. These are the kinds of questions I can handle. Dad's death and Rusty's childishness, those two things have always been tall enough and wide enough for me to hide behind. Even so, the way Dr. Monkton sits back in his chair and listens — it's like he's waiting for me to admit something tragic. Like he knows very well I'm concealing something.

That little box labeled *rape* — it's been cracked open.

I wonder whether it smells rotten.

"I'm sure it's a big adjustment," he says as we're wrapping up. "Being in New Harbor is bound to stir up a lot of memories about your father. How are you coping?"

I shrug. "As well as I can."

He scratches something into his notebook, wrinkling up the skin between his eyebrows. The action makes him look like Yosemite Sam. "Do you feel secure, staying with your uncle?"

What I want to say is that I don't know who to trust. That I'm terrified of everyone and everything. That my entire world is crumbling from the foundation up. Instead, what I say is, "Kind of." As the words twist their way out of my mouth, I'm struck by the clearest memory of Janna, years ago, when she confronted me about whether I had feelings for Owen.

Kind of.

I'm still skirting around the truth with her, still afraid of it, not quite lying to her, but not quite telling her everything, either. What happened that Labor Day weekend — it's wedged between us right now, arms spread wide, pushing us apart. I shut my eyes for a moment, and when I open them, I find my therapist watching, waiting for me to make the next move.

And so I do.

"We good?" I ask. "I need to go see a friend."

Thirty

Janna stands unmoving, a statue lit up in sharp relief by the McAllisters' patio light that evening, the hum of the living room TV behind her. Me, though — I'm a knot of kinetic energy, pacing from one end of her porch to the other, hands flitting in the air like birds' wings as I tell Janna what happened that Labor Day weekend.

I feel strangely as though I'm recounting a book or a movie or a shocking newspaper article. Someone else's horror story. But it's my horror story, and as Janna listens to it, as she begins to understand the truth, revulsion and shock pour into her expression. I don't know where my words are coming from, but they're coming, alarming and ugly and revealing, getting wrung out of my chest and wrenched up my throat without any assistance whatsoever.

And once I get all the way through it, I just keep on talking. I'm stalling, hijacking her chance to respond by repeating the same thing about a thousand different ways — "And then after that, Dad died" and "I didn't really have time to process it, because Dad died" and "I was going to confront Owen about it, but then Dad died."

The truth: I'm terrified that Janna sees me differently now.

It's silent.

So silent.

I can hear her breaths and the spaces between her breaths and even the spaces between those.

"Grace," Janna finally whispers.

I don't answer her. I don't even move. My legs are locked in place by an invisible force field.

It isn't the sexual assault that's so paralyzing. It's the shame.

I'm so tired of being ashamed.

Finally, I straighten my spine, draw in a breath and turn around. Janna's eyes are round and sad and swallowing, and I want to hurl myself into her arms. But I don't, because her arms are folded over her chest, hands clenched into fists.

I open my mouth to tell her *It's okay* and *I'm okay* but then stop myself because neither of those things is true and I'm not sure they will ever be true. "I'm sorry," I say instead. "I'm sorry for keeping it from you."

Tears spill down her cheeks, and her chin wobbles. "No, *I'm* sorry. I'm sorry that this happened to you, that you had to go through it by yourself. I'm sorry for acting so stupid and stubborn." She pauses. "I'm sorry you thought it was Owen."

We're quiet for the space of several heartbeats, the air between us thick with everything.

"I'm sorry for that, too," I whisper, picking at a loose paint chip in the porch railing.

"I understand why you'd think it was him, Grace. Really, I

do. But it's just — Owen is *Owen*. He would never do something like that."

I nod and whisper, "I know."

We stare at each other for a moment, a lifetime of friendship pulling us together and a couple of years of misery pushing us apart, and then Janna wipes the wetness off her face and walks the length of the deck. When she turns back around, her expression is fierce. "I can't believe that Rusty could —" She swallows the rest of her sentence, disgusted. "God, Grace. You have to go to the police. You have to get the hell out of that house."

It's the condemnation behind her words that bothers me most. Not once tonight have I mentioned Rusty, yet she's already convicted him. "Janna," I say, "Logan told me that he saw me talking to one of Rusty's coworkers outside. I'm sure he was the one who —"

Her eyes snap to mine. "You've got to be kidding me," she says, exasperated and angry. I miss having somewhere to direct my anger. Mine just flies out and arcs right back to me. She leans toward me, imploring, insistent. "Grace, he avoided you for nearly two years. You have to know that Rusty did this."

I used to think I knew it all, and it was easier then, because everything was black and white. Yes and no. Guilty and not guilty. I knew exactly who to blame, and it was Owen. Now, though, everything is ambiguous. Maybe deep inside I believe that Rusty is guilty, and maybe I don't. I can't even tell anymore. "I don't know, Janna. I just want —" I stop. Swallow. Wipe away an errant tear. What do I want? To heal? Forgive? Move on? All of those things sound stupid, because I feel like it's more than that. I feel like it's everything. "I just want my life back."

Thirty-One

Say what you will about Janna McAllister, but she's as protective as they come.

First thing the next morning, she barrels through Rusty's front door with the elegance and composure of a hurricane, eyes pinned distrustfully on my uncle as he eats breakfast. She calls me twice from work, nagging me to go to the police. And then, late that afternoon, she sends Andy over to drag me out of the house. I find him shifting his weight on Rusty's front porch, looking embarrassed and confused as he says, "Janna told me you might want to come with me to get an ice cream at Dream Cones? So here I am. Uh. To take you with me to Dream Cones."

I pinch my forehead. "Right. Okay."

And so: Dream Cones.

Where Andy takes a full five minutes to order one ice-cream cone.

I'm not even kidding.

"Most important thing is the toppings," Andy tells me, rather seriously — like he's imparting sage-like wisdom or something — as we stand at the counter to order. "Stick with cookies or candy bars, crushed, not chopped. Beware of gummies. They practically freeze into rocks when they're cold, and they don't work well with chocolate. Never mix gelatin with chocolate, Grace. Never. Ever." He pauses for an extended moment, scrutinizing the menu on the board overhead. The girl behind the register sighs and fishes her phone out of her back pocket, thumbing around on it. To me, Andy says, "You need a mix of three different chocolate-based toppings for the best blend. It's the perfect chocolate balance you want. Without the balance, your ice cream will lack oomph, and an ice cream without oomph might as well be plain vanilla."

"Oomph. Gotcha," I say, hoping to speed him along. People around here like their ice cream, so the place is packed — customers waiting in line behind us, kids milling around the pickup counter, tourists searching for a place to sit, employees buzzing back and forth behind the counter.

And then there's Andy.

Some sort of weird, endangered species.

Finally, Andy knocks twice on the counter and says, very intensely, to the clerk, "Okay. So I'll have a chocolate-vanilla swirl on a waffle cone, with crushed Butterfingers, Peanut Butter Cups and Oreos, please."

A million years and/or five minutes later we're finally walking out with our ice creams. As we step onto the beach-front, we nearly barrel over a bunch of guys from the track team. Front and center is Sawyer, naturally, wearing a back-ward baseball cap and a smooth, deliberate expression. Logan, the friendliest face in the bunch, is flanking his right side. There's also a skinny, long-legged kid whose name is Chase or Charles, maybe, and a few others I don't know, most of them decked out in board shorts and sunglasses and smiles, like there's no place they'd rather be but with their hero, Sawyer Simon.

Ack.

As we step around them, Sawyer glances at his brother and then back at me. "Ladies," he says.

One of the guys snickers.

Andy shifts his weight and flushes in embarrassment.

Is the annoyed part of your brain attached directly to your leg? Because right now I want to knee Sawyer in the —

"Janna with you?" Logan says, peering around me. Like many guys in New Harbor, like Andy, Logan has always had a thing for Janna.

I say, "She's working today."

"Ah," Logan says. And then he turns to Sawyer. "Dude. I think I'm hungry for pizza. You?"

Sawyer scratches his chest and rocks back on his heels, his eyes lingering on me a moment longer than necessary. Then he smiles. It's not a real smile. It's just a squint of his eyes and a twitch of his mouth. "Sure thing." And with a wave, the whole mess of them ambles away.

I glance over at Andy and say, "Don't let Sawyer get to you."

Andy shuffles around in his flip-flops. "It's — whatever," he says. He looks down at his feet. Fixedly. Nothing else comes out of his mouth till we've nearly made it back to Rusty's. And when he finally speaks, it isn't about his brother. Pointing at the lifeguard tower in front of us, he says, "Did you notice you have a new lifeguard by your house? He's a transfer from Siesta. We work opposite shifts, so I haven't actually met him, but I hear he's cool."

Shielding my eyes, I turn and peer toward the guy perched atop the lifeguard stand.

My breath goes still as stone.

Early twenties. Mop-top hair. Tan arms.

It's the guy from the bus. The guy whose wallet I stole.

"Shit," I say. That's my first mistake. Actually, scratch that. My first mistake was, oh, I don't know … something along the lines of STEALING HIS WALLET TO BEGIN WITH. Because what the hell was I thinking?

I wasn't thinking. That's the problem.

That's always the problem.

My eyes are still fixed on the lifeguard. Barefoot and relaxed, he looks like someone who inhabits the world informally, maybe even a little recklessly, not a worry to be found.

"Earth to Grace?" Andy says, and I can hardly hear him due to my stroke symptoms. "I asked if you're okay? You look pale."

I need to speak.

I need to speak.

I need to speak. Once I can figure out how to form words. Since that doesn't appear to be happening anytime soon, I do the only thing that makes sense: I start coughing.

I mean, my mouth needs to do *something*.

Andy thumps me on the back. "Are you all right?"

"Yeah," I say finally, forcing myself to start walking again. "My ice cream went down the wrong pipe, is all. I'm fine."

#

I'm not fine, though. I'm terrified.

Because suddenly this lifeguard — who works a stone's throw from Rusty's house — is right there in plain view almost every single day. And when your stupid, illegal mistakes wander too close to your front door, well, that's how you end up in a heap of trouble.

So by Saturday night I'm in a perpetual state of anxiety. Seriously. On the nervous-breakdown scale, I'd have to say I'm probably at a nine point five. I've barely eaten. I haven't set foot outside Rusty's in several days. I'm wearing a hoodie pulled tight over my head — in *July*, mind you — so that I'm disguised on the off chance Lifeguard Guy spots me as I stand by the living room window, trying to calm down.

Because what if this guy knows it was me who stole his wallet?

What if he recognizes me?

I slam my eyes shut. When they open again, I see Owen walking out of his house, dressed in that freaking dress shirt and those freaking khakis. I look at my watch. "Six forty-five, on the dot," I sing sarcastically under my breath, watching him climb into the Jeep. "Must be Saturday night."

He's hiding something. I know it.

The Jeep wheels slowly out of sight. I glance at Eleanor's car.

It's a nice night for a drive, isn't it?

It's an awfully nice night for a drive.

I tighten my hoodie till only my eyes remain uncovered and, with exaggerated casualness, stroll to the kitchen table, pluck up Eleanor's keys and head for the front door. My words come out clumped together, like a massive hashtag: "HeyEleanormind-ifIborrowyourcarforafewminutesokaythankyoubye."

#

If I squeal out of the driveway, make a lurching left on Sixth and disregard a speed limit sign or two, I can coincidentally find myself a couple of car lengths behind Owen.

Wherever he's heading, it isn't far away, because within a handful of minutes, he's twisting his way through a quaint New Harbor neighborhood and hooking a right into a driveway. Hanging back a little and ducking down in my seat, I come to a slow stop in the middle of the street, watching him in a manner that a passerby would probably consider stalking. Fortunately, no one's passing by.

Owen has a spring in his step and an expectant curve in his shoulders as he climbs out of the Jeep.

Gah. He's definitely here to see a girl.

This is a small town, small enough that I could've bumped into her at some point. Maybe I even know her. Maybe she's Owen's age, and the two of them are planning on going to the same college. Maybe they hang out every Saturday night to discuss where they'll get married and how many children they'll have and which suburb they'll live in. A lifetime of love doesn't just plan itself, you know.

My train of thought is interrupted as a minivan rolls around me, the driver holding an angry fist in the air, her lips forming a question that I can see clearly through her passenger-side window: *What the hell are you doing?*

Good question, I think. I may also say it out loud. And then I pull to the side of the road and resume my short, illustrious career as a detective.

The front of the house is nondescript, really, just a cozy place, splashes of red flowers dangling from planters on the porch and a rocking chair facing the street. Off to the side of the entry, a long wooden ramp leads to the driveway. My eyes linger on it for a moment as Owen rings the doorbell. The door swings open and —

There she is.

A young blonde girl — like, a *girl* girl, maybe nine or ten years old — screeches hello to Owen in an excited, high-pitched voice that I can hear even from where I am. She reaches up to hug him from, *oh God*, a wheelchair.

My heart drops straight out of my chest.

This is the girl from the car accident. Zoey Barnes.

I stare at her for a moment, frozen and struck dumb. She looks completely different from the girl I saw online. I'm not even sure I would've guessed she's the same person, actually — what with her bright smile and her leaping joy in seeing Owen — if it hadn't been for the blond hair and the wheelchair.

So Owen has made amends with her.

They're … friends.

And I'm an idiot.

Through the embarrassment I smile, just a little. Because it occurs to me that even if I never find peace with my past, I'm glad Owen's found peace with his.

Thirty-Two

The next evening, Mrs. McAllister, apron tied around her waist and private smile tugging on her lips, materializes on Rusty's front porch, singing, "Knock, knock," while simultaneously opening the front door. Spine straight and chin high, she barrels inside like she has free reign over the entire neighborhood, or something. Coming to a stop in front of the couch, where I've been playing the violin for God knows how long, she says, "We're eating dinner in ten minutes, Fettuccini Alfredo." She lifts a brow at me, because she knows very well it's my favorite meal. "I'd like you to join us."

"Uh," I say.

All right. First of all, I'm still feeling sort of guilty for following Owen to Zoey's house. It wasn't the worst thing I've ever done — clearly — but I'm not proud of it, either. Second of all, it's seven o'clock, which is exactly when a particular lifeguard gets off duty from a particular lifeguard tower. Best not to be showing my face outside right now.

"Don't tell me you're busy, because you're clearly not," Mrs. McAllister says. She's a walking bullshit detector. Lying to her takes planning and focus, both of which I'm currently lacking. So when she grabs my hand and pulls me upright, I helplessly follow her to the door. As she steps onto the porch, I trail behind her, my eyes scanning the beach. When I realize Lifeguard Guy is already gone, I exhale in relief.

In all the years I've stayed at Rusty's, I've never had reason to set foot in the house next door. Most of my life, it's belonged to the Simons. And because of my best-friend rivalry with Andy and my overall dislike of Sawyer, I've steered clear of this house on principle alone. Still, the place feels instantly familiar as I step inside, either because it's decorated à la Mrs. McAllister — all blue plaid and floral arrangements and hazelnut-scented candles — or because Janna is in plain view.

Pacing back and forth in the living room, Janna is reading from a sheet of paper, muttering to herself. This is Janna when she's cramming to memorize lines for a play. She claims that she remembers them best when her body is in motion, which has always been a point of contention between us, because she memorizes her lines everywhere, inside malls and at school and on sidewalks. I used to gripe that she was going to break her neck, and she used to grumble that I worried too much.

Mrs. McAllister says, sort of loudly, "Janna, honey. We have company."

Janna jerks around to face me, surprised.

Ah. So Janna didn't know her mom was inviting me over. Ten bucks says that this is a truth-finding mission for Mrs. McAllister — that she's aware I've been talking to Janna and Owen, and she wants to get a feel for what's really going on.

Basically, it's an ambush.

"Dinner's in ten," Mrs. McAllister says. "Grace, mind helping me with the breadsticks? Janna, you stir the sauce."

The kitchen smells like Parmesan cheese, garlic and some familiar spice that I can't quite name. Long ago, Janna's mom gave me the recipe for her fettuccini, although I always suspected that she left out an ingredient, because mine has never tasted as good as hers.

As I pull the breadsticks out of the oven, I find myself glancing around for Owen. This would be an excellent time for me to become — oh, I don't know — unconcerned about Owen's every waking, breathing moment. But the more I try not to think about him, the more I think about him, and the more I realize how overwhelmingly sad I am that he isn't home. I'm actually staring at the back door like a pining idiot when Owen opens it and strides into the kitchen, his father close behind him. "All I'm saying," Owen is telling his father, his voice sort of curt, "is that you should come to a complete stop, even if you don't see anyone else coming. It's just safer."

Mr. McAllister is about to reply when Owen sees me and stops short, causing his father to almost barrel into him from behind. "Grace," Owen says, his eyes wide.

Placing a huge bowl of pasta on the table, Mrs. McAllister says in an offhand way, "I invited Grace over for dinner."

Nothing for me to do here but smile and wave. "Hi," I say, super-originally, tucking a stray strand of hair behind my ear. When I first arrived, I twisted my hair up on top of my head, letting a few tendrils escape around my face. I used to wear it like that a lot, back when Owen and I were together.

Not that I want to get back together with Owen.

Because: awkward.

Still, I don't want to discount it completely.

Even though there's no way in hell.

I clear my throat and drum the pads of my fingers on my legs. Now seems like the perfect time to imagine my sunflowers. "Hi," I say again, like an Alzheimer's patient.

Janna's mom must've told her husband that she was planning to hijack me for dinner, because there's no surprise in his expression whatsoever. He gives me a quick hug and holds me by the shoulders at arm's length, smile lines creasing the sides of his eyes. "New Harbor looks good on you." He glances at his wife. "Honey, doesn't New Harbor look good on her?"

"It looks good on her," she agrees. "Now, sit down before everything gets cold."

The thing about Mr. and Mrs. McAllister is that they never really stop talking. And when they do, either Owen or Janna prompts them to continue. Tonight their conversation revolves around a girl on the track team, Gabby, who's one of those people who knows the history of everything — "Paper plates were invented in the late-nineteenth century by Martin Keyes" and "The first gasoline-powered American car on the road was the Duryea Motor Wagon" and whatever. And after that, they discuss Mrs. McAllister's experiences in college, going on and on about some music-appreciation class that she never actually appreciated.

Things are going well.

Possibly a little too well.

Owen's wearing this thin cotton T-shirt, and every time he reaches across the table for something, his sleeve slides up a little and I can see entirely too much of his flexed right biceps.

I try not to stare, but even when he barely moves his arm — BOOM — there it is. *Stop staring*, I keep telling my eyes, but they aren't listening.

Finally, Mrs. McAllister turns toward me, pats my hand and says, "It's so nice, having you here. How's Rusty? I'd ask him myself, but I hardly ever see him."

"He's doing great," I say, forcing a smile. "He got married last week."

Janna stares at me, totally aghast. "No shit?"

Her mom shoots her a look. "Watch your mouth, Janna."

"Sorry," Janna mutters. She puts both palms flat on the table and leans toward her mother. "It's just — Mom. Rusty's already been married, like, *five times*."

"Six," I correct, "if you count the annulment. The courthouse should probably start giving him marriage permits instead of marriage licenses."

Janna's dad snorts, shakes a breadstick in my direction and then turns to his wife. "I forgot how much I love this girl. I wonder if we could trade Janna for her?"

And so it goes. The best meal I've had since I came back to town. I'm helping to clear the dishes off the table when I grab a plate, spin around and find myself practically nose to nose with Owen. Is it possible for chests to cartwheel? I believe my chest is cartwheeling. Owen scrubs a hand over his hair and lets it drift to his side. I stare at his thumb, which, I notice suddenly, has a gigantic blue-black bruise. "Get into a fight with a piece of driftwood?" I say.

Owen glances down at his thumb. "Got distracted and accidentally hit my hand with a mallet."

"Must've been one hell of a distraction," I say.

"I was looking at you."

My lighthearted mood vanishes along with most of the muscles that hold me upright and also the ones I use to speak. The cartwheeling in my chest has turned into full-fledged backflipping. Um, how should I reply? With some sort of joke? No. Owen's expression is sincere. How do you joke with sincere? Hope and terror are mushrooming inside my chest in equal measure, squashing my heart and lungs flat against my rib cage.

Mrs. McAllister breezes past, shooting us an all-knowing look as she wraps up a plate of leftovers and slides it into the fridge. With a small smile, she walks out of the room, leaving us alone.

"Sorry," Owen mumbles. "Didn't mean to make you uncomfortable."

"No, it's fine. It's fine! I mean, you didn't — I'm just —" I grab a rag and wipe off the counter like my sole purpose in life is to bravely save thousands from *E. coli*. "Ack," I say finally, tossing the rag in the sink. "You have nothing to apologize for, Owen."

We wash dishes for a few minutes, Owen rinsing off plates and then handing them to me to slide into the dishwasher. I can hear the TV in the living room, and Janna, talking on the phone to Andy, who called at the end of dinner.

"Your neck sore?" Owen asks — fair enough question, I guess, because I'm rolling my head around in circles, stretching my neck muscles, as I wait for him to hand me another plate.

"Too much practicing today without a music stand."

He glances at me, surprised, his amber eyebrows arching just the slightest bit as he hands me a platter. "Did you leave it in Tampa?"

Putting the plate in the dishwasher, I say, "When I went into foster care, I was given only a certain number of my things. It wasn't the biggest priority to the state of Florida, I guess."

"So it's gone?"

There's a constriction in my throat. I speak around it. "Yeah. It's been two years. I'm over it."

The only sound in the kitchen is the clink of silverware in the stainless sink. "Careful — sharp," Owen says as he hands me a knife. "I'm glad you kept it up, the violin. Yesterday, I heard you playing that Brahms song ..."

"The Brahms violin concerto?" I supply. It's weird standing in the McAllisters' kitchen having a regular conversation with Owen. Also, it's not weird.

"Yes! Love that one. You're getting really good. Have you been taking lessons?"

"Nah," I say, shrugging a bit. "I mean — I've always taken orchestra at school, but orchestra teachers don't really teach individual lessons."

We're quiet for a few minutes as we finish the last of the dishes and start the dishwasher. When I turn toward Owen, I find him leaning against the counter, watching me. I can tell he's about to say something serious, because his eyes are solemn. "Look," he says in a low voice, glancing toward the living room and then back at me, "I know I should've said this the last time we talked, and I know it's probably way too late, but I want to apologize. For everything. For leaving you alone that night on Labor Day weekend. For not trying to track you down when you fell off the grid. I should've known you wouldn't walk away unless something huge had happened, unless something was really wrong. It's just —" He stops and fidgets with the cargo pocket on his shorts. "You were this awesome, beautiful girl, and I was a total disaster. I honestly thought I was dragging you down." His voice breaks on the last word, and my heart twists.

"Owen —"

He raises a palm. "Hear me out, please. I feel like an ass. I was hurt because I thought you were brushing me off. Not trying harder to get in touch with you after you went back to Tampa — it was shitty and it was wrong and I need you to forgive me, because I want to be part of your life again, Grace. You want to just be friends? Fine. We'll be friends. If you want something more, well, you can have that, too."

Is this real?

Is this actually happening?

I hedge uncomfortably, stuffing my hands in my pockets. Then I say, "I'm not the same person anymore, Owen."

He ducks down to meet my eyes. "Yes, you are. And I'm going to help you figure out who this" — he pauses, clenches and unclenches his jaw — "person is who hurt you."

I don't think I can do this. "Owen, I —"

"Grace," he says, his voice pained. "Please let me help you."

I stare out the kitchen window at Rusty's house, where Rusty and Faith and Eleanor have been buzzing around ever since I arrived — hummingbirds visiting flowers — busy with their own lives.

I'm tired of being surrounded by people but feeling so alone.

Owen and I can hang out, can't we? I'm not going to jump into a *relationship* relationship with him. I won't get in over my head. "Okay," I whisper.

Thirty-Three

The next day begins like any other day. I roll out of bed, shuffle into the kitchen to start a pot of coffee, grumble at the cat on my way to the bathroom, make a face at my reflection in the mirror, slouch my way back to the kitchen, drink too much coffee and attempt to make my hair presentable.

When I walk back to my room, though. That's when it happens.

I find Eleanor crouched over my desk, the top drawer slid open. She straightens up as I enter, smiling congenially. "I have to wonder," she says slowly, gesturing to the drawer, "whether you obtained those wallets in a legal manner."

Suddenly I feel like I'm sliding down the steep, gravelly slope of a mountain, arms flailing, unable to stop. Words start flying out of my mouth. "I can't even — I mean — those aren't — why were you going through my things?"

Eleanor rocks back on her heels. "Was going to borrow a pair of socks," she says, and she has a smirk on her face that tells me she finds this whole thing vaguely entertaining. "I have to admit — I didn't see this one coming. You, a thief?" She shakes her head back and forth in disbelief.

I shut my eyes so I don't have to look at her. But I can still hear the ghost of her words, echoing in my head. *You, a thief?* I want to feel angry with Eleanor for invading my privacy. But all I feel is humiliation, thick and tar-like. And all I see is Dad, looking down on me, his expression heavy with disappointment. *You, a thief?*

I'm sorry, Dad.

I open my eyes. I'm crying huge, stupid tears. Eleanor's form swims in front of me as she says, "Relax, slick. Your secret is safe with me."

I wait a moment for this to make me feel better.

It doesn't happen.

I want to tell Eleanor that I had my reasons for taking those wallets, that I'm not a bad person. But I'm not sure whether I believe that anymore.

Who am I? The criminal or the victim?

I don't even know.

Time and time again, I've told myself it was okay to steal from those men, because they made me uncomfortable, because they were disgusting, because they shouldn't have been looking at me like that in the first place. I felt like I was taking things back, collecting all the little parts of me that had been blown apart, putting myself together again so I wouldn't have to worry about footsteps behind me or leering eyes or creepy stares.

But what I should've been doing was finding the person who stole my trust in the world. I should have been looking for *him*, because he's still out there. And as much as I'd love to blame that on someone else, I can't.

I can't.

I'm the one who gave him his freedom.

I'm the one who let him get away with what he did.

I wipe my tears with the back of my hand. All these wrongs I've committed, well, I'll right them somehow. What matters most is stopping this monster before he hurts someone else.

#

"Do I remember a dark-haired kid who used to work with me a couple of years ago?" Rusty repeats as he uncovers a container of leftovers he's pulled from the fridge. He's still wearing his work clothes. I barely let him walk through the front door before I started asking questions. "Not specifically. I've worked with a lot of kids who match that description. They come and go all the time."

I square my shoulders and draw in a breath, steeling myself. "He came over to your house to watch the Gators' season opener a couple of years ago, that time I was sick."

A complex, unidentifiable emotion passes over Rusty's face. He puts the container on the counter and turns toward me. "Why do you ask?"

I tell him the truth, or at least part of it. "Logan told me he saw me outside that night, talking to that guy. I just thought it was weird, is all."

A little crease forms in Rusty's forehead. "You went outside that night?"

"Apparently."

Leaning against the counter, Rusty says, "Maybe it was when we walked over to the beach to watch the fireworks."

"You left the house to watch *fireworks*?"

Rusty shifts his weight. "I mean — most of us did? Can't remember who all went. I had a few beers that night." He lifts his hat and then crams it back on his head. "I think Andy hung back, though. Why don't you ask him?"

Thirty-Four

I leave a long, detailed voicemail on Andy's phone that night, but he never returns my call. So the next day, I leave another.

And then another.

And then another.

I look for him at the beach and downtown and in the library. I go to his house and knock on his front door. But I can't seem to find him anywhere. Which is upsetting in a sharp, visceral sort of way, because earlier this summer, I bumped into him practically every time I turned around.

Thirty-Five

The first thing Rusty says to me when I get home from my therapy appointment Tuesday night is, "Sorry it's so loud," followed closely by, "Want some orange juice?" I'm unbelievably exhausted, the past several days wearing on me like a toothache. All I want to do is curl up in bed and sleep an entire week away. But the sight of Rusty, wearing glasses, standing at the kitchen counter with Faith, a juicer and a mountain of oranges in front of him, makes me hitch to a stop.

Who is this person, even?

Rusty must see the question mark in my expression, because he says, "We're stocking up on folic acid. It's supposed to prevent neural tube defects in babies." He pauses a moment, waiting for me to respond. When I don't, he goes on, sounding like he's reading from a brochure in an ob-gyn office. "Women who ingest the recommended dose of folic acid can reduce the risk of neural tube defects by fifty to seventy percent. Also, folic acid helps decrease the chance of cleft palate and heart defects."

Pretty sure that even in Rusty's head, he misspelled the words "neural" and "cleft."

I say, "So you're trying to knock up Faith, and you thought it would be a good idea to make a year's supply of orange juice." I try to make the words come out rather seriously, but I feel the sides of my mouth creeping up as I speak, negating my tone completely.

"I'm a day late, actually," Faith says.

"A whole day?"

Clearly Faith doesn't speak sarcasm. "Yes!" she says, pointing at me. "Exactly! And so I said to myself, 'Faith, it's time to pay attention to your folic acid intake.'"

I turn back to Rusty and just stare at him.

"What?" he says.

"I mean, you're making juice," I point out. "And wearing glasses."

Faith pats his cheeks with both palms. "They look distinguished on him, right? I told him he should start wearing them. It's time for him to grow up. He just needs a nudge in the right direction."

#

I'm lying in bed that night, half asleep, when I hear a tiny tapping sound on my window. I jerk upright, completely startled, and find Janna peering through the pane. A scarf is hippie-wrapped around her head. In her hand is a rigid container filled with what appears to be tea. I throw her a questioning look as I yank open the window. "Sorry!" she yell-whispers. "I didn't want to ring the doorbell and wake everyone up."

This is Classic Janna, and it feels so familiar — a pair of old shoes that I slide my feet into. "What's the story?" I ask.

This makes her smile.

Long ago, Janna read a book about two sisters who hijack their mother's car and drive cross-country to see their favorite band in concert. Janna found it fascinating and empowering in this *it's a big, amazing world and we need to conquer it* sort of way, so she started converting the things we did to adventures.

What's the story?

It's shorthand for *What sort of awesome thing can we do today? Where should we go? What kind of fun can we have?* Janna has forever dreamed up fabulous stuff for us (e.g., the "I'm Too Sexy" thing at Island Pizza) and I have forever gone along with it.

Janna says, "The tide is low, so I thought you might want to go with me to The Point." She pauses dramatically. "Momma turtles. You. Me. What a fabulous time we'll have." Then she backs away to make room for me to climb out, not even waiting for my reply. I'll say yes, obviously. I've always said yes.

We hike out to The Point, a sandy jut of beach just north of Rusty's, and then settle shoulder to shoulder in the sand. It's a beautiful night, a small consolation prize for a horrible week. The sounds are all water slapping onshore and wind whistling through the dunes and Janna's quiet inhalations. Overhead the stars are spinning and infinite.

Janna offers me her green tea. I make a yuck face and grumble, "Nasty." But then I take a sip anyway and pass it back to her. Janna got into health foods right around the same time she started wearing mascara. I've always figured the two are related, but I've never quite deciphered how.

We sit in companionable silence for several moments. We've

wasted probably a hundred summer nights like this, watching a small stretch of shadowy beach, the only light coming from the moon. Ever since Owen built that turtle-nest enclosure, Janna's been enchanted with the idea of grown turtles returning to the exact place they were hatched to lay their own eggs. Mind you, we've never actually seen a turtle out here — our presence probably scares them all away — but that hasn't ever stopped us from coming. I think it's the idea of it, more than anything else, the notion that there's this essential order to the universe. That somehow, we all find our way back to exactly where we're supposed to be.

Or maybe we just like gossiping on the beach.

Whatever the case, here, now, with Janna, it's easy to pretend that the past couple of years never happened. This is the place where we've admitted crushes and complained about parents and whined about schoolwork. It's sacred ground, and its magic softens my anxiety a little. I draw in a breath and exhale, gazing out over the dark stretch of sand.

Janna says, "Seems like there are less stars out here than there used to be, back when we were little."

I think about this, then lean back on my elbows. "Really? To me, it seems like the sky just keeps growing bigger and bigger. Like any day now it's going to swallow me whole."

"Must be hard to sleep."

"You have no idea."

We're quiet again for a minute, and then Janna says, "So I found out that my *Grease* costar — Mr. Tall, Dark and Gorgeous — is taken."

"Ah. Well, I'm sure there's another eligible bachelor ready to take his place."

"Yeah? Who?"

Andy.

A couple of years ago, I probably would've told Janna about Andy's crush. Now, though, I understand that some things are best kept private. So I shove my toes into the sand and say, "Logan. He was asking about you the other day."

Janna turns toward me, lifting both eyebrows. "Was he now?"

"He was. I saw him that day you sent Andy to babysit me." I give her a pointed look, which she ignores completely.

"Where'd you see him?" she asks.

"Outside Dream Cones. He was with Sawyer."

"You don't have to say Sawyer's name like that."

"Like what?" I say. I see a shadow shift and I sit up, peering into the darkness, wondering if it's a turtle. It isn't, though — just the moon-shadow of a palm frond, dipping and swirling in the breeze.

"Like he's an arrogant ass," Janna says.

"But he *is* an arrogant ass."

"I suppose he is," Janna admits, and both of us laugh.

I use my toe to write my name in the sand and then squint at it, trying to examine my handiwork. Finally I say, "So I followed Owen to Zoey Barnes's house. I thought maybe he had a girl-friend." It's a little embarrassing, this admission, but I feel like I owe Janna some truths.

"Hm," Janna says.

"Oh, now you're just screwing with me. What are you thinking?"

She must see the same moon-shadow, because she straightens up like a prairie dog for a handful of seconds. Then she grumbles something unintelligible and slouches again. "What am I thinking? That you're still totally in love with my brother. That's what I'm thinking."

I blink. Am I in love with Owen? If I'm being honest with myself — something I generally strive to avoid — then the answer is yes. I try to even out my expression. I don't know why. Janna has always been able to read me, probably even better than I can read myself.

"Look," she says, her voice softening a little, "I know you've been through a lot. I get that. But you know what? So has he. And Owen is … he's pretty clueless when it comes to girls. And he's been stuck on you for so long that he's never looked twice at anyone else." She lets out a long sigh, glancing sideways at me. "I know you had your reasons when you walked out of our lives, and I get them. Honestly, I do. But you really hurt Owen, and he's too good a person to have his heart broken like that again. So whatever you do, be careful, okay?"

I feel like she's giving me her blessing. I sit there for a moment, silent and still, and then I whisper, "I will." Holding Owen's heart in my shaky, incapable hands is a tall order for me right now, but I don't know how *not* to be in Owen's life. I've tried to walk away from him, but — like the turtles that return here year after year — an overwhelming, invisible force always draws me right back.

Thirty-Six

Janna and I are silent as we walk home. Not particularly uncommon for me, but it's a long pause by Janna standards, so I know she's gearing up for something. And I'm right. "Have you gone to the police yet?" she asks as we trudge over the dunes.

"No."

She sighs, just a little. "Look, I know you think that too much time has passed, and that you feel embarrassed and humiliated and whatever, but the fact is that you need to *do* something, Grace."

"I am," I say. I want to be annoyed with Janna, but I sort of love her for pressing this, for standing firm beside me as I face my very worst fears, for reminding me that even though sometimes life is terrifying and messy, you can't cower away from it. "I keep trying to get in touch with Andy, because I'm pretty sure he either knows something or he —" I stop and swallow. I don't want to suspect Andy, but how can I not? He stayed behind when the others went to watch the fireworks, and he's clearly been avoiding me the past couple of days. But I don't want to jump to conclusions. I did that with Owen, and look where that got me. And anyway, Andy is Janna's friend — maybe even my friend now — so I weigh my words carefully. "I think maybe he knows something about that night. I've been trying to get in touch with him, trying to ask him about it, but he's been avoiding me."

Janna narrows her eyes. "*What?*" she asks. I tell her about my conversation with Rusty, and about Andy's sudden vanishing act. "That's —" she begins, but she stops and shakes her head in disbelief. She fishes her phone out of her back pocket. "I'll call him."

"At one in the morning?" I ask, suddenly exhausted, slipping on my flip-flops before I step out of the sand and onto the road in front of the McAllisters'. "Just give it a couple of days, and if he's still MIA, you can hunt him down and we'll talk to him together."

She twists her lips together in a way that makes me nervous. Janna is not exactly known for her patience. But before I can confront her on this, I spot Owen striding across the road toward us. "Where did you go?" he asks Janna. "I walked into your room and you were gone. I was getting worried."

I don't hear a word of Janna's explanation, because when I glance up at Owen, I find him looking at me. My eyes jerk away. I try to focus on what Janna's saying, but fail miserably, because I can still feel Owen's eyes on me. My gaze roams back to him. Our eyes lock.

Janna stops talking suddenly, blows out a huge gust of air and says, "Oh my God, will you two get back together, already?"

Owen looks away. I chew on my thumbnail. Janna takes me

by the shoulders and shoves me up close to Owen. "Grace, this is my brother, Owen. He'd like to take you out."

Then she spins around and walks off.

Leaving us alone.

Owen shoves his hands in his pockets, sending his shoulders nearly to his ears. Even in the dim moonlight, I can see that his cheeks are pink. He opens his mouth to say something but shuts it. Then he tries again. "So I guess we should ..."

"Go out?"

He shifts his weight. "Yeah. Like, even if it's just as friends or whatever? It's a good idea. And anyway, I was going to ask you to go with me to —" He clears his throat and stares at his feet. "Um. There's this place I go to sometimes, and I think you'd love it. So if you're free tomorrow night, you should come with me. Like, to the place."

"To the place."

"It's sort of a restaurant, but not really? The last time I went, all I could think was that you would love it there, and that it would take your mind off everything that's going on right now."

"Sure. Sounds perfect," I say. *Is this a date?*

I know the answer to this immediately. Of course it's a date. With Owen, it's always a date.

Thirty-Seven

What the hell was I thinking?

Thirty-Eight

Let's see. My current life in a nutshell: My rapist is still at large.
I'm relatively certain that Janna is going to hunt down Andy
on her own and broadside him with questions. Lifeguard Guy
is probably getting ready to report both me and the charred
remains of my dignity to the cops. Eleanor is likely out shopping for a billboard to advertise my criminal activity. I can
hardly walk past the spare room without sweating out a kidney.

And yet.

Here I am, going out on a date with Owen McAllister.

I find Owen leaning against the Jeep, arms folded casually
over his chest and one foot propped up on a tire, waiting for me.

In another thin cotton shirt.

Tan biceps everywhere.

Green-green eyes.

He's not making this easy for me.

I squint at him, shielding my eyes from the setting sun,
coming to a slow stop in front of him. "Hey," I say.

His face cracks into a smile. "Hey, yourself."

Owen's mom opens the kitchen window and leans toward the screen. "Owen Tyrone McAllister, don't you dare leave this house without telling me where you're going." Her eyes shoot to me, and by way of greeting she says, "Grace, honey."

"Mom," Owen pleads, his face flushed. She squares a look at him, and he sighs. "We're going to Marisol's."

She brings both palms together in a prayer position, resting her chin on the tips of her fingers. "Lovely night for Marisol's," she says, and then she smiles, looking back and forth at us. "I've always known that the two of you would end up back togeth —"

Owen clears his throat. Now his face is basically purple. "*Mom.*"

"What?" she says.

Before Owen can reply, his dad appears in the window as well. To his wife, but loudly enough for us to hear, Owen's dad says, "They look cute together, don't they?"

Owen pinches his eyes closed. "Goodbye, guys."

After we pull out of the driveway, and after we turn onto Ocean Drive, I glance at Owen and say, "Your middle name is *Tyrone*? How did I not know this?"

Owen keeps his eyes pointing straight in front of him. There's a tiny twitch in the corner of his mouth. "You. Shut. Up."

I smile out my open window as we turn toward town. It's gorgeous out, one of those nights so thick and so perfect that you can almost breathe it into your lungs and keep it there. The sun is dipping low in the western sky, casting a pink, dreamlike glow over the palm trees and turning the puddles in the street into blush-colored pools.

"So you followed me last week," Owen says, taking me totally off guard, "when I went to see Zoey. I saw you in my rearview mirror."

Hoo, boy.

Fiddling with a loose thread on my sundress, I say, "Well, you leave every Saturday night, and —" I stop and clear my throat. "I mean — your clothes are *ironed* when you go. I thought maybe ..."

"I had a girlfriend," he supplies. "Yeah. Figured as much."

"Are you mad?"

"No. I wasn't trying to keep the Zoey thing secret. It just never came up." Smiling with one side of his mouth, he says, "I actually find it kind of cute that you were jealous."

"I was not jealous," I sputter. "I was just *clarifying.*"

He snorts.

I give him the stink-eye.

After a few seconds I say, "So how did that happen — you and Zoey?"

"Well, I was miserable. You know that much. Nothing seemed to bring me out of it. For months, the guilt was —" He breaks off, glancing toward me for a quick second and then jerking his eyes back to the road. "Anyway, I got to the point where I just couldn't take it anymore, so I went to Zoey's house to apologize to her and her family. It was a last resort, really." In the edge of his next pause, I can hear all the things he isn't saying. How difficult it was to knock on Zoey's door. How it tore his heart out to see her in that wheelchair. "Her parents yelled at me," he admits. "Zoey cried. I wanted to run. God, I wanted to run out of that house and never come back." Tears prick at my eyes and I blink several times. "It's okay," he tells me. "I got through it. It was rough, that first time, but I got through it, and then I asked if I could visit again. I've seen her once a week since. It took a while, but we're good now. We hang out. Sometimes we just talk. Sometimes we play video games. Sometimes I teach her how to draw or carve."

"I'm happy for you, Owen. Really, I am." Owen parks in front of an antique shop that I've seen probably a thousand times. "Wow, you shouldn't have," I say as I climb out.

Owen ignores my statement, opening the door and ushering me inside the store. One of those old homes that has been converted into a shop, the place is clean and old-fashioned, with wood paneling on the walls and an ancient silver cash register on the counter. Furniture and collectibles are scattered everywhere. On a vintage coffee table in front of me, fire-red zinnias lean from a mason jar. "Marisol?" Owen calls, and a woman with short gray hair springs up from behind a desk, a feather duster in her hand.

Plucking a pair of headphones from her ears, she says, "Good God, Owen! You scared me half to death." She smiles and waggles a finger at him. "I had a feeling I'd see you tonight."

"Well, it's the second Wednesday of the month, isn't it?"

"Sure is," she says, gesturing to the back of the store with a tip of her head. "C'mon."

We snake our way around the furniture, following her through a plain wooden door and into a tiny kitchen. A riot of smells assaults me as soon as we walk in. They are butter and sugar and cinnamon, as warm and as comforting as the sun. Every horizontal surface holds cooling racks, all dotted with croissants. "Marisol moonlights as a baker," Owen explains.

"She makes pastries for some of the local B and Bs. And also for me. Because she loves me."

Marisol laughs and swats him with a hand towel. "Actually, I owe Owen's mother my life, so I'm reimbursing her family in baked goods." She snatches a large ceramic plate from the cupboard, piles it with croissants and hands it to Owen. "Dig in," she says. With a loaded look at Owen, she spins on one foot and heads back up front.

Plate in hand, Owen leads me through a pair of French doors, where I jerk to a stop.

"Whoa," I say.

"Yeah."

I'm standing on a miniature terrace, where plants climb the side of the building and hang off the eaves and crawl across the concrete. The air smells flowering and exotic — like something you'd stumble upon in a remote, foreign village. Overhead is a web of tiny white lights, crisscrossing randomly and isolating the patio in a soft, luminescent glow. A metal bistro-style table sits in the middle of it all, an island in a sea of flowers. I feel like I'm not even in New Harbor anymore. I'm across the continent. Around the world. In one of my old posters — somewhere I always wanted to visit.

The table is so small we almost bump heads as we sit. Beside me, a bright pink hibiscus lies open as though waiting for me to whisper my secrets. I lean toward it, inhaling, and then fall back in the chair. Releasing a sigh that feels like it's been imprisoned in my chest for centuries, I turn to Owen, who has a private smile playing on his lips. "What?" I say.

He shrugs. "Nothing."

I give him a wary look. "So," I say, pointing to the pastries, "croissants, huh? I didn't even know you liked them."

He leans back in his chair, folding his arms across his chest. "Sometimes I mingle with the commoners."

I look dubiously at the croissants until Owen prompts me to take one. The pastry is still warm when I pick it up. Should've been my first clue. Owen watches me as I take a bite.

Jesus God.

This croissant.

"Holy shit," I mutter. "There's apple-pie filling inside." Owen starts to say something, but I hold up my hand and take another bite. And then I fall against the back of the seat and close my eyes.

"Her regular apple pie is even better," Owen says.

I look at him with one eye. "What day is apple-pie day?"

"Only once a year, the day before Thanksgiving. Haven't missed it in years."

I toast him with the last of my croissant. It's weird how, when your life sucks, you think something huge has to happen to make you feel better. Really, though, it's always the smallest things that improve your mood — laughter and the setting sun and flowers and an apple-pie croissant.

"So," I say, "what did your mom do to save Marisol's life?"

"She found a tumor in Marisol's mouth while she was filling a cavity. I guess it was in a weird place, or something? Crazy, right? Makes me wonder whether some things are just meant to happen."

"You mean, like, fate?"

Owen tips his head a little, considering. "Yeah. Something like that — some sort of Big Out There that's pulling all the strings."

Big Out There.

I like that.

We eat in comfortable silence. I'm overwhelmingly at peace underneath the twinkling lights, plants whispering in the breeze, apple-pie filling sticky on my fingers. I breathe in the night, listening to tourists murmuring on the sidewalk and thunderheads rumbling off in the distance.

"What are you thinking?" Owen asks. "You're smiling."

"That's because I'm happy," I say, and then I make a face, because *happy* is the sort of word that's so general its meaning gets watered down.

"Thought you might like it here," Owen says, "which is exactly why I brought you here for —"

I point at him. "Don't say date. This isn't a date, Owen McAllister."

Owen is beaming. "Totally not a date. If it were a date, I'd take you to eat peanut-butter-and-pickle sandwiches on rye at the Engine Room Deli instead of taking you here, to this gorgeous, private area." He turns his chair toward mine, resting his elbows on his knees. His eyes hook on mine. I'm acutely aware that we're just a few inches apart, his face so close that we're breathing the same air. The space between us crackles like it's filled with fireflies, like I can just reach up and grab one with my hand. His voice is hypnotic as he goes on. "If this was a date, right now I'd be kissing you." He pauses, glancing down at my lips and letting his gaze linger there for a long moment. "Which I'm not going to do, because we never actually declared this a date."

It's entirely possible that I'm going to spontaneously combust.

Just burst into flames and disintegrate, right on the spot.

I swallow, closing my eyes for a quick second. Longing, fiercer and more powerful than ever, is a hand on my back, propelling me toward him. I clear my throat. "So if we *were* on a date," I say, trying my best to keep my voice light, "where would we go after this?"

"I'd take you back home to my garage," Owen says. "To impress you with one of my projects."

"And if it wasn't a date?"

He flushes, sweat on his temples, looking at me like he has the best secret. "I'd take you somewhere else, to impress you with one of my projects."

"Where is this place?"

He stands up, offering a hand to me. I hesitate for half a beat before I take it. "Come on. I'll show you."

Thirty-Nine

Owen drives to the back lot of New Harbor High School, holding up the *wait* palm every time I question him. When we get out, he directs me toward a tall metal door in the back of one of the buildings. Fishing a single brass key out of his front pocket, he holds it up. "The shop teacher gave me this," he says, as though that explains everything, as though it makes perfect sense that we're trespassing on school property just because he has a key. "So, anyway," he says, and his voice has a little hitch in it all of a sudden, like he's nervous, "I've been working on something for the past few days." He gives this awkward little laugh-chuckle that's so endearing I almost melt. "I was going to give it to you for your birthday," he goes on, "but then I went and opened my big mouth tonight, and now I'm not sure if —"

I touch his arm. "Owen. I'll love it, whatever it is."

"Right," he says, shifting his weight. "Right." He fumbles with the lock for a couple of seconds, and then, shouldering the door open, he motions me to step inside, flipping on the lights after he crosses the threshold.

My footsteps echo as I walk into the room. I come to a slow stop and look around. There's a profound, church-like silence here, even though the place is a high school shop in the very worst possible way — scratched-up tables and piles of lumber and bulky machinery.

This is the second before I see it. The tiny splinter of time where my toes pause right on the edge of the moment, where all I know is the cluttered chaos of the room and the smell of polyurethane and sawdust. I hear Owen breathing, feel the warmth of his body behind me. I see a line of abandoned projects on a table against the wall, stacks of wood and building materials, and —

"Owen," I say, but it's just a whisper. Almost not even that. It's more of an emotion than a word. My whole body sways. I have no bones. They've all liquefied or collapsed or fallen to wherever bones fall when people go into shock. My knees tremble as I stumble forward, reaching out to touch my old music stand.

I remember that Christmas morning like it was yesterday, like I could crawl into the memory and just become the early morning sunlight slanting through our living room window. Become the wayward tuft of hair that rocked side to side on my father's head as he carried the tall, bulky gift across the room to me. The present itself was sort of pitiful-looking, lopsided and sloppily wrapped with Santa paper and a bright red bow slapped on with piece of Scotch tape. But my dad's writing was scrawled in black ink across the tag, transforming it into a work of art. I glanced up at Dad just before I pulled off the paper. The absolute joy I saw in his expression — that memory — it was a physical thing. Just as real as the music stand in front of me right now.

One of my hands is at my side, shaking uncontrollably. The other one traces the tiny grooves in the stand. Dad brought this home with the same hands that taught me to tie my shoes, the same hands that taped Band-Aids over my knees and packed my lunchbox. The same hands I held when he died.

This is the most tangible piece of him I have left.

I clap a palm over my mouth, my spine unzipping and all my emotions tumbling out — sadness and elation and hope and grief and delight and joy and helplessness.

This is everything to me.

I hear Owen take a step forward. His breath is in my ear. "Are you okay?" he whispers, but I don't answer. The tears just keep coming.

"I made a few calls," Owen explains. "I found it at a pawn-shop in Saint Pete. It was in rough shape, and I had to take it here to refinish it; there's too much humidity in our garage. I just — I wanted to feel like I was doing something that might help you ... I don't know, feel better, I guess? That sounds stupid, because you aren't sick. But you're hurting, and I feel so useless."

He rests his clean-shaven chin on my shoulder and wraps his arms around me. And I close my eyes, praying for time to stop right now, in this perfect moment. With this music stand in front of me and Owen behind me — with their sturdiness holding me upright.

"It's perfect," I say, and I'm not sure whether I'm referring to the music stand or not.

"I'm glad you like it."

His arms are still encircling me when I turn around. "Also," I whisper, "thank you."

His expression melts. "You're welcome."

I draw in a deep breath, just looking at him, and allow myself to hope. More than I want to admit, even now, I want *us* again. I want it so badly that it makes my stomach ache.

I remember standing next to him after we dragged that turtle-nest enclosure onto the beach all those years ago. I remember his concern, the earnest set to his jaw, the way he looked at me that day. I remember sitting across from him in Voodoo Pastries, knee to knee, arms touching. I remember every kiss we've ever had, every laugh we've shared, every time I've slid into his arms. I remember us.

Walking away from Owen was a huge mistake.

I can't go another second with that in my head.

We're so close. Just a breath apart. He's staring at me in a way that leaves me feeling light and untethered. My heart is slamming out of my chest. "Owen?" I say. It's a plea, really. I'm trying to tell him to be careful. I'm trying to tell him how much this means to me, how much *he* means to me. I'm trying to tell him that I'm damaged. That the best and the worst parts of my life are suddenly woven together as one. That this part — here, now — this is the one I want to pay attention to.

His lips are soft at first, just a whisper on mine. They taste like brown sugar and cinnamon and promises. And then he pulls back, cups my face with both hands and kisses me again. It's calm and turbulent, blown apart and smashed into creation, all at the same time. I stand outside myself, watching in wonder as the barn doors of my heart burst open with massive force, and just for a moment, just for that one fragile blink of time, the world doesn't seem like a dangerous place.

#

I'm completely useless after I get home that night. I lie in bed, a book propped in my lap, reading the same paragraph probably twenty times but still not comprehending it. The events of the evening circle inside my head in a loop, a refrain from a favorite song.

Finally I give up and wander out to the front porch, where I settle in my usual spot, turning sideways a little so I can lean against the banister. Offshore, a strobe of lightning flashes upon a bank of approaching thunderheads. The rest of the sky is dark and infinite — a secret whispered too quietly to hear.

I swallow, suddenly overcome with the strongest sense that all of the moving parts of my life are hurling toward one another, that everything is going to collide in a single cataclysmic explosion, and there's nothing I can do to stop it.

Just then, the front door flings open, and Eleanor, wearing an abundance of purple polyester and hairspray, bumps gracelessly across the porch and collapses beside me, emitting a loud grunt. She looks young and uncomplicated, despite her wrinkles and gray hair and graceless gait. In her hands are a pack of cigarettes and her phone, the latter of which she places beside me with flourish as she says, "There you go, slick."

I just look at her.

"I got a new phone," she explains. "Giving you my old one." She pauses again, presumably waiting for me to reply. When I don't, she goes on. "I don't want you to get desperate and steal one. Oh, don't get all pissy. We both know you have sticky fingers."

My ears burn. Enunciating my words, I say very slowly, "I would not steal a phone."

She shrugs. "If you say so." Shaking a cigarette out of the pack, she flicks her lighter several times before a flame gasps to life.

My eyes lingering on the phone, I say, "What's the catch, Eleanor?"

She leans back on her elbows and glances at me. "No catch. Just thought you could use it, is all. Take it. It's yours."

I pick it up, but I feel sort of spineless. Accepting this phone is like giving Eleanor a free pass for all the crap she's pulled since I moved in, all the little jabs she's aimed in my direction. But I do it anyway, pressing the little round button at the bottom and making the screen light up. "Thanks," I say.

She turns toward me, nods and says, "No problem, kid."

It's just a tiny bottle bobbing across the ocean that separates us. Not large enough to carry an important message, but just the right size to show that she cares.

Forty

I awake the next morning to find Janna, in full costume for a
Grease rehearsal, banging into my room. Her hair is wild and
she's faintly sweaty. She's wearing black leather pants and a
shiny Pink Ladies jacket. Her eyes are wide and virtuous. It's
a dignified expression, despite the fact that her wig is teased
straight up on her head and she's dressed like a hooker.

"Wake up, get dressed and come with me," she says. "I found
your rapist."

Forty-One

For a fraction of a second, a sliver of a breath, I don't understand what she said. Then her words snap through me like lightning, and I sit straight up in bed. "Right. Okay," I say. My voice sounds weird, tinny and shrill.

Janna doesn't speak while I get dressed and follow her to the Jeep. I don't know why she's silent, but I'm grateful for it. I need all my concentration just to make it outside. The ground seems tilted, pitched sideways, so I grip the seat cushion after I shut the passenger-side door, working to keep myself upright.

"First off, promise me you won't get mad," Janna says, glancing over her shoulder as she backs out of the driveway, her hair bouncing stiffly on top of her head. She doesn't give me a chance to reply. She just slams on the brakes, shoves the car into gear, hits the gas and goes on. "I talked to Andy about Labor Day weekend. I swear I didn't tell him any of the gory details. I promise, I — oh, my God, breathe, Grace. *Breathe*." That's when I realize my hand is on my chest and my mouth is open and I'm struggling to suck air into my lungs. I lean back in the seat and force in a breath as she goes on. "So I called Andy this morning, and I was like, 'Hey, do you remember a couple of years ago, when Rusty had a million guys over to watch the Gators' season opener on Labor Day weekend?' and he was like, 'Um,' and I was like, 'Did you see anyone go into Grace's room that night?' and he was like, 'Um,' and I totally knew he was hiding something, so I was like, 'Dude, I know what happened. Stop protecting him,' and he was like, 'He's not anyone, he's my *brother*.'"

Janna jams on her brakes at a stop sign but doesn't make a move to start driving again. Her mouth is set into a tight line. In the side mirror, I can see cars starting to stack up behind us. Janna turns toward me and grabs my arm like she's trying to wake me up again. "*Sawyer*, Grace — it was *Sawyer*. Andy said he caught him coming out of your room that night, looking guilty as shit. And when Andy questioned him about what he was doing in there, he said Sawyer freaked out on him and threatened him into keeping quiet. Andy is under the impression that Sawyer stole something from your room. Which I guess he did. The asshole."

"But Sawyer," is all I can get out before my voice disappears. I inhale and start over. "But Sawyer isn't the sort of person who …" I stop again, because what am I planning on saying, even? That Sawyer isn't the sort of person who's used to getting whatever, whomever, he wants? That Sawyer isn't the sort of person who thinks he's entitled to every girl in Florida?

The car behind us honks, and Janna stomps on the gas and takes off, making a hard right on the next street. "As per my dad, track practice starts in fifteen minutes at the high school," she says, all business. "We'll be waiting for Sawyer when he arrives."

Her hands tighten on the steering wheel, and she turns and meets my gaze. Her expression is fierce. "I swear to God, Grace, I'll kill that sonofabitch."

I shut my eyes. "Janna, I don't want a scene." I can hear her drumming her fingers against the steering wheel. "Janna —"

She says, sort of loudly, "I won't cause a scene."

Except when we pull into the parking lot beside the school's practice fields, and we see that Sawyer is already there, getting out of his car, she blasts out of the Jeep like a nuclear bomb, dragging me behind her and stalking toward Sawyer in a way that would probably be considered running if you were to count how much ground she's covering per second.

As we approach, Sawyer turns in our direction and tosses us his trademark smile. A searing stab of anger shoots through me, because here he is, with his perfect hair and perfect face and perfect life, and here I am, a complete disaster.

Sawyer's eyes slide to Janna and he says, "Love the getup, McAllister."

"Shut up," Janna says, pushing his chest.

Sawyer staggers backward a little, into his still-open car door. He looks at me, then at Janna and then back at me. His grin fades and is replaced by something else. Something uncertain. But then just as quickly, that stupid smile spreads across his stupid face again, and he coolly props his arm on top of the door. He says, "What's your problem, Janna?"

"That question isn't at all appropriate for what's going on right now," Janna says, sort of through her teeth.

"And what exactly is going on right now?" he says. "Because I'm lost here."

Janna leans toward him and bellows, "You telling us the

truth about what happened on Labor Day weekend two years ago! *That's* what's going on right now!"

Just like that, Sawyer's confident demeanor vanishes. The color drains from his face. He goes completely still.

The entire world stops. No sounds. No movement. Nothing.

I turn to Janna. "Go wait in the Jeep, please." When she opens her mouth to protest, I say, *"Please."* For a moment, I think she might refuse, but then she gives me a quick hug, tosses a vehement glare at Sawyer, turns on one heel and stalks away.

Then it's just Sawyer and me. I stare at the wooded area that borders the school, shift my weight, wrap my arms around myself. I don't know what to do with my body right now. It's this strange, clunky bit of flesh that isn't quite attached to my head. I look up at Sawyer. His eyes are wide and anxious. Everything in his stance screams *guilty*.

I self-consciously yank down the hem on my shorts, wishing I wore a turtleneck and jeans and a hat and boots. Am I supposed to feel this humiliated right now? I don't know the rules.

I close my eyes. A tear slides down my cheek. I have no clue where it came from — I don't feel sad. "When I woke up the next morning, after —" I stop and scrub my face with the back of my hand, and then I begin again. "It was pretty obvious that — I mean, my clothes had been — and I was —" I cut off, unsure of why I'm trying to relive this for him. Maybe I want him to understand how damaging it was. Maybe I just don't know what else to say.

I open my eyes but don't look at him. I stare at the pavement, where the heat is coming up in waves, making the lines on the parking spaces appear convoluted and warped. When I think of him with his hands all over me, something inside me warps as well.

There's a beat before Sawyer speaks, the silence hanging charged in the air. Then: "It wasn't me."

His denial is so ridiculous that my eyes jerk up to meet his. I say, "Did you go into my room that night?"

He clears his throat. His eyes are darting everywhere. "Yes, but only for a second. And then I —" He swallows and shifts his weight. It's surreal, seeing him so utterly uncomfortable. "I walked right back out. I swear to God, Grace, I didn't touch you."

"Then who did?"

Suddenly, we're two points on a long, thin black line, staring at each other. And then Sawyer says, "A bunch of us went to watch the fireworks off Holmes Beach. I came back early because I had to take a leak. I walked into your room by mistake, thinking it was the bathroom." He pinches his eyes closed with a trembling hand. "You have to believe me. He forced me to keep quiet. He said he'd tell everyone about the drugs. That I'd lose my chance to run track for Clemson."

It's like he's speaking a foreign language.

"Drugs," I repeat.

Sawyer paces in front of me, holding his head like he's trying to keep it from detonating right off his shoulders. "Why do you think I'm breaking all these records in track? Don't you think my coach might question whether I'm taking steroids? Dig a little deeper?"

My coach.

I feel like I'm falling off a rocky cliff, tumbling with no ability to stop, falling through two years of confusion and pain and denial, slamming into the jagged, stony truth.

Coach McAllister.

Forty-Two

I stand there, frozen and disoriented, staring at Sawyer for I don't know how long. I'm not sure I breathe. I'm not sure of much of anything, to be perfectly honest. I hear a truck rattle by on the street, the hiss of a sprinkler on one of the athletic fields.

"Grace."

Sawyer is walking hesitantly toward me. I want to scramble backward, get away from him, but my feet have grown into the pavement and they won't move. I'm dead quiet inside — the eye of a hurricane, everything else spinning around me.

"Grace."

I think, *Is this what it feels like to be in shock?*

I think, *What am I going to tell Janna when I get back to the Jeep?*

"Grace."

I blink several times as Sawyer stops in front of me. His voice pleading and stripped bare, he says, "When I stepped into the room and saw him, you and —" He stops, closes his eyes and shudders like he's trying to knock the memory out of his head. "He was —" He swallows and bends over, planting his palms flat on the hood of his car, his head hanging low. "And it was obvious you were out of it. Jesus, he threatened me. He told me he'd expose me to Clemson if I told anyone. I'm so, so sorry." He waits for me to speak, and when I don't, he straightens up. "Grace, please say something."

It takes me several moments to open my mouth.

Several more to attempt to speak.

And several more to spin around and take off running, careening from the parking lot to the wooded area beside it, trying to escape the truth, trying to escape Sawyer and Janna, trying to escape the riot of emotions chasing after me.

Coach McAllister.

For two years, he's gotten up and had breakfast with his family and laughed with his wife and hugged his kids and gotten into his car and driven to work — while rolling emptiness swallowed me whole.

The toe of my shoe catches on the uneven ground, and I stumble, plunging to my knees. I scramble back up and lurch away.

Owen and Janna.

I will lose them.

Because if I don't tell them the truth, how can I ever look them in the eye? And if I do tell them the truth, how can they ever look me in the eye?

I can hear Sawyer calling after me, his voice growing fainter and fainter the farther I run. I'm crashing through the shrubbery, the sun strobing through tree branches, blinding me for small increments of time. My mind keeps flashing back to that dinner at the McAllisters', when Owen's dad sat across from me at the table, laughing and shaking a breadstick at me.

He's like family to me.

I stagger against a tree, clapping a hand over my mouth to stop myself from screaming. I wish I could rewind time. Rewind everything, so I could not be at Rusty's that Labor Day weekend. Not take Ambien. Not pass out. Not get raped.

But I can't.

I can't.

I reel away, bursting out onto the beach about fifty yards from Rusty's house, barking a loud, humorless laugh, because I've run as far and as fast as I can, and yet I've ended up right back where everything started.

Forty-Three

Janna knocks on my bedroom door a half hour later.

She says, "Grace? Are you in there?"

I say, "Yes."

She says, "Why did you run away? I was worried about you."

I say, "I need to be alone."

She says, "Can I come in?"

I say, "I need to be alone."

She says, "Grace?"

I don't answer. A couple of minutes later, I hear her walking away.

Forty-Four

I'm sitting on the floor in my room late that afternoon, my back flat against the wall, the hardwood slats cool and rigid underneath me. I can hear Rusty in the living room, in front of a baseball game, snoring loudly — the sound of a simple, uncomplicated life.

I cry for a while, like some pathetic female character on the Lifetime Channel, feeling stupid and ashamed, because — *Jesus* — there are girls on Mr. McAllister's track team. And I've wasted almost two years by not stepping forward. Who knows how many of them might've gotten hurt by now?

Also, I'm trying to gather the courage to talk to the police.

Talk to Owen.

Talk to Janna.

It can't wait, really.

My violin is on the other side of my room, propped against my bed. For the first time ever, I don't want to play it. I don't even want to look at it, actually. It's the window I keep glancing at, like there's some sort of magnet attached to it, drawing my attention from across the room, again and again. Finally I haul myself upright and step toward it. My feet, as I walk, feel heavy enough to crash clear through the floorboards.

I brace both hands on the windowsill and look out. Mr. McAllister's car is in the driveway next door. I don't know why I find this surprising, but the sight strikes me dumb for a second. All I can think is, *Why did he move here, of all places?* I mean, the *balls*. To live and eat and sleep and love right next to the house where he raped me, right next to my uncle. Right next to me.

It's almost like he's flaunting it.

I'm crying again, everything inside me ripping open and spilling out, the humiliation I've clutched so tightly the past couple of years, the anger I've stuffed into my rib cage, the fear that's cleaved to my cells. God — fear of *everything*. Of living and dying, of loving and desertion, of friendship and loneliness. The stupid truth of it all is that day after day I've been trying to protect myself from things that have been out of my control. I've been worrying about getting hurt or getting sick or getting abandoned. But the fact is, people like me get raped every day. People like Dad die every day. People like Owen are involved in accidents that are out of their control every single day.

The world, with all its beauty and wonder and love, is a frightening place.

I'm still staring out the window when Owen swings open his back door and steps outside. I freeze — trying to hold back my thick press of tears — and watch him walk into his driveway, toward the garage. It's clear that Janna told him what happened this morning. He's hunched and pale, his tension evident even in the waning daylight. Glancing my direction, Owen's eyes meet mine. He jerks to a stop. For a heartbeat, we just stare at each other. Then he gestures for me to come outside.

My chest constricts, suddenly and painfully. I nod once.

This is it: the beginning of the end.

And I'm propelled toward it, because I can't be the person who gives Owen's dad the freedom to hurt another girl. I can't turn my back on this. Not anymore.

So at long last, I scrub the tears off my face. I wipe my palms on my clothes. I draw in a deep breath. And I walk out of my room.

I used to think bravery is something you're born with, like blue eyes or big feet or a good sense of humor. But that isn't the case at all. Bravery — it isn't something that you have. It's something you use. A bridge that you walk across when you want to get somewhere, no less accessible than the wooden planks of Rusty's porch as I step outside.

Lifting my chin, I stride down the steps. Suddenly I'm Faith, walking fearlessly into the unknown. I'm Eleanor, ready to speak the truth without filter. I'm Janna, writing my own story. I'm every girl, every woman, every female who has ever walked this planet in fear. I'm me, prepared to face the truth.

Forty-Five

Owen's eyes are hooked on me as I approach. "Hey," he says. His voice is scratchy and rough, like he scrubbed his throat with Brillo pads. Though he looks pale and strung out and stressed, I know I look much, much worse.

"Hey." I stand there for a moment, my hands dangling at my sides, wondering what to do, wondering what to say, wondering what the protocol is for destroying someone's life in a couple of seconds flat. There might be proper words for this particular situation — a tactful way to lead up to the truth — but I don't know what they are.

The concrete is warm under my feet as I stare up at Owen. I can hear a plane whirring overhead. A dog barking somewhere down the street.

You can do this, I tell myself, fully aware that once Owen knows the truth, it will be permanent. I look up at him, reach out and give his hand a brief squeeze. It's probably the last time I'll touch him, so I memorize everything about the moment.

The shocking color of his eyes. The earnestness in his jawline. The half-moon shadow under his collarbone.

I don't have a clue what I'm going to do with my life or the wallets I stole or my smashed-up heart. All I know is that I'm the one in charge of it. Just me. So I look into Owen's eyes.

I take a big breath.

I open my mouth.

And I tell him everything.

#

Owen blinks. And blinks some more. His face is blank. I don't know what's happening inside him. Maybe he's gone into shock. Then he says slowly, almost like the words are too big to fit in his mouth, "My dad was the one who …"

I watch the color leach from his face. His right eye is twitching. I want to flatten a palm on it to make it stop, but I know that my days of touching Owen are long gone. There's no way to fix this. No chance of stitching it back together. I try to draw in a breath. The air doesn't make it past my throat. "Yes," I say.

Owen just keeps staring at me. "My *dad*," he says.

I can see pain in every angle of his face. He looks completely demolished, like I crammed a lit explosive inside his rib cage and blew him apart.

I've done it. I've hurt him again, and this is something I can never help him through. Guilt kicks in, flooding my chest. I want to take my confession and shove it right back to where it came from. "I'm sorry," I say, not even trying to stop the tears from coming, waiting for him to jerk around and look at me in disgust. But he just keeps on pacing.

I feel so responsible for all of this. Why? I haven't done anything wrong. For once, I'm doing something right. I fold my arms across my chest. "Owen, please," I beg, although I don't know what I'm asking of him.

He seems to understand, though, because he straightens up, jams his hands in his pockets and says in a cold, closed voice that I've never heard before, "This is a lot to take in." Then he turns toward me and our eyes meet. The moment lasts so long that I have to look away. "You're the only girl I've ever loved," he says in a voice so heavy that my heart collapses under the weight of it. "How am I supposed to deal with that?"

But I don't have time to reply, because just then, to my utter shock, Mr. McAllister opens the back door and steps outside.

I can't —

I'm —

Oh, God.

I inhale quickly, the sight of him cold and sharp and painful. The instinct to run is overpowering. I wedge my feet together, locking myself in place. My legs are shaking so badly that the bones in my ankles knock together.

I'm humiliated. Ashamed and embarrassed.

But I'm also furious.

Mr. McAllister doesn't seem to notice. He's twirling his keys around his index finger as he heads to his car. "What's up?" he says, as casual as a pair of Chucks, sliding to a stop in front of us.

Jesus, he's smooth. I have to give him that. He looks like the epitome of a perfect father, standing here with his brows furrowed in mild concern. His eyes slide to Owen and linger there a second, assessing the confusion and rage in Owen's expression, and then they finally make their way to me. A prickle of revulsion skitters up my spine. I fold my arms over my chest, all of a sudden feeling completely naked.

I remember watching him clap in the closing moments of one of Janna's plays. I remember watching him hug his wife that day I went to the river to feed the ducks.

I remember waking up bruised and bloody and terrified.

Nauseated, I turn away, wishing I could slip right out of my skin and disappear forever. But in this moment, with the truth pressing down so hard on me, all I can do is whisper, "How could you?"

His expression falters for a fraction of a second before it reassembles itself. Then he gives me a perplexed smile. "How could I what?" he asks, all earnestness and fatherly sincerity.

His acting could give Janna's a run for its money.

Owen's hands are balled into fists. His breaths are ragged enough to make his whole body lurch backward with each one. Pressing a knuckle to his forehead, Owen says, very distinctly, "You raped her."

Mr. McAllister's eyes dart to me and then back to Owen, his face turning as ashen as the eastern sky above. Giving Owen a plastic-looking smile, he says, "What are you talking about, son?"

"Don't call me son," Owen says, his voice disturbingly even. His father's composure is starting to falter. I can see it in the tenseness of his muscles and the defensive way he plants both feet apart from each other as Owen goes on to say, "Let me refresh your memory. Two years ago, when Rusty had a bunch of guys over to watch the Gators' season opener, you went into Grace's room and raped her while she was knocked out on Ambien."

"That's ludicrous," Mr. McAllister sputters.

Owen opens and closes his hands several times, and then he leans toward his dad and says, "Cut the crap, all right? Sawyer already told Grace everything, how he walked in and saw —" Owen stops for a moment and gulps, then begins again. "How he walked in and saw what you were doing to her, and how you threatened to expose him for steroid use."

Mr. McAllister shakes his head fervently. I can see a vein in his temple pulsing, the faint sheen of sweat on his forehead. He says, "That boy is disturbed. All those drugs he's been taking — his mind is completely fried. He doesn't know what he's talking abou —"

"Sawyer walked in the room and saw you having sex with Grace without her permission! I think it was pretty goddamn clear!" Owen bellows. It's so sudden and so out of character that I flinch and cover my mouth with my hand.

Mr. McAllister holds up a palm. "Look, why don't we go for a walk, so we can clear this up without making a scene?"

Owen's expression is brittle. "Here's what's going to happen," he says. "We're going to get into the car, pick up Sawyer and then we're all going to drive to the police station and talk."

Mr. McAllister swallows. He glances toward me, his eyes shooting away before they can meet mine. "Owen, think about this for a moment. Going to the police would be a mistake."

It isn't exactly a confession, but it isn't a denial, either. And it feels surreal, a movie scene playing out in front of me.

"Really, Dad? How would it be a mistake?"

Mr. McAllister crosses his arms. "It was so long ago. There's no evidence that bears weight. People will just think Grace is crying wolf. That could be dangerous for a girl's reputation."

A flicker of indecision passes through Owen's expression.

And that's when I find my voice.

"That's a load of horseshit and you know it," I shout. Oh, I'm talking now. My voice is getting louder and louder with every word. I have no idea how I've gotten there, but I'm standing right in front of him, my finger in his face. "You aren't worried about me or my reputation — all you're worried about is saving your own goddamn ass. What you did to me — it was sick and it was brutal and it ruined me. Don't you get that?!" Out of the corner of my eye, I see Owen turn away. I'm overwhelmingly aware that he can't look at his father. Can't look at me. "You were *family* to me," I go on, and the enormous injustice of what he did, his absolute betrayal, has me sobbing and yelling at the same time. "And you went into my room that night and stole my life."

With my last words, I hear Rusty's front door fly open. Rusty leans over his porch railing, hat in his hands, a bare look of confusion on his face. He says, "What's going on? Everything okay?"

Nobody speaks. Nobody breathes. We're statues, staring at Rusty, who's now taking the steps two at a time, who's now walking quickly toward us, his brows crammed together.

For the first time this evening, Owen's father looks terrified. He takes a step toward his car, glancing at the door handle.

"What's going on?" Rusty repeats as he comes to a stop.

Suddenly we're four corners in a boxing ring, three of us looking at Owen's father.

I turn toward Rusty. I swallow hard, my mouth dry. "Owen's dad —" I stop. Close my eyes. It's easier, not having to look at him. It's like whispering a secret in the dark, like lying in bed, muttering an embarrassing truth over the phone. The dark — it makes you bolder. I say the words slowly and carefully, so there's no mistaking them. "He raped me."

Rusty doesn't reply, and for a moment I wonder whether I only thought the words and didn't speak them out loud.

I open my eyes.

Rusty's hands are frozen in the air. He's staring at me, pale and dazed. "What?" he says. There's a quiver in his voice that makes me want to take off running.

I can hardly breathe. There isn't enough air out here. I say, "He came into my room that night I took Ambien, when ..." My voice breaks and I clear my throat. "It was a couple of years ago, during that party you had for the Gators' season opener."

Rusty blinks at me. *"He what?"*

Every time this secret is shared, its horror seems to quadruple in size.

I try to keep my voice even. It takes a lot of effort. My words, and all the truth and tragedy in them, come out softly, almost in a whisper. "Owen's dad raped me, Rusty."

This time they seem to find purchase in Rusty's head. They just ... snag on something and stay there. Every muscle in his body tenses, and he turns toward Owen's father, who takes another step backward. Rusty, though, he's a mountain of still-ness — except for the infinitesimal motion of his jaw tightening. To Owen, he says, "Take Grace home, please."

Owen just looks at him.

Rusty closes his eyes for a quick second and says, *"Now."*

Taking me by the elbow, Owen leads me toward Rusty's porch steps. I look over my shoulder just in time to see Rusty yank his phone out of his pocket and call the police.

#

I wake around two in the morning, curled up at the end of my bed, facing the window. After the deputy talked to me, and after Owen's dad left in a police car, I lay in bed and watched Rusty and Mrs. McAllister as they stood in the driveway, wrapped up in quiet discussion.

Now, as I wander toward the kitchen to grab a glass of water, I find Rusty, still dressed in the same clothes, standing at the living room window in a rectangle of moonlight. I come to a stop beside him. We stay like that for a while. Finally Rusty says, "How are you holding up?"

"I don't know. I'm not sure of much of anything right now." Rusty reaches toward me with one burly arm and pulls me close. Looking up at him, I say, "Thank you for believing me. For calling the police."

His eyes widen a little, surprised. "No thanks needed, kid."

"I know, but it's just —" I sigh and give him a small smile. "It's nice to have family behind me, is all."

He closes his eyes, his expression distorting a little. "That's something you should never have to thank family for, G. Real family — they're supposed to be there for you. Always." He seems to be deflating, right in front of my eyes. His shoulders sag. His mouth falls slack. And for the first time in my life, I see him break down and cry. It takes a long time for him to start speaking, and I wait him out. Wiping his eyes with the back of his hand, he says, "I want to tell you something, and I want you to hear me out, okay? And when I'm finished, if you hate me, well, that's my cross to bear." I nod once. Everything inside me goes still as I look up at him. His chin is wobbling as he says, "Your dad's death. It was my fault. He told me that weekend, Gracie. He told me when we walked over to watch the fireworks that he was having chest pain. And you know what I told him? I said it was probably heartburn. His death — that's on me, kid." He's really sobbing now. He swallows and pinches his eyes closed with his fingers. "How could I even look at you, knowing it was my fault? How could I bring you into *my* home, knowing that it was me who caused you so much pain? So I didn't. I was a coward. I left you to rot with those strangers." He blinks several times and looks up at the ceiling. "Fact is, I didn't deserve you. And I still don't. I'm not a good person, G. That's what I found out. Your dad, he was the good one."

Heartache and heartbreak grip my chest. "Rusty, no. No. It wasn't your fault. It wasn't. You didn't know any better, and neither did Dad. What happened to Dad — it was devastating, and I miss him every day. But I'll never blame you for it. You shouldn't, either."

He gives me a weak smile. "Maybe someday."

"And you came for me eventually," I whisper.

He exhales and rubs the back of his neck. "Day late and a dollar short," he mutters. Even in the dim light, he looks pale. "And look at you," he goes on. "You're still a good person. The adults in your life have either deserted you or hurt you, and you walk out of it like you're fireproof. I'm proud of you, kid." He squeezes a little harder on me, pulling me closer. "And I want you to know — I'm here for good."

Forty-Six

I was four years old when I first met Janna. It was a fluke, really, that our paths even crossed. Back then she lived on the other side of New Harbor. But she just so happened to know Andy, and he just so happened to be having a birthday party on the lawn, and Dad and I just so happened to be arriving at Rusty's that day.

As I helped Dad drag in our bags, I glanced up and saw Janna standing on the grass next door, a mess of boys wrestling and shouting behind her. She looked supremely out of place in her bright orange dress, twirling a daisy between her thumb and first finger, staring at me.

I gazed back at her. "Hey," I said after a moment, using my heel to scratch my opposite ankle. Then I pulled a foil package out of my shorts, ripped it open and held it out in her direction. "I have lemonade fruit snacks. Want some?"

When you're four, that's how friendships are born.

Now, thirteen years later, as I look out Rusty's front window,

I feel like I've fallen back in time. Janna is standing in almost the exact same spot on the lawn, staring at me.

My legs heavy with the weight of our impending conversation, I wrench open the front door and step outside. Gripping the porch railing for balance, I watch her approach.

She looks so, so sad.

This is her goodbye is all I can think.

It's her chin that gives her away. She has it pulled down clear to her chest. And the way she walks — slow and tentative as she steps across the grass. She stops at the bottom of the stairs. Tears spill furiously down her face, but she doesn't move, not even to wipe them away. I want to hug her, but I don't dare. Instead, I watch her unload on the steps, wrap her arms around her legs and look out at the shoreline. I sit down hesitantly beside her, all my words tangled together into a thick ball in my throat.

"I don't know if it's okay to talk to you right now," she says, her voice raw and broken, "so tell me to go home if it's not."

I flick a clump of sand off the step. "It's fine."

Janna nods once, a quick, jerky motion. Then she inhales, and in her exhale she says, "I just wanted to come over and say that I'm sorry, for all of this, for my dad, for everything, and I wanted to make sure you're okay."

"Janna, you don't need to apologize."

She's really crying now. Completely hysterical. "It was *my dad*, Grace."

"Which means it isn't your fault. It isn't anyone's fault but his," I say. After a short pause, I repeat the last sentence, hoping she'll understand. Hoping *I'll* understand, because I've been blaming myself, too. I've spent a lot of time over the past couple of years, thinking about all the little things I might've done differently, and how altering just one of them could've changed the outcome of everything.

Janna slaps the tears off her face. "My dad confessed to everything — did you know that? He's in jail until his arraignment, and he'll probably stay there for at least six months, until his trial, because Mom already said that she won't bail him out. And Owen — you know what he does when he's upset. He shuts down. Won't talk to anyone. He'd rather carry it all on his shoulders until he finds a way to unload it on his own. He took off last night and we haven't seen him since."

"Do you have any idea where he is?"

"Logan's."

I nod, trying not to think about the beautiful boy who's avoiding his family, avoiding his life, because I just stomped all over it. I focus desperately on a stray weed in the flower bed, because I know the million-dollar question is coming, I can feel it, thickening the air as it rolls and gathers like a thunderstorm in Janna's head. When it comes, though, it's so quiet I barely hear it: "What happens now? With us?"

A stark sort of silence falls between us.

I feel so bare, in this moment.

I don't look at her, but I'm honest. "I'm not sure. Everything has changed," I say. I feel like I'm untangling, spinning away into a different version of myself, and I don't know where I'll land when I finally stop.

#

Two weeks pass before I talk to Owen. By then, I've already spoken to his mom, who materializes on our front porch late one afternoon holding a huge dish of lasagna, like she's consoling me for a death in my family or something. I stand there, staring at her red, swollen eyes and her devastated expression, feeling as though I should be offering *her* lasagna. Or at least offer to divide this one in half. I invite her in, barely getting the chance to put the dish on the counter before she crushes me in her arms, muttering, "I'm so, so sorry, honey," over and over, her cheeks wet with tears.

I've done a lot of crying, too, mostly with my therapist. Sometimes, Rusty sits beside me, bawling as well. Sometimes I'm on my own, staring at the most heavily mustached man in the history of the world, spilling all my secrets. He's a weird caricature of a guy, this therapist of mine, but he's patient and kind, and I sort of love him for it. I don't need someone to yank me toward wellness. I need someone to walk beside me as I find it on my own.

I told him about the wallets I'd stolen. That was a weird day. I walked in, sat down across from him, said hello and said his suit was a good color for his complexion and said — oh, by the way, I had a bit of a criminal past.

Yeah.

He took it like a champ, though, not even blinking. He told me that I was doing the right thing, talking to him about it, that it takes courage to admit mistakes.

Now, it's one in the afternoon, and Rusty, Faith and I are walking through the hospital's parking lot, toward the entrance. I need a physical assessment, something the courts requested for their investigation, something I've been dreading. But I'm here. Which feels like a small victory.

I'm weaving around a car when I see Owen, shuffling

toward us, head down, shoulders low. I freeze, a pang of sadness piercing my chest, because he looks so miserable. It's followed by another pang, because I feel guilty for his misery.

An ache as big as the planet swallows both of us as he makes his way toward me, stopping just a couple of feet away. His face is peppered with stubble and his eyes are puffy and red.

I glance toward Rusty and Faith, who are waiting for me a few yards away. Rusty points at the hospital's front doors like, *We'll wait for you inside.*

I nod.

And then it's just Owen and me and a million unspoken words. I start with the easiest one.

"Hi."

"Hi," he says quietly, his eyes on his shoes.

I swallow. "How've you been?"

"I'm still here. You?"

"Same."

Silence falls between us like a screen.

I clear my throat and shift my weight. A raindrop lands on my arm. I glance up at the gray, rolling clouds tumbling across the sky, and then back at Owen. "What are you doing here?"

"I needed a meningitis shot for college before our insurance changes." Then he drops the bomb: "We're moving to Illinois — Mom and Janna and I."

I don't say anything at first. I'm not even sure that I breathe. I don't want to lose Owen again. I know what that feels like, how much it hurts. Fate has always been pulling at us, trying to separate us, trying to worry one of us free.

I suppose it was only a matter of time.

I say, "Are you still going to University of Florida?"

He shakes his head no. "Mom is making some calls, trying to get me into a school up north."

"Were you even going to say goodbye to me?" His eyes shoot down to the asphalt, and I have my answer. "Why, Owen?"

His voice is soft. "I didn't think you'd want to see me."

The rain is coming down harder now. My T-shirt is sticking to my shoulders, my stomach, my back. A car to my right pulls out of a nearby parking spot, revealing the McAllisters' Jeep. I say, "Why would you think that?"

His words tumble out all at once. "Because my dad is a monster. Because I left you alone the night you were sexually assaulted. Because I ran away the past couple of weeks, when you needed me most. Because I couldn't help you."

This is what it always comes down to — blaming. Me blaming myself. Owen blaming himself. "None of this is your fault, Owen. You didn't know who your father really was. You couldn't have predicted what was going to happen that night. And staying at Logan's? I get it."

"And moving away? Do you understand that?"

I glance at the Jeep. It breaks me a little, looking at it, knowing that he and Janna will be driving away from me for good. A single crystalline raindrop dangles from Owen's eyelash. "Yeah. I get that, too," I say. And I *do* understand. How can I expect his family to stay here after everything? And who am I to tell anyone how to grieve? Because that's what we're doing — grieving. We've all lost so much. I've lost my innocence and my dignity, and Owen has lost his father. Owen and I — we were hit with the same wrecking ball, but we flew in opposite directions. I can't blame him for how he picks himself back up any more than he can blame me.

In my heart, I know he should go.

I need some time to move beyond this, too. I've hidden the rape inside myself for so long that it's grown roots. I'm not sure I can remove it without cutting out a piece of myself.

"Why did he do it, Grace?" Owen says, his voice cracking. "Why? It just doesn't make any sense. He's known you practically your whole life. You're like a daughter to him."

"I don't know."

Owen glances away from me, his throat working. I can tell that he's trying to untangle the mess his father made, trying to smooth it out into a straight line that leads to the truth.

I start to shiver. Every part of me is soaked. I wrap my arms around my chest and rub them with my palms, trying to warm up.

"You're cold. You should head inside," Owen says, and I nod.

I can see our goodbye stampeding toward us.

So this is how it will end this time. At one in the afternoon, standing in a hospital parking lot in the pouring rain.

I force myself to look him in the eye. There are no guarantees that I'll ever see him again. And if this is the last time, I want to remember everything about this moment. Because life is hard and it's messy, but it deserves to be lived. And if you're always turning away from it, you aren't really living it. Living, really living, is standing on the very tip of the moment — right on the leading edge of now — no matter how heartbreaking or beautiful or terrible it might be.

Still.

I hate goodbyes.

And I don't know how to let him go. It was so much easier to walk away from him when I thought he was a monster. Here, now, with our shared pain, with our past and present so matted together, saying goodbye feels unnatural.

"Owen," I begin, and my voice cracks. I pause, trying to find the right words. Owen doesn't need my permission to leave town, but he needs my blessing. And so I give it to him. "Your leaving — it's what you need right now, and I'll never hold that against you. Please don't feel guilty. Your family deserves to get past this. You deserve to get past this. You deserve to have a life. You deserve happiness. You deserve love. Real love. And if you can't have it with me when this is all said and done, if you just can't move beyond what your father did, then I hope you find it with someone else." The last sentence strangles me a little bit, but I get it out.

It isn't clear who reaches for whom. The space between us is gone and we're kissing. His hands frame my face, and I don't know what is rain or what is tears, because both of them are everywhere as he says, "I'll miss you," and I say, "I know," and he says, "This is killing me," and I say, "I know."

And just like that, he's gone.

Forty-Seven

I'm standing outside on the porch the next day, a couple of hours after sunrise. It's a cool morning by Florida standards. There's a hurricane off the coast of Texas, and it's kicking up the waves into choppy white peaks. In the McAllisters' driveway, backed up to the house, is a large U-Haul truck, which evidently arrived yesterday, while I was at the hospital.

Eleanor comes bumbling out the front door, wearing both a one-piece swimsuit and a somber expression. She probably weighs only a hundred pounds soaking wet, but the deck groans loudly under her feet as she stops beside me and says, "I had a dog once — did I ever tell you that? A shih tzu. Yapped all the time. The vet found a tumor on him when he was only five years old. Killed me to have to put him down, but I didn't have much choice." She blows out a breath. There's a long pause punctuated by the caw of a seagull. Then she says, "The day I had to let him go — that was the day I loved him most."

I turn toward her. She looks sincere and honest and maybe

even a little bit sad. I didn't realize how accustomed I was to her sarcasm. Now that it's gone, I actually miss it a little.

We stay there like that, silent for I don't know how long. Then she nods at me, walks down the steps and crosses the road to the beach. I watch her wade into the water and then dive under, paddling out past the swim buoys. She stays there for a moment, just bobbing, and then she ducks under an oncoming wave like it's nothing, as easy as breathing, only to come to the surface and get blasted full-force with another massive wall of water. Reflexively, I suck in my breath and hold a hand over my mouth. But within seconds, her head bursts through the water. I can almost swear I hear her laugh.

#

Eventually, I wander inside, where Faith is dumping white flour into a mixing bowl. "Pancakes," she tells me. "With extra vegetable oil." She swallows and forces a smile. "I got my period today."

"I'm sorry," I say, and I walk across the kitchen and hug her, spontaneously and hard. She stiffens for half a second, surprised, and then she wraps both arms around me. It occurs to me that this is the first time I've hugged her on my own. Even so, she smells familiar, like vanilla and flour and clothes that have been hanging out on a line.

I hang around the house all morning, one ear on next door. Strange as it sounds, I want to spend as much time here as possible with the McAllisters still living next door, still in my life. So I eat breakfast with Faith and curl up on the couch with a book while Rusty watches TV.

When the moving truck fires up, I inhale sharply, hit all at once with this weird instinct to burst outside and tell them to get back in their house, as though I feared for their safety. Instead, I sit perfectly still, listening to the truck bump down the driveway. All I can think is, *Nobody came over to say goodbye*, even though that's all we've been doing the past several days, just by acknowledging how screwed up everything is.

Still, though, it hurts like hell.

As the noise of the engine grows quieter and quieter, Rusty gives my shoulder a squeeze and says, "You want to go see a movie or something?"

I shake my head no, my rib cage crushing my heart into a tiny grain of sand. "I think I need to stay right where I am."

#

That evening, someone shuts the door to the spare room. And it remains that way, a two-inch-thick wooden barricade, safeguarding us from the things we can't change.

Forty-Eight

Sarah visits me one afternoon in early August. She tells me that she wishes I had confided in her, that everything will be okay, that she'll help me in any way she can. That Mr. McAllister is still in jail, awaiting his trial.

Even so, I'm restless. Late at night, when the house is quiet and everyone has gone to sleep, I tiptoe into the kitchen, slide Eleanor's car keys off the counter and slip off into the night. I drive in circles, down the coast, through Bradenton Beach, past Longboat Key and then back to New Harbor the long way. Just before sunrise I arrive home, where I pad quietly into the house and collapse in bed, finally able to sleep. And that's how it goes for days on end. Drive. Come home. Sleep. I feel like I'm looking for something, looking to get away from something. Just … looking.

Currently, it's four thirty in the morning and I'm pulling Eleanor's car to a stop at a gas station in Sarasota. I slide the car into park and just sit there for a moment, staring down the street. Mr. McAllister is in a jail cell somewhere. I know this should make me feel better, safer.

It doesn't.

I pull my phone out of my purse and check it for messages. I don't know why. I guess I keep hoping that one of these days I'll find a text from Owen or Janna, even though I fear in a real, bruising way that I'll never hear from them again.

I'll understand, but it will still break my heart.

I take a shuddering breath, blinking until my eyes clear, and then I open the door and climb out. The gas station looks washed out and dingy in the blinding fluorescent light. I stare through the windows of the station's convenience store, wondering whether I should walk in and buy something to eat.

That's when I see him. The guy whose wallet I stole. The life-guard. He's standing at the counter inside the store, holding a to-go cup of coffee, his feet kicked out in the same casual stance I've gotten used to seeing lately. He waits, unaffected and idle, for the woman behind the counter to ring him up.

I shift my weight, a swirl of apprehension in my stomach. I haven't been hiding from him. Not for several weeks now. The weird, confusing truth is that there's a part of me — and I'm not sure how big a part it is — that actually wants him to recognize me. To figure it all out. To just storm on up to me and demand his wallet. But he hasn't so much as looked at me, or maybe he has and I just haven't seen it.

Anchoring myself to the car with one hand, I watch him put his coffee on the counter and reach into his pocket, pulling out a wad of money. He gives two bills to the cashier, holding up an easygoing palm and shaking his head when she tries to give him his change. With a tip of his head, he gestures to the little plastic dish that customers use when they're a few cents short, and then he ambles away.

I'm not quite sure I've ever felt so ashamed.

I wonder whether I overreacted that day on the bus, whether I jumped to assumptions too quickly, whether my past warped my perceptions of the present.

Finally he saunters outside, toward a banged-up Honda parked in front of the shopette, and within seconds, he's driving away.

It isn't until I'm in Eleanor's car, turning onto Route 41, that I realize I'm following him, just trailing the faded red of his taillights for a couple of miles until he turns right, down a shabby street full of potholes, and pulls into a driveway. I hang back, not quite in front of his house, staring at his mailbox, which reads *Luke Simmons, 1243 Brighton*.

Luke Simmons.

I shake my head, completely disgusted with myself. Because I didn't even know his name. Didn't bother to look at his driver's license when I stole his wallet. Or any of the wallets, for that matter.

Those people — they weren't even *people* to me.

Embarrassment cresting like a tidal wave in my chest, I put the car into drive and pull away. When I get back to Rusty's, I stride into the house, grabbing a stack of notepaper and envelopes on the way to my room, feeling lighter with every step I take. Outside my window, the sky is red and orange: morning, bursting through the night. Crashing to the floor, I lean against the futon. And I start writing.

I tell those men everything — everything that happened to me and everything that happened *because* of me. I want them to understand what I did and why I did it. It's my story, after all, every screwed-up piece of it, and they need to hear it because I've yanked them into it. When I'm finished, I grab their wallets, using money from my purse to replace what I stole.

As I'm pulling out their IDs to find addresses for the envelopes, I feel it. The terror. Because what will they do after they've read my letters? Will they tell Rusty what I've done? Materialize on my doorstep, screaming and ranting? But I don't stop. I just keep on going until the feeling passes.

#

For the record, I don't return Owen's wallet, because I didn't actually steal it. And even if I *did* take it, I couldn't have sent it back to him, because I don't have his new address.

Besides, when I'm having a particularly tough day, I pull it out of my desk, slide out his old driver's license, stare at his picture and remember.

#

Weeks slip by, and not one of those men shows up on my doorstep. Luke Simmons doesn't so much as glance in my direction as I come and go from Rusty's. Has everyone forgiven me for what I've done? It appears that way as time trudges on, summer vacation bleeding into the first several weeks of school.

Sawyer, who's promised to testify in court about what he saw that Labor Day weekend, quits using steroids and sends a letter to Clemson, explaining why he won't be attending their school next year. I pass him in the hallways sometimes, and we nod at each other — awkward yet strangely familiar.

I spend my free time doing the therapist thing and the homework thing, or else holing up in my room with my violin. I'm staying above water — I am — but I miss Owen and Janna. Their absence is deep and gaping, a hole I tumble into, time and again, and the longer I go without a phone call or a text from them, the more I wonder whether they've moved on. Even though I've never said as much to Faith, she peers at me over a magazine one Thursday evening in late September, and says, "I'm sure they'll call you soon."

I blink at her from the couch, where I'm bent over an English paper. "Who will call me soon?"

She sighs and flips the page.

Forty-Nine

The thing about Eleanor is that it's easy to believe all the ridiculous stuff she says, but also it's impossible to believe all the ridiculous stuff she says. She's so garish it makes perfect sense that she's capable of outlandish things, but then she's such an obnoxious old crow that you can't really trust a single thing that comes out of her mouth.

"You're getting a tattoo," I say, jacking up an eyebrow as our waitress hustles past us with a tray of drinks.

Eleanor takes a noisy sip from her soda, peering at me over the rim of her cup. "That's what I said."

Leaning back in my seat and crossing my arms, I give Eleanor a dubious look. Island Pizza is crowded, packed with the usual cast of characters — tourists and locals who've dragged in from the beach, sunburned and relaxed. "Why are you getting a tattoo?" I ask.

"Eh." Eleanor shrugs. "Always wanted to."

"You've always wanted to."

"Why do you always repeat everything I say?"

I pinch my eyes shut with my thumb and forefinger, sighing. "I was just wondering," I say slowly, measuring my words, "why a sixty-nine-year-old woman would want to get a tattoo."

She holds up her spoon and makes a horse face at her reflection, picking something out of her teeth. When she puts it down, she says, "I don't know, because it just feels like something I want to do, I guess?" She cocks one eyebrow at me. A dare. "Want to get one, too? I'm buying."

My answer comes quickly, before I even have time to fully consider her question. And as we walk out of the restaurant that day, my heart might be thrumming double-time and my mind might be whirring. But for once, I'm not afraid.

#

I need to scream in the worst, eye-bulging, mouth-pursing, mind-cursing sort of way. But Eleanor is standing at my side, arms crossed and eyes challenging me, so I draw in a deep breath and let it out through my nose, willing my heartbeat to slow.

I will not have a heart attack in Sorry Mom Tattoo Parlor.

I will not.

I can feel the backs of my thighs sweating against the vinyl seat as Tom, the tattoo artist, who has — no shit — a dragon tattoo creeping up his neck and around his eye, makes me doubt every decision I've made today, particularly the stupid, spontaneous, irrational one that led me here.

Tom straightens up and swaps out his ink vial, and then he bends over me again, moving the needle to a different part of my foot.

Turns out, I know a lot of cuss words.

I glance at Eleanor, my hands gripping the sides of the chair. "Why didn't you tell me that this is one of the most sensitive places to get a tattoo?"

Eleanor's eyes trail to the tattoo, hanging there for a moment. If she has questions about my artwork selection, she doesn't voice them. She simply says, "You've got this, slick. You're a criminal, remember? Embrace your inner badass."

Tom eyes me with sudden interest.

Eleanor smirks.

I smirk back at her.

On the way here, Eleanor gave me one of her side-looks and said, "How're you holding up, kid?" I stared out the window for a couple of beats, trying to put together a reply.

I hadn't seen Mr. McAllister, and I probably wouldn't until his sentencing, whenever that happened. But earlier that week, I'd learned that two other girls had stepped forward, claiming he'd sexually assaulted them as well. I'd also found out that he'd told the police he'd been molested as a child. This was his excuse for raping three girls. It didn't make me any less angry with him. That was the hardest part for me — the forgiveness. I kept trying, because I felt like I should, because I felt like it would help me get over everything, but in the end, it seemed like forgiving him would be like granting him a favor, excusing what he did.

Finally I turned to Eleanor and said, "I'm still pretty angry."

She nodded. "Me, too. The guy's a dick." I laughed out loud and tipped my head at her, like *Well said*, and then she went on to say, "Choosing to think otherwise would be a tall order for you."

Sitting in this chair with my foot basically on fire, I keep thinking about that conversation. Because it's never occurred to me that I have a choice. I've always felt helpless to the things life has thrown my way. And I guess, in a way, I've chosen to feel helpless, again and again and again.

I close my eyes, draw in a deep breath and exhale, releasing my death grip on the chair, just letting go, letting go of everything, listening to the buzzing of the needle and the sound of my slow inhalations. It seems like only seconds later when I hear Tom say, "What do you think?"

I sit up and blink a couple of times. Is he finished? He's finished. I glance at my foot and then back at him. I smile, because I feel a little better. Or different. Like I've reached the top of something. Or else, the bottom of something. I look at Eleanor, who nods at me, grinning, and then at Tom and then again at the top of my foot. It's red and puffy and sore as hell. It's foreign in the best possible way. "It's beautiful."

Fifty

By the time I arrive home that afternoon, I feel lighter and happier. Rusty is standing at the kitchen sink, filling a glass of water. He turns and says hello, his gaze skimming over my face in an assessing sort of way that I've grown accustomed to lately: *Does she look like she's been crying? Is she hurt in any way?* I guess I pass his evaluation, because he smiles and says, "Want to go grab an ice cream? We could drive down Longboat to that place on the —"

"Actually, I thought maybe we could go visit Dad."

"Yeah. Okay," Rusty says without even thinking, as though I've just asked him if he wants to settle into the couch and watch a TV show. "That's a great idea."

We don't go to the cemetery where Dad is buried, though. That's the thing. We go to the river.

Even though it's within walking distance, Rusty drives us in his truck. He stares straight out the windshield, tapping his thumb to the music on the radio. I can tell he's lost in thought, so I let him be, resting my head against the back of the seat and gazing out the window until the tires crunch on the gravel parking lot.

Rusty gestures toward the riverbank as we climb out of the truck. "Have you been since you came back to New Harbor?"

"Once," I say, grabbing a bag filled with bread slices and shutting the door. "You?"

"Nearly every day since your dad died."

I blink at him. "Really?"

He nods once and adjusts his hat. "It was your dad's favorite place. We used to fish here all the time," he says quietly, squinting at the tight knots of mangrove lining the water like there's no place in the world more important than this tiny pinprick of southern geography.

We settle on the riverbank, both of us quiet for several minutes. Somewhere behind me, frogs call out to one another. A family of ducks swims past and I toss them a handful of bread. They flap and splash as they scoop it up. It's a knife in my chest, the way they make me think of Dad, but I watch them anyway. Moving on, I guess, isn't about glossing over the past. It's about choosing happiness. And sometimes, choosing happiness means acknowledging painful things and then letting them go.

"Lucky ducks," I murmur.

Rusty smiles softly. "Your dad told me once that people tend to put their stock into one of two things, luck or hope. But that when it really comes down to it, luck and hope are the same thing — a wish, thrown up to the universe." He's quiet for a second, and then he goes on. "He said the world is built on those wishes."

My breath hitches and my eyes blur, because it feels a bit like

Dad is speaking to me from the grave. Like he's telling me to hang in there, to keep wishing and hoping and rebuilding my world. I send him a silent thank-you. I think maybe Rusty is talking to him, too, because his face is about as serious as I've ever seen it. Finally Rusty says, "Your dad would want you to be happy, you know."

"I know."

Rusty looks up like maybe the answers to everything are skywritten above. His brows furrow. "And you'll be more than happy. I'll damn well see to that."

I'm not sure what *more than happy* would even look like. Won't I always be That Girl Who Was Sexually Assaulted? I throw another handful of bread to the ducks. "Do you still think of me as the same person?" I ask, my words tumbling out before I can catch them, revealing all my hopes and fears.

He gives me a surprised look. "Of course. Why do you ask?"

"I feel like people see me differently now. Kind of like —"

Damaged goods.

Rusty says, "I don't think you've changed as much as you've learned. And you've learned things about trust and cruelty that a girl your age ought not ever learn, and it would please me if you never learn anything that brutal again." He exhales heavily, like he's just exhausted himself, and stares at the water. Then he goes on. "And anyway, it doesn't matter what people think. This is about you. It's your life. Your story. You just need to figure out where your next chapter will lead you."

It's my story.

I always passed this off to Janna. *What's the story?* I've asked her, time and time again, never once taking the time to decide this for myself.

What do I want?

I think about all the things I've wished for, farfetched or not, and I think about all the people I've wanted to share my life with, farfetched or not, and I realize: I've never asked for any of them.

"Do you think we could afford to hire a private violin teacher?" I say, fast and loud. I've never spoken those words, and now that I have, it's cathartic and empowering. It makes the entire world seem possible.

Rusty blinks. "Sure. Yeah. Anything else on your mind?"

I smile at Rusty. It's a hesitant smile, maybe even a little bit fearful, but it feels more genuine than ever. "Yeah," I say. "I think I'm going to call Janna and Owen."

Fifty-One

It takes a little while for me to figure out what I'll say to Janna when she picks up her phone. By a *little while*, I mean five hours. Possibly six. Whatever the case, it's nearly midnight when I finally punch in the number I've known by heart since middle school, praying it hasn't changed. When she answers, I open with the only line that seems to fit.

"So I got a tattoo."

I can tell this throws her a little, because she doesn't reply right away. After a hiccup of silence, she says, "If you tell me it's a butterfly, Grace Cochran, I'm hanging up on you."

That's how I know we'll be okay.

I'm so relieved I almost drop the phone.

Keeping it light for the first few minutes, we talk about Janna's new school and the weather in Illinois. And then we grow quiet, the phone heavy with everything. Janna clears her throat and says, "How are you doing, Grace? Are you okay?"

No.

I'm not okay.

I know this without a doubt. But I also know that I will be. I'm already on my way.

I'm sprawled out on my bed, hair everywhere, a chorus of cicadas chirping outside my bedroom window. Wedging the phone between my ear and shoulder, I spin sideways on the futon so I can plant both feet on the wall. "Actually," I say, "I'm screwed up beyond measure. You?"

"Total train wreck."

"High fives," I say with a snort.

And so it goes. Neither of us mentions her father, yet the tone of Janna's voice is a little uneasy and hesitant and something else — sad, maybe. Or else wistful. So I give her all the positivity I can muster, telling her stories about my therapist and Eleanor and Andy. Finally Janna sighs and says, "I'm so glad you called. I've missed you terribly. Have you talked to Owen?"

Owen.

The name wobbles unsteadily inside me — a loose wheel on a shopping cart. I swing my legs over and sit up on the edge of the futon. "No. I'm calling him next."

Janna's silent, and then says, "Um."

I jerk to my feet, all my worries suddenly mushrooming inside me, pressing against my skin, trying to get out. "Um, what?"

"It's just — we're all so messed up right now, Grace." Janna stops and exhales, long and slow. "I don't know. I mean, what are you looking for? From him?"

"I want to —" I break off abruptly, not knowing how to end my sentence, not knowing what I really want. To make sure he's okay? To talk? To rekindle our friendship? To resume something more?

Maybe. Maybe to all of them. Maybe to just one or two of them. I don't even know.

I just want a chance for a Maybe.

Fifty-Two

After we hang up, I dial Owen's number, but click the END button before it even rings. I stare at my phone for a while. I clean my room. I go to the kitchen to get something to eat. I walk back to my room. I stare at my phone again. I stick my tongue out at it. I call Janna. I have never made so many phone calls in my life.

"Here's the thing," I say as soon as she answers. "I'm worried that Owen doesn't want to talk to me."

"Grace, it's two thirty-seven."

"Two thirty-eight," I correct without a pause. "Don't you think he would've contacted me by now if he wants me in his life?"

"I don't know," Janna says. "But you could find out IF YOU CALLED HIM."

I chew on my thumbnail, pacing across the room. I'm jittery and jumpy, like my body isn't made up of tissue and muscle and bone, but motion. "Does he ever mention me?"

"Two thirty-nine."

"Janna —"

She groans all over the place. "I mean — of course he's mentioned you. But I haven't heard from him lately because he went away to college."

This gets my attention. "Where did he end up going?"

She yawns, an unsubtle reminder that I've woken her up. "University of Florida. He missed the application deadlines for the other schools."

I bolt to my feet. My free hand explodes up in the air as I say, "University of Florida is only like three hours away! Why hasn't he come to see me?"

"Maybe you should ask *him* that."

My heart is racing, and I've gone sweaty all over. "Um. Do you think you could call him first? Just to find out if he needs more time, or if he's had too much time. If —"

"Grace. Do whatever you think is right. Drive to Gainesville and talk to him for all I care. Goodnight." And she hangs up.

Well.

I didn't even consider talking to Owen in person until Janna mentioned it. But now I want to see him in an obsessive sort of way.

So I'm standing in the middle of my room, muttering to myself. I'm giving myself reasons why I should talk to Owen in person, while simultaneously producing about a gallon of armpit sweat.

"I still have his wallet," I say, lurching from one corner of the room to the other on wobbly knees, "which I really should return. It probably isn't right for me to keep it."

I yank open my desk drawer and pull out Owen's wallet.

Holy effing hell. I can't believe I'm actually considering this. I swallow. "Also," I tell myself, rather convincingly, "Owen isn't much for talking on the phone. It would be more comfortable for him if I showed up in person. So it only makes sense that I go see him."

Did I say a gallon of sweat? Make that fifty gallons.

I call Janna back.

"OH MY GOD GRACE I AM GOING TO KILL YOU," she says instead of hello.

"Don't hang up," I say superfast. "I just need Owen's address."

Fifty-Three

Three hours and forty-five minutes later, I'm in Eleanor's car, Owen's wallet in my purse, over halfway to Gainesville. The sun is bursting up from the east. Birds are soaring everywhere. Traffic is practically nonexistent. The radio is playing my favorite song.

I don't know whether I'll be able to stand myself for another ninety minutes.

Putting my phone on speaker, I call Andy. The two of us have been hanging out a lot lately — eating lunch together at school and going to movies — both of us suffering an immense loss when the McAllisters pulled out of town. Andy has been kicking himself for never having made a move with Janna. He told me philosophically last week in the cafeteria, over a shared pile of fries, "The biggest regrets in life are the risks you don't take."

Pretty deep for the guy who once told me, "I've only had two thoughts today, and one of those thoughts was 'I wonder if this is a thought?'"

As soon as Andy answers, I say, "I need you to distract me right now. Any sort of idle chitchat will do. Tell me about your dog. Your grade in bio. Anything."

"Why do I need to distract you?"

I blow out a breath, puffing out my cheeks. "If I tell you, it would totally defeat the whole purpose of calling. Distraction, Andy. Distraction is what I need. Did I wake you?"

"No. I was online, shopping for a jerkin."

"A jerkin?"

"It's a sleeveless jacket. I need one for the Renaissance festival next month."

I feel the sides of my mouth tugging up a little, because you have to travel pretty far into the Dork Forest to get to the guy who buys jerkins. "Andy," I say, "this is why you've been single all your life."

He snorts once. And after a short pause, he says, "Are you in a car? Where are you going? What's happening, Grace?"

Shit.

There goes my distraction.

"Goodbye, Andy," I say. I reach across the dash and hit the END button.

#

A half hour left till I get to University of Florida, as long as I don't get snagged up in traffic or, say, have a stroke.

#

I sing loudly and horribly to exactly six songs, which brings me to the parking lot in front of Owen's dorm.

#

Seven thirty a.m., on the dot.

Standing in the hallway in front of Owen's dorm room.

Gathering my courage.

I slipped into the building without ceremony or incident. Like, I didn't have to bribe my way inside or sneak in after a student or anything. I just slid right on in because the door, which, I have no doubt, is typically locked to those without a key, was propped open with someone's old sneaker.

And now, minutes later, here I am.

Emitting a shaky breath, I put my hair up into one of those messy ponytail buns, then let it fall back down, then put it up again, because this is what normal people do when they're about to knock on someone's door, right?

I swallow.

This is where Owen lives.

I glance down the hallway. It's nondescript, with off-white walls covered in posters advertising various upcoming events — sort of quaint, actually, once you get over how ordinary it is. I turn back to the door. Nerves buzz in my stomach, a hive of bees. I'm sweating and shaking and short of breath, but I square my shoulders. I straighten my spine.

I am not a disaster. I have overcome so much.

This is my story.

I knock twice. And I wait.

Fifty-Four

"Grace? What are you doing here?"

Owen blinks at me, completely bewildered. His hair has grown out a couple inches. It looks more like it did when we were younger. One side is adorably flattened from sleep, and the other side is sticking straight up.

I open my mouth and then clamp it shut.

I've planned a hundred different versions of this moment in my head, but now that I'm here and he's standing in front of me, I have no clue what to say. I don't know how much he's changed the past couple of months, and I can't tell by looking at him. He's —

Oh, God. He's still gorgeous.

I meet his eyes. I want to hug him forever and smile until my cheeks hurt and bawl my eyes out. I don't do any of those things, though. There's this hesitance in his posture that keeps me a step away. "I just —" I begin, but then I stop. The reasons that led me here seem flimsy all of a sudden. *I have your wallet.*

Just thought I'd drive three hours first thing Sunday morning to return it. Also: *I'd like you to be part of my story. Think we can make that happen?*

"Janna told me you ended up going to school here after all," I say finally, and then I pull his wallet out of my purse and shove it into his hands so quickly that he nearly drops it. "I've had your wallet since forever, so I thought I'd swing by and drop it off." Swing by? How do you swing by from New Harbor? "I also thought we could talk. I just want —"

— a chance for a Maybe.

I wipe my palms on my clothes. Steel myself. "We've gone a long time without talking." I wait a moment for him to reply. He doesn't. I soldier on. "And I think it's time we do. I think we can help each other. I know that everything has changed, but I want us to be — something. Friends. Or more than that. Or less than that. I don't know, exactly. All I know is that I want whatever sort of us we can have after — after everything. We've known each other too long to throw it all away."

His chin goes a little slack, like he wasn't expecting this much honesty from me. For the record, I wasn't expecting this much honesty from me, either. Even so, speaking the truth so boldly pushes open some sort of dead bolt inside me — metal sliding against metal, a door swinging free.

I feel like I've just handed him my heart.

Everything we've gone through reflects back at me in his expression — pain, joy, sadness, isolation, caring, heartbreak, longing.

It's there.

But he still seems so far away.

"I'm not — I wasn't throwing it away," Owen begins, his eyes big and green and heartbroken. Then he sighs. "I was trying to sort everything out."

I glance past him, into his room. Every inch of wall space is covered in artwork — sketches, paintings, drawings, doodles. You name it. There's hardly any furniture. Not that I can see, anyway — it's concealed by carvings and sculptures.

For some reason, it's one of the saddest things I've ever seen.

I blink a couple of times, my eyes blurring.

Pull it together, Grace.

I gesture to his room. "Love the college-chic decor," I say, trying to make light of it. Trying to make light of everything.

Owen flushes and presses his bare toes against the door-jamb, bending them backward a little. "Helps me untangle my brain," he mutters.

"Ah." I rock back on my heels. "Far be it from you to funnel your angst into something common, like a frat party."

For a fraction of a second, he smiles. But it vanishes almost instantly.

A knife twists in my heart.

Sometimes the tragedies aren't the hardest part. It's the aftermath that's excruciating.

A sleepy-looking guy in a struggling goatee shuffles down the hallway, yawning, barely giving us a second look. Suddenly I'm acutely aware that Owen hasn't invited me in. That I'm still standing in the hallway.

Owen says, "How are you, Grace? Are you okay?"

I want him to see the changes in me. I want him to know that they're good changes. "I'm hanging in there. I'm going to school. I'm seeing my therapist. I'm …"

"Moving on," he says, sagging slightly.

"*Carrying* on."

"But you're okay?"

"I'm getting there."

His exhale is half relief and half surprise. It spills out of him like a rug unrolling. I'd like to think that there's some affection in his breath, too, but lack of sleep might be clouding my perceptions.

"I'm really worried about you, Owen," I blurt. "Your family is so far away. You're here by yourself. I don't think you should be going through all this on your own."

He blinks at me. "I'm not. I mean — I've been seeing a therapist."

Wait. What? He's actually talking to someone? A flicker of hope warms my entire body. I say, "Is it helping you?"

"A little, I guess? My therapist keeps telling me that I need to talk to my father to move past all this, even if I just write him a letter. But I can't." Owen stares at me and looks away. "I hate him, Grace," he admits, his voice breaking. "I hate him with every part of me. I hate what he did to you and what he did to my family. I hate that he led everyone to believe that he's this great guy, when he's really a vicious asshole who ruined everyone's lives."

"Remember how much it helped you when you finally talked to Zoey? Maybe if you just try to —"

"I am *not* talking to my father," he says, enunciating every word.

"Okay, then talk to me."

He swallows. "I'm not going to dump my problems on you."

How can I get him to understand? "You wouldn't be," I say. "We can help each other."

He drags in a breath. His body twists in misery. He says, "I don't think you can help me, Grace."

The words are like a door slamming in my face. I stagger backward a little. The floor feels unsteady underneath me. Then I reel myself back in, remembering all those times Owen hit a brick wall with me, and yet he never gave up. Remembering every time he was strong when I couldn't be.

I lift my chin. I look him dead in the eye. My words come from everywhere, from every part of me, because I already have too many regrets in life and I'm not about to make any more of them. Not with Owen. Not anymore. I say, "Well, I'm going to try."

Fifty-Five

The next day, I sit on the very edge of my bed, grab my cell phone and call Owen. He doesn't pick up. Sighing loudly, I slide a sand dollar off my nightstand and roll it around in my hand.

I think of my dad's words about luck and hope.

About wishes being thrown up to the universe.

With a small smile, I search around for an envelope. Once I find one, I slip the sand dollar inside and seal the package shut, scratching a quick address on the front.

Owen needs more than luck to get through this, but luck is a damn good start.

And right now, it's all I can give him.

Fifty-Six

I'm almost home from school the next afternoon, completely immersed in thought, mentally practicing the violin for my upcoming lesson and also considering my next step with Owen. When I hear someone holler, "Hey!" I spook like a cat, my books flying everywhere, and jerk around. And there's Luke Simmons, standing on the edge of the road.

Yeah. Luke Simmons.

The guy whose wallet I stole. The lifeguard.

That's what I'm saying.

I suck in my breath before I can even stop myself, because it's like turning around and seeing a lion stalking toward you.

This particular lion is smiling hesitantly.

I can tell that he's figured out who I am — that he's taken my letter and my return address and connected them to my face — because he has this expression like he's just come up with an answer to a particularly difficult *Jeopardy* question. "Hey," he says again, jogging toward me in his yellow lifeguard T-shirt.

He doesn't appear angry or ready to rat me out, but even so, my heart has leaped into Tampa Bay, and whatever has filled its vacancy is rattling inside my rib cage.

I stoop down, grab my books and stand back up, humiliation warming my face as Luke comes to a stop in front of me. "Look, Grace," he says, and I cringe when he says my name, "I just wanted to come over and say —" He breaks off suddenly. His John Lennon hair swirls around in the wind for a few seconds. "God, this is strange, right? This is super strange. Anyway, I just wanted to say thank-you for your letter and stuff? You must be a helluva thief because I had no clue you stole my wallet that day." He gives me one of those weak soft-punches on my shoulder, like *Atta girl, way to steal*, then he lets his hand drop awkwardly. He clears his throat. "I also wanted to say that I'm sorry. I mean, I know you're the one who jacked my wallet, but —" He stops again. His ears are pink and his nose is wrinkled. He won't even look at me. "I *was* actually looking at your —" He coughs a little and starts to point to my chest, but then changes his mind and points to his own. "I mean — I'm a guy. Kind of a shitty excuse, but it's true. And you didn't do anything to deserve me gawking at you. So I guess what I'm saying is that I'm sorry for looking at you like that, that I'm sorry for every-thing you've gone through." Suddenly he's walking backward, both palms facing me like he's afraid I'll spray him with mace or something. I still haven't said one word to him. "We cool?" he asks as his feet hit the sand.

I nod once, and he spins away and jogs toward the lifeguard tower. I feel colossally thankful, yet about three inches tall.

#

That afternoon, I breeze into FedEx with a bamboo plant, a four-leaf clover and a box of Lucky Charms. "I need to send this to a friend in Gainesville," I tell the clerk.

She stares at me like I'm a total crackpot.

I shift my weight. I don't want to explain Dad's luck thing to her, so I say, "This isn't really all that weird."

She puts everything in a box and starts punching numbers into her computer. "It's pretty weird," she mutters.

Fifty-Seven

I can't sleep that night. Which really isn't all that uncommon. What's uncommon is that I'm not the only one awake. I walk into the hallway and find Faith standing in the spare room — like, *the* spare room — her back to me and her hands propped on her hips. I have no clue how she knows I'm behind her, hovering in the doorway, but she does, because without even turning around, she says, "I had Rusty take it out. I can't imagine how hard it's been for you all these weeks, knowing it's still here."

It only takes a second for me to realize she's talking about the bed. Which is gone. Actually, everything's gone. The furniture, the decor, all of it. The room has been completely gutted. I have no idea how long it's been this way. The door has been closed for months.

I take one step into the room but don't go any farther. I stand very still, waiting. Though my mind is heavy with images, my spine is straight. My breath is steady.

I'm a sexual assault survivor.

Keyword: *survivor.*

"Thanks," I say to Faith, and it's not just about this room. It's more than that. Faith is gifted, it seems, at nudging us all toward what we need — even before we know we need it. I wonder, for a moment, if this is what it feels like to have a mom. A swell of emotion fills my chest and I blink several times.

A couple of seconds pass where all I hear is the steady drone of the air conditioner, and then Faith turns around, gives me a small smile and jerks her head toward the kitchen. "Herbal tea," she says finally, clicking off the light and brushing past me.

While she fills the kettle with water, I slide into a chair at the kitchen table. We don't talk at first, but there's something comfortable about the silence.

Faith puts a steaming mug in front of me, sits down and says, "Should we paint it? That room?"

"Yeah," I say, without even having to think about it. "Yeah. I think we should."

"What color?"

I smile. "Sunflower."

Fifty-Eight

The next day, Rusty lugs a couple of gallons of eye-bleedingly yellow paint into the house and unloads them onto the counter with a grunt. Then he says, "Faith told me not to even bother coming home tonight unless I'm carrying two gallons of sunflower-colored paint." He stares at them for a moment, totally perplexed. "Women are strange."

Fifty-Nine

"Dinner," Andy tells me as soon as I answer the phone. He says it so fast that I can tell he's been pacing in his room, waiting for me to get home from my violin lesson, just so he can call and inform me of his hunger.

I prop my phone between my shoulder and ear, unloading my purse and violin on my bed and then toeing off my shoes. "By 'dinner' do you mean three meatloaves?" I ask, because Andy's appetite is huge and unprecedented.

"Three," he scoffs. "I would never eat an odd number of meatloaves. Also: I would never eat meatloaf. Too loafy for my taste. We'll find something glorious to eat. I'll pick you up in ten." And then he hangs up.

It's late November, so the weather is perfect — more warmth than humidity, more sky than clouds. We keep the windows down in Andy's car as we look for somewhere to eat. I'd suggest Island Pizza, except I just went there a couple of days ago. Also, it reminds me of Janna, and once I start thinking about Janna, thoughts about Owen will likely ensue. Then I'll get weird and obsessive about all the crap I've been sending him, and I'll end up skipping dinner altogether.

So we end up stopping for fast food and then heading over to Marisol's for her renowned day-before-Thanksgiving apple pie, which Andy basically swallows in one bite without even chewing. Then he bounds to his feet and marches around the patio, poking around in the greenery and sniffing at the plants. He looks profoundly out of place here, a skinny, awkward predator pacing among flowers and twinkle lights. I'm convinced that he's going to break something or trip on something or squash something.

"Andy," I say. "Please sit down. You're making me crazy."

He flops into the chair beside me and spins a fork on his empty plate. "How'd you do on the calc test?" he asks.

Calc is the only class we have together, so this is a common question. "Calc — that's the one with all the numbers and symbols, right? Did we have a test? I don't think I did particularly well."

He squints at me. "Clearly you need my tutelage."

Tutelage. Good lord.

"Andy, you say the weirdest things sometimes."

He balances his chair on its back legs. "It's a particular talent of mine," he says, and then he points to the last couple of bites of my pie. "You going to eat that?"

Mind you, in the past hour I've watched him inhale Big Macs — like, *plural* — two orders of fries, a shake and a piece of pie. I've come to discover that Andy eats in much the same way that Doc Brown fueled the DeLorean at the end of *Back to the Future*. He just dumps in a bunch of crap and calls it good.

I point my fork at him. "Touch it and you'll lose a finger."

I look around. Nothing has changed since I was here with Owen. Everything is still green or sprouting or flowered. There's still a web of lights overhead. The chair is still cool metal underneath me. I can still smell the hibiscus. My fingers are still sticky with apple-pie filling.

Yet everything is so different.

I fidget with my napkin, trying not to feel heartbroken. Over the past month, I've sent Owen God knows how many texts, left him a dozen voicemails and mailed several boxes of random luck-related items. And I have yet to hear back from him.

Maybe I should stop trying.

I close my eyes and try to shove the miserable thought out of my mind. With a sigh, I glance at my watch. Seven o'clock. Thanksgiving is tomorrow, and I told Faith I'd be back early to help her with food prep. I should be getting home.

Home.

My breath hitches, hard and sudden, an engine starting to turn over. When did Rusty's become home? My mind scrolls back over the past several weeks, running through all those times I've sat in the living room or walked into the kitchen or taken a shower. Every time I've bounded up the porch steps and burst through the front door.

It's been home for a while now.

Something catches in my throat, and I press into my eyeballs with my fingers.

Andy says, "Are you okay?"

I wipe my eyes. "You know what, Andy? I'm getting closer every day." Finishing my pie, I stand up. As I reach for my purse, I hear a familiar voice that makes me freeze, perfectly still, like a deer.

"Grace?"

I don't turn around. My heart is suddenly sprinting so fast that I can feel my pulse in my throat. I close my eyes and say, "Owen?"

The night is impossibly silent.

"Hey," he says.

I want to let out a victory whoop and jog around the patio, maybe even scramble up on the table and do a little touchdown dance. But I don't. I'm not sure what's running through his mind right now, or where he stands. Swallowing once, I turn around. He's hovering in the doorway to the kitchen, wearing jeans, a white T-shirt and an uncertain expression, a plate of apple pie in his hand.

Our eyes lock.

I've completely forgotten that Andy is there until he clears his throat and says, "Well. I'll just go inside and look for a vase. Or, like, a spittoon. A guy never knows when he'll need a spittoon." He claps a hand on Owen's back as he walks past him, muttering, "Nice to see you, man."

Then it's just Owen and me. Silence presses in on us from all sides. Owen leans against the doorjamb, his eyes still hooked on mine.

"You're here," I say, rather brilliantly.

Owen says, "I come here every year, the day before Thanksgiving. It's apple-pie day."

I fold my arms across my chest. "This year is different," I point out.

His eyes flutter down and his mouth twists a little. "Yeah," he says softly. His gaze slides across the plane of the patio to my foot. It stays there for an extended moment. I know exactly what he's going to ask. It's a question everyone has been asking me over the past several weeks. "Why did you get a sunflower tattoo?" he says.

I hold my arms out wide, almost like I'm introducing myself. Maybe I am. "To remind myself that no matter what, I'll be okay," I tell him.

It feels hugely powerful, saying this.

Owen nods. "A good thing to remember."

A seagull calls out overhead, and I look up. After a moment my eyes drift back to his, and I say, "Tomorrow is Thanksgiving. Shouldn't you be home?"

"I'm catching a red-eye home tonight," he says. Then, evidently realizing he's standing in the doorway with a plate in his hand, he walks toward me. Putting his pie on the table, he says, "So I talked to my dad."

I'm shocked, but I try not to show it. "Yeah? How'd that go?"

He barks a laugh, and it's so unexpected that I flinch. "Oh, it was epic," he says. "I've never screamed so loudly in all my life."

"Did it help?"

The sides of his mouth tug up a little. "It helped me decide that he's done enough damage. That I won't let him win. That he's already taken so much from me, and I sure as hell won't let him take any more." I feel the heat of his gaze clear down to the backs of my knees. "That whatever we are — whatever we can be — is more than the sum of his mistakes."

Whatever we can be.

Translation: he wants our Maybe.

My heart.

It's pumping pure hope.

Owen goes on. "So I came here hoping to find you. Hoping to

talk to you in person. Hoping to catch you without your family around. I wanted to —" He breaks off and smiles with one side of his mouth, hooking a hand on the back of his neck. "I wanted to tell you about all the crazy shit I've been getting in the mail."

I do my best to appear nonchalant as I say, "Crazy shit, huh?"

Owen rocks back on his heels. His cheeks are flushed pink in a way that makes me want to smile. "Yup," he says. "I'm wondering what it all means."

I bite my thumbnail. "Well, hypothetically speaking, the person sending those things might have some theories about luck, about throwing wishes up to the universe."

"Oh yeah?" he says, faux-casual. "That so?"

"Um-hm," I say.

"That person might be onto something."

Owen draws in a slow breath and stares across the balcony at the tangle of flowers and plants, or possibly even beyond that, clear through to the past, to the time we put that turtle enclosure on the beach or when the two of us snuck off to eat bacon donuts. Or possibly he's thinking about all the things we've gone through together. First kisses and last kisses. Tragedies and celebrations and tears. Then he smiles as though he's decided something. When his eyes slide back to me, they're soft. He reaches out for my hand and pulls me to him, wrapping his arms around me. I rest my cheek against his shoulder and he props his chin on top of my head, and we just hold each other. Not like friends, not like boyfriend and girlfriend, but like something solid.

Who knows where we'll end up? I'd like to think we'll find our way to something big and bold and beautiful, and if I were a betting sort of girl, I'd place everything I had on it. Thing is, though, nobody really knows where their stories will go. We can only write so much of them, and the rest unfolds on its own as life gets in the way, as we lose people, lose our way, as we become victims and criminals, as we tumble away from each other and fall back together, as we discover ourselves, escape ourselves, grieve, forgive, change, grow. Because it isn't just a story, it's *life*. It's the chaotic everything. It's the Big Out There.

"I don't have classes on Fridays," Owen whispers into my hair, his voice a jumble of gratitude and relief. "I was thinking maybe we could make Marisol's a Friday night tradition? Meet here once a week to talk?"

And I smile.

Sixty

Like so many years in the past, I find myself taking a seat at Rusty's kitchen table for Thanksgiving dinner. This is the exact place that comes to mind whenever I think about this particular holiday — the table my family has always gathered around, the table where I sat next to Dad year after year, our elbows brushing.

When I look up, I half expect to see him there beside me.

And I guess, in a way, I do.

He's in the late-afternoon sun slanting into the kitchen. He's in Rusty's smile as he hands me the bowl of mashed potatoes. He's in my every breath, my every move, my every decision.

All the windows are thrown open, so I can see Luke Simmons in his lifeguard tower, hands curled around the railing, one foot casually kicked to the side, watching a couple of kids chicken-fighting in the waves.

"Want some stuffing?" Faith asks, offering me a dish.

I glance down at my already-full plate, considering whether

I should throw a scoop of stuffing on top of everything, or start eating so I can make room on my plate, or skip it altogether.

Then I consider another idea.

I drum my fingers on the table. I glance at Luke again. I pick up my fork, shove aside my turkey and throw a heaping scoop of stuffing onto my plate.

My chair makes a scraping sound as I stand.

Do I really want to do this?

Yes.

This is my life. This is how I want to live it.

Picking up my plate, I spin toward the door before anyone can question me. "I'll be right back," I call over my shoulder as I burst out of the house, my steps quick and light and free, the ground blurring under my feet.

If you told me a couple months ago that I'd offer a plate of food to Luke Simmons on Thanksgiving Day, I probably would've peed my pants laughing.

That's the thing, though.

You just never know.

Who knows whether this shaggy-haired guy will become a friend? Who knows where the story goes from here? The only guarantee is that there is no guarantee — just the now, and whatever truth or tragedy it holds. Just the perfectly imperfect moment, the next thirty seconds or whatever second I'm paying attention to. The little gasp of story I'm living, right here, right on the verge of everything, right on the leading edge of now.

I come to a halt under the tower, grinning up at Luke, big and bright and happy.

This life, this terrifying and beautiful life. And this now, this terrifying and beautiful now.

It's mine.

"Hey," I shout up. "I brought you some dinner."

Acknowledgments

The Leading Edge of Now is a story I was compelled to write, a story that grew out of a painful experience in my past. And while my circumstances were vastly different from Grace's, the feelings were the same, so please understand that this book carries a little bit of my heart.

That being said, writing this story was a lot like jumping off a cliff. The second my feet left the ground, I was praying, hyperventilating, imagining my own demise, screaming, laughing, crying, wishing I didn't eat those nachos for lunch. It was the best thing I've ever done. But also, it was the most terrifying thing I've ever done. And there was a huge, magnificent cast of hundreds who were either brave enough or foolish enough to grab my hand and leap along with me. While I'd love to thank all of you by name, space doesn't permit, so please forgive me for keeping this brief.

First and always, thank you to my family. To my husband, Paul, I've loved you since the beginning. You never cease to amaze me with your sense of humor and generosity of heart and spirit. I cannot thank you enough for your constant, unrelenting strength. To my kids, Talon and Blaise, I'm so grateful for your bottomless laughter, your biggest and most beautiful Nows, and your constant reminders of what really matters. I love you two to forever and back. You are, and always will be, my heroes. As for my parents, Janet and Merle, I'm enormously thankful for your boundless love and support. Thank you for what you do for the foster kids who have been lucky enough to live under your roof. This book is better because of you. This world is better because of you. I am better because of you. And to my sister, Cari, eternal thank-yous for your carefree sense of humor and unending encouragement. You are a gorgeous gem in my life.

I also owe unbounded appreciation to Kathleen Rushall, my agent, whose talents are legion and who resolutely stood by me and this book's sensitive subject matter. Grace's story would not exist without you. There aren't enough thank-yous in the universe for that. And while I'm thanking agents, buckets of recognition and acknowledgment to my foreign agent, Taryn Fagerness, for scattering *The Leading Edge of Now* across the ocean and beyond.

Next, I owe tremendous gratitude to the Kids Can Press and KCP Loft team, who have made me feel like a member of their family since the very beginning. Ceaseless thank-yous to Kate Egan, my amazing editor. With your guidance, brilliance and tolerance, you've helped me blow the dust off the heart of this novel. Your talent and insight are truly magical, and I now understand why you've charmed and enchanted this entire industry. And to Lisa Lyons Johnston, I have no idea how you saw potential in that first draft of mine, but I thank my lucky stars that you did. I'm so very grateful for your faith in me. To all the others who have worked behind the scenes at KCP on my behalf, I'm endlessly thankful for your support, earnestness and dedication to this story.

A massive shout-out goes to my publishing friends, far and wide. To my critique partners and early readers — Lola Sharp, Lindsay Currie, Jan Gangsei, Laurie Flynn, Sharon Huss Roat, Samantha Joyce, Shannon Parker and Marley Teter — all of whom had to endure my struggling (and by *struggling* I mean STRUGGLING) draft of this story. Thank you in every way for your encouragement, talent, love, expertise and reassurance. You are goddesses.

To my extended family and friends, too many to name here, but you guys know who you are: You're the ones giving me constant encouragement when I'm battling a deadline. You're the ones out there shoving my books into strangers' hands. You're the stampede of love that follows me everywhere. I'm forever grateful and honored.

Loads and loads of thanks to the librarians, bloggers, booksellers and teachers who have advocated this story. I'm so blessed to have you all in my corner. You're thoughtful and kickass, and I'm not sure what I ever did to deserve you.

And as always, thank you to my readers worldwide. I count my blessings every day because of you. I love you epically and infinitely, and am so very thankful to be trusted with your hearts.

Lastly, I'm most appreciative to the one in six — *the one in six* of you who have experienced sexual assault in your lifetime. It means more than I can say that you read this story, because I wrote it for you. Please remember that you are survivors, that you are not alone, that you are not to blame.

The past is in the past. Go live your Now.

Author's Note

The statistics of sexual assault are extremely alarming. According to the Rape, Abuse & Incest National Network, the nation's largest anti–sexual violence organization:

- women the ages of 16–19 are four times more likely than the general population to suffer sexual assault

- one out of every six women has been the victim of an attempted or completed rape in her lifetime

- every 98 seconds, someone experiences sexual assault

- seven in ten rapes are committed by someone the victim knows

- two out of three rapes go unreported

If you are a victim of sexual assault, please reach out. There are so many resources waiting for you. The National Sexual Assault Hotline is always ready for your call: 1-800-656-HOPE (4673). RAINN (the Rape, Abuse & Incest National Network) is the nation's largest sexual violence center, and it offers help in every way at www.rainn.org. NSVRC (National Sexual Violence Resource Center) offers a breakdown of resources by state at www.nsvrc.org.

WHAT ARE YOU READING NEXT?

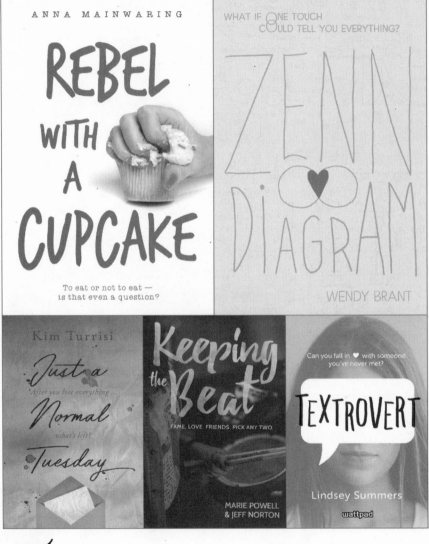

MORE GREAT BOOKS

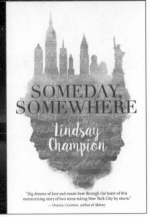

KCP Loft

kcploft.com

 @KCPLoft